Entitlement

Jessica White is a novelist and researcher, and the author of *A Curious Intimacy*. She was raised on a property in north-west New South Wales, and is now based in Brisbane.

JESSICA WHITE

Entitlement

VIKING
an imprint of
PENGUIN BOOKS

VIKING

Published by the Penguin Group
Penguin Group (Australia)
707 Collins Street, Melbourne, Victoria 3008, Australia
(a division of Pearson Australia Group Pty Ltd)
Penguin Group (USA) Inc.
375 Hudson Street, New York, New York 10014, USA
Penguin Group (Canada)
90 Eglinton Avenue East, Suite 700, Toronto, Canada ON M4P 2Y3
(a division of Pearson Penguin Canada Inc.)
Penguin Books Ltd
80 Strand, London WC2R 0RL, England
Penguin Ireland
25 St Stephen's Green, Dublin 2, Ireland
(a division of Penguin Books Ltd)
Penguin Books India Pvt Ltd
11 Community Centre, Panchsheel Park, New Delhi – 110 017, India
Penguin Group (NZ)
67 Apollo Drive, Rosedale, North Shore 0632, New Zealand
(a division of Pearson New Zealand Ltd)
Penguin Books (South Africa) (Pty) Ltd
24 Sturdee Avenue, Rosebank, Johannesburg 2196, South Africa
Penguin (Beijing) Ltd
7F, Tower B, Jiaming Center, 27 East Third Ring Road North,
Chaoyang District, Beijing 100020, China

Penguin Books Ltd, Registered Offices: 80 Strand, London WC2R 0RL, England

First published by Penguin Group (Australia), 2012

1 3 5 7 9 10 8 6 4 2

Design by John Canty © Penguin Group (Australia)
Cover photograph by Lori Andrews/Getty Images
Typeset in 11.5/16 Adobe Caslon
Printed and bound in Australia by McPherson's Printing Group,
Maryborough, Victoria

National Library of Australia
Cataloguing-in-Publication data:

White, Jessica.
Entitlement / Jessica White.
9780670075935 (pbk.)
A823.4

penguin.com.au

FOR HADLEY

I

It was a small train station with a single line of tracks, a stuccoed building painted white, and two wooden benches, the sign 'TUMBIN' nailed to the wall between them. The heat of the January day hung in the air, trapping the smell of asphalt, while the lowering sun glared.

Blake had come home early and sponged dust and sweat from his skin in the shower. He'd pulled on his moleskins and a red checked shirt Leonora had ironed. She wore her navy-blue linen dress, belted at the waist, and red sandals. Next to the handful of others at the station in dusty jeans and T-shirts, they looked out of place.

Blake shifted his weight and clasped his hands behind his back, as though he were meeting the Tumbin mayor. He nodded to the man next to them in khaki shorts and shirt, a trucker's cap shading his face.

'Rellies coming to stay?' the man asked.

'Cate's coming back for a bit.'

'Haven't seen her for a while.'

'No.'

'You never had any word?'

'No.' Blake directed his gaze back to the tracks.

The man folded his arms.

Leonora stepped close to Blake. 'Who was that?'

'MacPherson. Grain trader.' Blake began to limp stiffly down the platform.

Leonora wrapped the thin straps of her handbag around her fingers and swallowed. A fly persisted at her face, trying to get at the moisture in her eyes. She waved it away, ran her hand through her dark-brown bob and fiddled with her pearl earrings.

Blake returned and placed an arm around her shoulders.

'Train's coming,' he said.

Their daughter, when she stepped onto the platform, looked to Leonora as hard and weary as a soldier. There were blue circles beneath her eyes and she was scrawny, her hair dull. Leonora embraced her. The girl's body was like steel, but her mother didn't care. It was Cate, and she was home.

Blake bent and awkwardly kissed his daughter's cheek, then took her bag to the car. He made an effort to walk naturally.

'Did you have a good trip?' Leonora asked, as they pulled away from the station.

'Not really. I took a sleeping pill and woke up past Kynidia.'

'I still don't understand why you couldn't have flown.'

'I didn't want to get here in a hurry.'

'Oh. Did —'

'I don't want to talk, Mum. I've got a headache.'

'I've got Panadol in my bag.'

'I've had some.'

'Well, it's not too long —'

'Nora, leave it,' Blake said.

Cate sank into her seat, unable to stop herself looking out the window. They passed the red-brick primary school, its grounds dry from the summer, jacarandas dripping purple flowers onto the concrete paths, the steps to the classroom swept clean. When they'd been children, they had lined up in front of those steps, she in one row, her brother in another, each trying to make the other laugh by crossing their eyes or curling their tongues. To Cate's admiration, Eliot could twist his into the shape of a three-leaved clover.

The car crawled by the pub with its wide verandah. Men and women sat on white plastic chairs in thongs, shorts and T-shirts, their bottles of beer glowing in the last of the light.

Blake sped up once they reached the outskirts of the town, where most of Tumbin's Aboriginal population lived in fibro shacks built in the fifties and newer brick houses. Kids were playing handball on the hard, compacted earth of a driveway, and dogs barked at the car as it passed.

The light faded as they left the town behind and reached the irrigated paddocks of cotton. Wild turnip weed sprawled across the roadside. Cate hated its oily-smelling yellow flowers, which made her eyes itch and her nose run. Bigger, deeper dams had been built to service the cotton since she'd been here last. She closed her eyes and leaned her cheek against the seatbelt.

She was woken by the slowing of the car. Darkness had fallen, but the light on the verandah shone the way it always had. For a moment Cate was a little girl again, arriving home late after Blake and Leonora had been at a party. She almost glanced to her right to see if Eliot was still asleep.

Her parents had new dogs; they jumped up and left dusty paw prints on her jeans as she climbed out of the car.

Silently, Blake carried her bag indoors.

Her bedroom was just as she'd left it eight years before. The toys and dolls were arranged according to height, starting with an enormous, under-stuffed pink bear Eliot had won at the clay-pigeon shooting stall at the Tumbin Show, and ending with a lilac

My Little Pony. In the bookcase was her complete set of *Anne of Green Gables* and innumerable volumes of *Sweet Valley High*. Her jewellery box with the red satin cover still sat on the dressing table. She lifted the lid, and the tiny ballerina inside twirled to 'Over the Rainbow'.

The adjoining door to Eliot's room was open.

Leonora hovered.

'I need to be alone, Mum.'

'Okay, love.' Her mother looked disappointed, but she closed the door.

Cate took off her shoes. She padded into Eliot's room. His glow-in-the-dark stars were still on the ceiling, his soft-toy troll lay against the pillows. The house shifted in the wind, its rafters clicking.

'Cate?' An hour later, Leonora rapped lightly on the door. There was no answer, and the light was out. She twisted the brass knob and her heartbeat vaulted. The room was empty. Then she stepped forward and saw, through the doorway, Cate curled up asleep on Eliot's bed, her arm wrapped around the troll.

Something settled inside her.

2

Mellor rocked gently in the saddle, reins loose in his hands, comforted by the smell of his horse. Blowies dipped and settled on his sweaty back. He was on his third day of checking and mending the boundary fences: it would take him another three days to finish the circuit. He enjoyed the sun on his shoulders and listening to his country.

Before they'd moved into town when he was nine, Mellor had ridden alongside Stanley, his dad, to check the fences during school holidays. It had taken them a week back then, as the property had been almost a third bigger. After the war, Blake's dad had sold part of it to the government, who gave it to returned soldiers.

He and his dad had slept under rough wool blankets, the fire crackling, air sharp with the smell of smoke. In winter the cold had sliced their nostrils as they breathed. Every night, Mellor had fallen asleep to the burr of his father's voice, as it described their ancestors scooping out rivers and making hills with their hands. One cool summer evening they had tied up their horses to walk into those hills. This, his father explained, was where their land traditionally began. It had been too rocky to turn into farming country, so it was left largely untouched. The rest had been ploughed into the soil by Blake's grandfather.

Mellor stopped and slid off the horse. One of the traps he'd set had caught a fox. The animal lay stiff, eyes empty and teeth bared. Mellor prised back the jaws of the trap and shook the fox loose, then threw it over the fence. If it were up to him, he'd have done away with the traps; all those years working in the abattoirs made sure of that. Instead, he reset it, mounted his horse and set off again.

He'd only been told of the changes the week before, when he'd stopped by the house to pick up eggs for his aunts and give Leonora some news he'd found.

'Hello?' he'd called out, opening the front door.

'In here,' Leonora had replied from the living room. She'd been crouched against the wall, wiping the skirting boards.

'The Queen's coming to visit, Mrs Mac?'

'Close.' Leonora had pushed herself up, her eyes shining. 'Cate's coming home.'

'Mrs Mac, that's good!'

He'd forced a smile, among all those clamouring ghosts in the room.

'How'd you do it?' he'd asked.

Leonora had looked at the rag in her hands. 'Let's have a cuppa, Mellor.'

Mellor and Blake always had their conversations about the day's work on the patio out the back, but when Blake was out, Mellor sat with Leonora in the wicker chairs on the verandah.

He eased himself into one, listening to the clink of cups and whirr of a boiling kettle in the kitchen. The verandah looked out to a smooth lawn that stretched to a fence, beyond which was a road and paddocks. Lining the fence were leafy shrubs and, in one corner, a cedar tree, while along the house and beneath the verandah were terracotta pots full of plants. In the middle of the lawn was a massive gum tree, around which wrapped a thick jasmine vine.

Mellor shifted a cushion behind his back as Leonora appeared and placed the tray on the small table between them. She poured the tea into her thin china cups, and he took his from her carefully. He wouldn't want to see her face if he broke one.

Leonora had started inviting him in after his wife had died: she and Joss had often had tea together, after they'd got back from CWA meetings, or Joss had finished cleaning. Leonora chatted, as she had with his wife, about people she'd met, their children, or about Charlie and Sally, her brother-in-law and his wife. She didn't seem to mind that Mellor let her talk flow around him, with just an occasional nod, or a 'That so, Mrs Mac?' in reply.

This time, though, she was silent, with a small frown between her eyes.

Mellor tipped half a spoonful of sugar into his tea and took a sultana biscuit from the plate Leonora held out. The sprinklers were on, twisting water across the lawn.

'We want to sell up, Mellor. That's why Cate's coming home, to help make a decision, although we've got someone who's interested.' Leonora tucked strands of hair behind her ears. 'Which puts you and your aunts in an difficult position, of course, but we'll try and sell to someone who is sympathetic to keeping you on.'

Mellor sipped his sweet tea. Sympathy. It was an easy word to use.

'I appreciate that, Mrs Mac.' He took another bite of his biscuit.

Then he drained his cup and stood. 'Better let you get back to your cleaning, Mrs Mac.'

She looked up, that frown still on her face. 'I'll get the eggs for you.'

~

Mellor walked carefully across the eerily green lawn, the cartons under his arm. When he repeated Leonora's words to his aunts, May didn't want to use the eggs.

'Don't be ridiculous!' her sister Kath replied, taking them from him.

After dinner, May appeared in the living room of his shack, where he was reading another report.

'What will we do, Mellor?'

He gazed at his aunt, her long grey hair pulled back from her face into a ponytail, her eyebrows drawn together with worry.

He tossed the report to the floor. 'I don't know.'

3

Cate opened her eyes and sought the red gleam of the clock – 4.30 a.m. The birds weren't awake. She was glad; she didn't want to hear the apostlebirds in the apricot tree outside her window. She pushed down the thin cotton sheet and pulled a T-shirt and pair of shorts from her bag, slipped her feet into running shoes, tugged the laces tight, and laid her feet one at a time against her old desk to stretch her tendons. Then she padded out, avoiding the floorboards that creaked. The screen door still screeched. It mustn't have been oiled in the last ten years.

Leonora had mown the lawn the day before; grass clippings, sticky with dew, coated the edges of Cate's shoes. At the start of the driveway, she saw Eliot throwing rocks into the beehive in the old gum to stir the bees up. She began to run.

The cool air bit her cheeks. Out past the drive, she clambered over the rusty iron gate and dropped into the Wedge-tail Paddock. Wiregrass brushed her calves.

She'd hoped that if she ran before dawn, there wouldn't be enough light to recognise the places where they'd rounded up cattle, shouting and driving the horses hard, or to see the dirt tracks they'd followed, dragging sticks behind them to make patterns in the soil. But it was midsummer, and the sun was already peeling away the night to reveal spindly eucalypts lining the fences. Light slammed against the side of a water tank, blazing gold.

Cate ran harder. She reached another gate, fitted her foot into the mesh and swung herself over. She crossed the dirt road and continued up into the hills. Heat began to coil around her ankles. The smell of the pines brought Eliot again – singing and weaving in and out of the trees while their grandparents, staying for Christmas, sawed down a small tree to take home and decorate. Here were the rocks they'd climbed over, grazing their hands on the sandpapery surfaces on their way to the top. Here, two broody magpies had warbled warning notes before diving at their heads.

Near the top of the hill, where the pine trees made way for eucalypts, Cate stopped and sat down on a slab of rock, pressing her fingers against her eyes, fighting the old pressure of tears. Her head ached from lack of water and sleep. She wanted to keep running, but her muscles were protesting.

The rising sun warmed oil in the eucalyptus leaves, coaxing their scent into the air. Once her ragged breathing had slowed, she rose. From here, she could see their whole property, nestled between two sets of hills. At the bases of the hills ran two roads, and between them curved a creek. The land was cut into squares of rust-coloured sorghum, tawny wheat stubble, or dark, ploughed soil, while pockets of sheep and cattle rested in the shade of trees. Each handkerchief of paddock and hollow of the creek was as familiar to her as Eliot had once been.

She began walking back downhill along a track made by wild goats. At the bottom, she saw a ute by the road, a man standing next to it, and her breath caught in her throat. But he was stocky, his shoulders too hunched.

When he heard the snap of sticks beneath her shoes, he turned, and she broke into a jog. 'Mellor! It's so good to see you!'

He clapped her on the back and pulled her into a hug. His smell of tobacco and perspiration was just the same, but his hair had gone completely white.

'It's been a while, Catie.'

'Yeah.' She stepped back, suddenly uncomfortable. 'Did they tell you why I'm here?'

'Yep.'

In a flash of green and red, two rosellas flew into a stand of gums. Cate watched as they settled in the trees.

'How are Rachel and the boys?' she asked, cautiously.

'The boys stayed up north. Don't see them much. She's in town.'

'Is she well?'

'Yeah.' He squinted against the sun. Heavy lines fanned from his dark-brown eyes. 'You staying long?'

'I don't know. They're already driving me crazy.' Cate smiled wryly.

'They missed you.'

She became conscious of her aching head again.

Mellor was silent for a moment. Then he slapped his cap back on his wavy white hair.

'Time to get moving,' he said.

'I'll see you round?'

'If you hang about, yeah.'

'Right. See you, then.' She crossed the road back into the Wedge-tail Paddock, crushing clumps of soil beneath her feet.

4

Blake held the thin tractor wheel lightly, his other hand resting on his worn jeans. The driving seat bounced as the plough behind the old tractor tore earth into furrows. The radio played, but he didn't pay it much attention.

Thick clouds bunched over the low hills. On walks with his father along the fences when he was young, he learned the names of clouds: *cumulus, stratus, cirrus, nimbus*, and the combinations that altered according to their shape and level. *Cirrus* sounded softest in his mouth.

The seat jolted and his hands spasmed around the wheel. Leonora had tucked a packet of painkillers into his shirt pocket but he refused to snap them from their tight silver foil.

He never thought he'd grow tired of starting work in inky-blue dawns, watching the skies blush as he pulled milk from a cow's teat into a tin pail. Yet these last few months, the cold seeping into his joints and the ache emanating from his hip meant he barely registered the warmth of the cow's flank, or her calf stepping impatiently nearby.

His father had remained in fine health well into his eighties, until he keeled over from a heart attack at the mailbox a few years before. When their grief had faded, the family joked it must have been his sister's letter announcing a visit. Aunty Fay would run baths that wasted precious rainwater and left her frilly smalls on the washing line, while his wife bought underwear in packets of ten from Parker' s and dried them in the hot-water cupboard.

It was a good way to go, they all said, at the funeral, in shops, at the school fete – for an event in Tumbin was circulated and chewed over for months. *He loved his life right up to the end.*

Although it had taken Blake's father fifteen minutes to pull on his socks and lace his boots with thick, fumbling fingers, and although he drove the ute at five Ks an hour, the engine chugging unhealthily, it was true. In lambing season he'd drive around looking for strays and, even with his unsteady gait, would catch motherless lambs and swoop them into the passenger seat where they tottered and bleated.

'Better that than the crows,' he told them on the way home, although for some it was too late. They lay in the soil, their eyes pecked out.

Even though it took him three times as long as it once had, Blake's father could still tighten a loose fence and check the thresher for weeds as it sifted harvested wheat. Blake, however, knew his crumbling hip would interfere not just with physical motion, but with his pleasure in method and routine.

His brother Charlie worked the property with him, living a few kilometres down the road with his wife, Sally. After their mother died in a car accident in 1976, Blake had asked Charlie, then married to Sally for a few years with still no kids on the scene, to move in and take care of their father. Charlie took forever to do anything, though, and they both knew it was Blake who made the money.

Their grandfather had bought the property nearly a century before. At first he'd just kept on with cattle and sheep, but as his son, Blake's father, began to help out, they realised the land was good for farming, and planted wheat, sorghum and oats. They had a couple of milking cows as well, to save them always going into town for fresh milk. Blake had liked that things were mixed; it meant that he was rarely bored.

He turned up the radio. 'Campbell beat Masterton twenty-five to fourteen in one of the best games for 1999! Stay with us for more updates in an hour. Buy Hartigan's tyres, the region's best!'

He spun the wheel of the tractor, looking behind to check that the plough was properly aligned.

Now Cate was home, filling the house with her silent resentment. She barely spoke to them, but ran off into the hills or stayed in her room. It was like living with a teenager again, one that looked exactly like Eliot. Leonora didn't seem to notice it. If she did, she didn't care.

'Coming up next: Tumbin Primary School student Andrew Kearne comes second in the district's Mathematical Challenge.'

Usually, Blake's thoughts meandered through the broadcasts and he tuned in when something interesting came on, but today it was difficult to concentrate.

'Does it hurt?' Leonora had asked him a year ago, as he shifted in bed, unable to sleep.

'Yes,' he replied automatically.

'Which part?'

He couldn't answer.

'You can't keep this up, Blake.'

Her words stayed in the room, drifting into the corners of the pressed-metal ceiling.

He had ignored them, just as he had overlooked Leonora's pitying gaze as he tried to jump the motorbike into life after breakfast each day. Then, that evening when he bent to place the dogs' bowls of biscuits on the lawn, something gave in his side and he fainted.

'There's no tricking me, Blake McConville,' Leonora had said, perched on the edge of the hospital bed, her jeans stretched tightly over her thighs.

He'd forgotten the woman could read his thoughts, and reached for her hand, the soil of a day's gardening still beneath her nails. After the disappointment the kids had dished out to her, it wasn't fair.

The doctors arranged for him to be put on the list for a hip replacement.

'How long will we have to wait?' Leonora asked, voicing his own anxiety.

'At the least, a few months; at the most, a year. Depends when the specialist can come in from the city.'

The doctor left. They felt deflated. The room darkened with evening.

'You can't hack it for much longer, Blake.' It was both an observation and a threat.

'Charlie can help,' he said lamely.

Leonora snorted. 'Your brother's too bloody lazy.'

Blake turned the tractor again. The clouds were beginning to gather themselves, stacking in the sky. Soon they would become cumulonimbus, broody with rain.

That was six months ago, and since then the pain had dug its fingers in further. Some things he'd given to Leonora to do, such as heaving grey blocks of salt licks into the middle of the paddocks, or throwing the rubbish out at the tip in the gully. He and Charlie bought a quadrunner that could be turned on with a button rather than a jump.

Sometimes he did jobs he wasn't supposed to, like throwing bales of dried lucerne to the cattle. Although he nearly flaked, it meant he could recall his old father lifting the small, confused lambs without feeling chastened.

When the paddock was finished, crossed with neat, parallel lines, Blake switched off the engine and climbed down from the cabin. The effort left him sweating and he leaned back against the tractor tyre. If Leonora had seen him, she'd be scolding, 'Why do you have to be such a man all the time? It's ridiculous. Who's there to impress?'

It surprised him that she couldn't see it: the older, more acute pain that obliterated the one emanating from his hip. He limped to the ute and whistled for the dogs.

5

Rain clattered against the corrugated-iron roof. Cate lay on the pale-green sun lounge as she had when she was a girl, watching the tiny squares of gauze fill with water. In Sydney, at this time of the day, she'd be walking home after work through Centennial Park, watching dogs bound alongside their barely sweating owners. The collective effort of the Eastern Suburbs, she often thought, was to look cool at all times, even if the humidity was so thick you could cup it in your hands and squeeze out moisture. As she walked, she would automatically canvass the men jogging past, not for their compact torsos or strong legs, but for dark-brown hair and freckled skin.

Her gaze refocussed on the gauze. Clinging to it on the other side was the cream belly and feet of a green tree frog. Eliot, his hair plastered flat with rain, peered at it curiously. He stroked its damp back with his index finger, then carefully peeled it from the mesh and carried it to the apricot tree. It crawled over the rough bark and stopped, blinking.

Eliot smiled at Cate. 'It's safe, now.'

Cate stood abruptly, the rush matting bristly beneath her feet.

There was nowhere to go. If she spoke to her mother she would snap.

Two weeks earlier she'd come home from work to her apartment in Randwick. As she sifted through the impersonal collection of bills from her mailbox, she noticed a message blinking on the answering machine.

Quickly, she pressed play, but her shoulders sagged when she heard her mother's falsely cheerful voice. Unlike the rest of the family, Leonora persisted in the belief that they were still a unit.

Cate poured herself a glass of water and picked up the phone.

'Hallo, Nora McConville speaking.'

'Mum, it's me.'

'Hallo, darling —'

'I haven't got long. I've got work to do tonight.'

Her mother paused. 'We need you to come home.'

'Have you found him?'

'No, Catie. No. We want . . .' The silence lengthened. 'We're thinking of selling. We need to discuss our options.'

'Sell the farm? You're fucking joking, Mum —'

'Cate, please, listen to me —'

'Why do you want to sell?'

'Dad's hip is too bad. The waiting list is at least a few months and he can't really work —'

'Why didn't you tell me before? I could have got him moved up the list, or paid for private care. Besides, that's a stupid excuse. Charlie can manage, and you've got Mellor.'

'It's not just that.'

'What is it, then?'

'Everything.'

'That isn't what you would call a specific explanation.'

Leonora sighed. 'Even when his hip is fixed, he'll still be too worn out to work.'

'The hip should work perfectly, Mum. Otherwise, I can pay someone to do his work on the farm.'

'How much would that cost?'

'I don't know, less than what I'm earning. I could afford it. Why haven't you discussed this with me?'

'That's why I'm calling —'

'What about Eliot? What if he comes back and he doesn't have a home?'

'He's gone, Cate —'

'He has *not* gone —'

'You need to give up!'

'Fuck that for a joke, Leonora.' Cate slammed down the phone. She changed into her running clothes and headed up the road to Coogee Beach.

The air was muggy and salty. Having grown up inland, where the only bodies of water were those that were still, such as dams or swimming pools, Cate had been suspicious of the sea. She didn't like the insistent tugs of rips, or the danger of sharks. Gradually, though, she'd come to enjoy the feel of her feet against compacted sand, the ruffle of foam at her ankles and the gentle, briny air. Now, instead of looking for snakes as she ran, she watched for embedded shards of shells and the poisonous tendrils of bluebottles.

She ran one length of the shore and returned, then unlaced her shoes and banged them together to release sand from the soles. She waded in, waves nibbling her legs. Out at sea were the leaf shapes of surfers' boards and, beyond them, the bright lights of cargo ships.

Back at the flat, she phoned her father's sister Natalie, who lived in Melbourne. When they were kids, she and Eliot had only once visited their aunt. Cate had been awed by her fine brick house with its white porch and coloured glass windows that left red and green squares on the cream carpet in the afternoon. In Natalie's bedroom, a string of pearls hung from the corner of an ornate mirror on a stand. In the kitchen were plates with gilt edges and bowls patterned with roses. Cate and Eliot passed most of the time curled in cavernous armchairs in the living room, poring over the fresh-smelling, shiny books Natalie had bought them.

Always awake before anyone else, they would sit in the kitchen, waiting for her. Unlike their mother, she was chirpy in the mornings. Crisp and slick in her suit with her light-brown hair pinned into a French roll, she would make them warm Milos while her coffee machine heated. When the coffee was done, they would sit at the small kitchen table, discussing the dreams they'd had and laughing at their milk moustaches.

In the evening she came home wan and exhausted, disinclined to conversation. She went to bed early and read reports. Cate would pile pillows up and lean against her, reading her own books. She loved her aunt's rich perfume, her silky kimono, and the rise and fall of her tummy as she breathed.

There was a pile of books on the opposite side of the bed, on embroidery and beading, topped by a novel by Maeve Binchy with a picture of a woman in a white hat sitting by a lake.

'Aunty Nat?' Cate asked.

'Mmmm?'

'Those books aren't yours, are they? You hate sewing.'

'They're Veronica's.'

'Who's Veronica?'

Natalie's pen paused in its underlining. 'My friend.'

The only time they saw Natalie after their Melbourne visit was when she came to the farm. However, Blake disapproved of his sister, and the time between her visits became longer.

On the few occasions Natalie had visited them, her expensive perfume and wit made Leonora self-conscious. Leonora dressed in basic blouses and corduroy skirts and was forever dusting and vacuuming, hanging out sheets or bending over pots of boiling vegetables. Cate ignored the tension between them and went riding with her aunt, their laughter carrying through the still, dry air. When she came home, flushed and flicking her riding crop against her legs, springing on the heels of her boots, she averted her eyes from Leonora's reproachful gaze.

When Cate began university, she flew to Melbourne regularly for visits, but once Eliot disappeared, she stopped travelling.

The phone connected.

'Hallo?' Natalie said.

'It's me. Mum wants me to go home.'

'Yes, she asked me too.'

'Are you going?'

'We have to work out what to do. It's a partnership, after all.'

'I don't want to sell the farm, and I don't want to go back. There's too much memory.'

Natalie was silent. Cate braced herself.

'If you want to persuade them not to sell, it would be more effective if you did it in person. When was the last time you saw them?'

'Mum, when she came down three years ago. Dad, not since I left.'

'And you've not been back once in what, eight years? If you go home now, they'll be beside themselves.'

'Dad won't.'

'At the very least, though, he'll be pleased that Leonora's happy.'

Cate was caught out by Natalie's logic. 'I want you to be there.'

'I'm not taking sides, Cate.'

'But you'll have to, eventually, because we can't reach a decision without a consensus.'

Natalie laughed. 'Maybe you should have been a lawyer too,

Cate. I'll book a flight.'

Cate had hung up, feeling lighter.

Cate found Leonora's oilskin coat and a pair of gumboots in the laundry. Stepping outside, the intense smell of a nearby lemon verbena mingled with the coat's chemical odour. She tilted her head, rain slipping down her cheeks.

6

Finch switched off his computer and stepped through the French doors, flicking on the garden lights. They shone against the long curving leaves of the lilies. He lit a mosquito coil and pulled out a chair, its iron legs scraping over the pavers. It was often at this time of day, when Jack was out boozing and Oxford Street's traffic had petered away, that he wished for a cat or a dog. He never understood how his mother had borne the isolation when she wasn't working and he was asleep.

Smoke from the coil drifted upwards. Jack had asked him to the pub to meet the friends of his latest girlfriend.

'I've met enough women,' Finch said.

'You've had what, three girlfriends ever? And you're ready to give up?'

'Not every man needs sexual conquests to validate himself.'

Jack, offended, hadn't spoken to him until the next day. That was a record for Jack.

Insects flew in and out of the beams and his kentia palms clacked in the breeze. He saw the doctor's shapely legs stepping up the stairs to her consulting room, her calves heavy with muscle and her backside curving pleasantly against her brown woollen skirt. She wore a jumper with a wide-eyed face knitted into the back. It watched him as he followed her up.

'I like your jumper,' he said, as they reached the landing, air forcing itself in and out of his infected lungs.

She didn't answer, but smiled tiredly and closed the door behind them.

She was small and lean, only reaching his shoulder. Her hair was the colour of dark chocolate, as Aubrey's had been, and her pale skin was dusted with freckles, her arms stippled with moles. Her eyes, a strange greenish-yellow, looked at him intelligently as she questioned him about his medical history.

'Take off your shirt,' she said, then stood behind him and placed her small hands on his chest. 'Sorry, they're cold. Breathe in.'

He inhaled against her firm palms, then she tapped his back.

'I'm listening to see how hollow it is. If there's fluid, it sounds dull.' As she spoke, he felt her breath against his skin.

'You can put your shirt back on. It's pneumonia,' she said, sitting at her desk.

As she typed a prescription for antibiotics, Finch admired the line made by her spine curving down to her buttocks. She turned to the printer and he glanced down at his hands.

Then she asked, 'You wouldn't happen to be from Tumbin, would you?'

'Near there. My mother lived in Kynidia, but I was at boarding school in Sydney from age six. Why?'

'A woman in Tumbin with your surname lived next door to my brother's friends. Billy and Russell Wakeley. She was married to a man who worked in the mines.'

'Carlotta Accorso and Dougie Nelson – my aunt and uncle.'

Her expression became keen, a hound pricking its ears.

'Small world, huh?' he said.

'Yeah.' She quickly rose and opened the door.

'They must work you hard in this place,' he joked as he stepped past, catching a mouthful of her sweet perfume. 'You look like you could do with a decent kip.'

She shook her head, attempting a smile. 'It's chronic insomnia. Sometimes doctors can't even solve their own problems.'

'That inspires me with confidence.'

Her smile widened, becoming more real. 'You'll be fine.' She closed the door.

The crickets began their songs for the night. Finch went inside to find a beer.

It was three in the morning when Jack crashed through the front door.

'Shhhh!' he whispered loudly. A girl tittered.

Jack, noticing the line of light beneath Finch's office door, repeated, 'Shush! He's working.'

Shoes rang in the hallway until they were dulled by the floorboards in the kitchen. Finch heard the fridge's seal unsticking as the door was opened, then the clink of bottles.

He and Aubrey used to come home like that and fuck on the kitchen table. Her thick hair ran through his hands like liquid. She spent a great deal of money, she said, to get it looking like that. When she left for England, the house was so lonely he asked Jack, an old mate from Brisbane who'd just landed a job in Sydney, to move in. With his ball scratching and slovenliness, Jack quickly dispelled the scent of perfume trapped in the couch. Finch learned not to expect vases of oriental lilies on the hallway table, but rather pizza boxes leaking grease onto his polished floorboards. Instead of Aubrey closing the door gently before breakfast to buy coffee for them from Café Brioso, there were random girls with messy hair and smeared make-up sneaking out.

Jack led the girl up to his room, her laughter fluttering down the stairs. The floor creaked beneath their unsteady feet. Soon it would be the bed, and it would last six minutes precisely. It never surprised Finch that the girls left so early in the morning, stilettos dangling from their hand as they waited on the kerb for a taxi.

Finch had loved it when Aubrey straddled him, hair slipping over her breasts, but she liked haste and drama, forcing him to be rough. Not like the year when he was seventeen and he'd locked himself and the new geography teacher in the stationery room at school, boning her hard and quietly.

Finch flicked through a report, emailed to him from the headquarters in Holland, on the successful salvaging of a container full of whitegoods off the coast of Japan. He worked for a maritime emergency response service and was on call for two weeks at a time, waiting for the adrenalin hit of a collision. If a ship ran into difficulties, it was up to him to work out how to salvage it and the cargo by using his engineering and naval architecture background, logistics, and a healthy dose of common sense.

Jack grunted furiously in the room above, then stopped. Finch grinned with relief, until the silence crept under the door and settled around his shoulders.

7

Leonora woke to the calls of a pair of crows in conversation, and sparrows twittering in the banksia rose swathed around the tank stand. Blake slept on beside her, twisted at an awkward angle to relieve his pain.

She remembered Cate, and sat up. If her daughter was awake, she might like a cup of tea. She buttoned up a blue blouse and pair of jeans that were soft from years of wear, and pulled on her tattered sandshoes.

Cate's door was open, the bed empty. Leonora checked Eliot's room. The bed sheets were drawn tight and flat.

Leonora breathed sharply, pulling morning air into her lungs. She returned to Cate's room and noticed her cotton pyjamas on the floor and roll-on deodorant on the marble-topped dressing table. Her daughter was out running, then.

She sank onto Cate's unmade bed and picked up the frayed teddy bear caught among the covers. Often, she had sat and sniffed that bear to find some trace of Cate's scent, though it had been years since her daughter had held it. Now it smelled sweet, probably from Cate's moisturiser.

She peered into Cate's open suitcase, not daring to touch anything. There was a pile of neatly-folded T-shirts, two pairs of jeans, a stack of Bonds undies, also folded, and a bundle of white ankle socks. The items were all purely functional. Leonora wondered if this was how her daughter always dressed, or if she had only brought practical clothes to wear on the farm. It didn't look as if she had packed enough clothes for a long stay. Then again, perhaps she was a light traveller and was intending to wash them.

Leonora made a cup of tea and took it out to the verandah, which was shaded by a thick wisteria vine. Tank, the half-feral ginger cat, sat in the garden. He leapt up the stairs and, in a rare gesture of affection, rubbed his cheek against her jeans. Built like a tank, he picked off mice and rabbits like a military machine. He came home for food but spent most of his time prowling the paddocks.

Cate used to scoop him up and plaster his head with kisses while he struggled violently. When he was tired, he sometimes sat in her lap, but the rest of the time he bit anyone who interrupted his existence.

'I don't know why you like that cat so much,' Blake complained. 'He's a bastard.'

'He doesn't answer to anyone.'

'Except you,' Eliot sneered.

'Yes,' Cate replied, as if it were obvious.

Leonora liked having him around. He reminded her of what Cate had been like before Eliot disappeared. She reached to stroke him but he sauntered away.

From the bedroom, she heard Blake's groans as he slid himself from the bed.

The tea stung her lower lip. The kids' wide smiles had been identical, their skin stippled, even when they were tiny. She liked to joke that she'd found them on the banks of a creek one day and that sunlight, dappled by ti-trees, had fallen onto their skin and marked them. 'You were my two naked babies, nestled in the grass.'

Cate had pretended to spew, but Eliot beamed.

Leonora closed her eyes. When she finished her tea, she dragged the old, battered vacuum cleaner from the cupboard. It roared when she switched it on and Tank bolted across the lawn. She moved from room to room, though barely any dust had settled. When the children were small, she used to shout that they weren't to bring their dirt indoors, and they learned to leave their muddy gumboots in the laundry. She decided she wouldn't say anything, when Cate came back, about the grass seeds brought in on her shoes.

She began on the wooden floorboards of the hallway and the machine screamed from the hollowness beneath its mouth.

Blake walked past on his way to the kitchen.

'Good morning!' she called.

He didn't answer.

She pulled the machine into the lounge room. Feeling as vivacious as she had in the days after she first met Blake, she thrust the vacuum's head under the couch and pushed it back and forth with vigour.

8

Mellor drove his clapped-out ute to the southern end of the property. His dog Sparks barked in the tray, skipping over coils of fencing wire as he bounded from one side to the other. Mellor parked in the shade of a stand of gums. Sparks, who sometimes forgot he was old, leapt off, put his nose to the ground, and galloped after a trail.

Mellor hauled the circle of wire over his arm and dragged the wire strainers to the sagging fence. He snipped the loose wire of the fence, clipped the tool onto either end and worked the handle back and forth, drawing them together.

Years ago now, there'd been sagging fences like these around the fibro shacks in town. The government was starting to take Aboriginal kids away from their families in the late forties if they weren't sent to school. Even though they were excluded because they were out of town, Mellor's mother, Nance, was still worried. She wanted to move into town so that the kids could be educated and the authorities wouldn't trouble them. Mellor's parents understood that the land would always be there, but the kids might not. After the stories they'd heard, they couldn't risk it.

Stanley and Nance had rellies in town who'd been forced onto a settlement on the outskirts of Tumbin by the Parkinsons, the whites who'd squatted on their country from the 1850s. When they turned up, the Parkinsons paid the government for leasing the land, shot a few of Stanley's rellies and starved the rest by forcing them off their hunting grounds, so they had to go to the settlement to stay alive. Then the Parkinsons called the country their own place. Stanley's family had only been allowed to stay because Mr Parkinson, who'd been partial to Aboriginal women and must have been a bit sentimental, had kids growing up in the mob.

Blake's grandfather had bought the land from the squatters in 1905. He, and later Blake's father, were better than the Parkinsons and took care of Stanley's family, especially during the Second World War when labour was scarce. There were a couple of Italian POWs working with them too. They were all needed then, but after the war, the government wanted jobs and land for the returned soldiers. What with the worry about his son's education as well, Stanley decided they should join his rellies in the settlement.

Their shack was one of a number at the end of a gravel road. Families fitted as many as they could into the houses, then added lean-tos and tarps for the rest. During hot summers, dogs sprawled in the shade, panting and snapping at flies, while kids shrieked and jumped into the nearby river.

Mellor, longing for evenings by a fire and the fresh smell of wind, walked the streets after dark. He listened to lizards slipping through the grass and mice scuttling beneath houses, but the sounds were thin compared to the mass of call, answer, chirring and warning in the bush.

One evening he'd walked through the front door and found Carol, his father's cousin, in tears at the kitchen table. His mother jerked her head towards the bedroom. Mellor sat on his bed, head bowed, listening through the flimsy walls.

They'd come in a shining black car. Carol, peeling potatoes onto the newspaper at the table, didn't notice the silence until a door slammed. She glanced out the window, saw the car and shouted to her daughter. Mary, who was too young to be at school, had never heard such sharpness in her mother's voice. She came running. Carol shoved her in the cupboard among the pots and pans and told her to keep quiet.

The men looked Carol up and down and walked through the rooms in their stiff wool suits, sniffing like foxes. The rooms were tidy, the potato peelings heaped on the newspaper and she'd wiped down the benches, but then they opened the cupboards.

'What's this?' they asked, when they opened the last door and found Mary, her eyes huge.

'That's Mary, my littlest. We was playing hide-and-seek before you came. Come here, Mary.' The girl jumped out. Carol held her tightly.

'What kind of mother are you, Mrs Spencer, to let a dirty little girl play among the cooking vessels?'

'She's not dirty!' Carol said, but her voice shook.

'Even with all the washing in the world, you'd never get her clean.' The man who spoke had blue eyes, hard as glass. 'Mrs Spencer, you aren't fit.'

They pulled the little girl away from Carol. Mary, her eyes big and wild, screamed like she were being cut with a knife.

Mellor had pushed off his shoes and crawled under the blankets of his bed, not wanting to hear anymore.

'She was my last baby. I can't have no more. The doctor says I'll bleed.'

~

Holding the strands in one hand, Mellor cut a piece of wire, hooked it through the loops and tried to twist it all together, but the wire was too stiff and wouldn't yield. The strands sprang apart and one gouged his palm.

Mellor swore, grabbing his wrist. Blood welled out, bright and swift. He pulled a handkerchief from his pocket and knotted it around the tear. He gritted his teeth, staring at the heat haze that blurred the horizon. When the pain receded to a heavy throb, he picked up the strainers again.

9

Cate slept fitfully through the day, curtains drawn against the light, and emerged in the kitchen after lunch. Leonora was at the table, tailing beans.

She beamed. 'Would you like me to make you a sandwich?'

Cate shook her head. 'I can do it myself.'

'There's a leg of roast lamb in the fridge, and tomatoes and lettuce.'

As Cate assembled a sandwich, she looked beyond the kitchen windows to the pool, as she had one morning in the weeks before her final school exams. She saw something black in the pool, flailing, and was unsure if she was awake, or still dreaming.

She was about to investigate when Eliot shuffled in.

'Why're you up so early?' she asked. 'It's six o'clock.'

'I dunno.' Eliot scratched his balls, wincing against the light. 'I woke up. I couldn't go back to sleep.'

She pointed out the window. 'There's something in the pool. It looks like a bird, but I don't think it is.'

Eliot squinted. 'Let's go outside.'

The grass beneath their feet was saturated with dew. Later, dry heat would pound against the lawn and Leonora would turn the sprinklers on.

Cautiously, they approached the pool. The creature, sensing their approach, flapped across the water.

'It's a bat,' Eliot said. 'It can't get out.'

'We'd better get the net.'

From under the decking, Cate pulled out the net attached to a long pole and handed it to Eliot. He lowered it into the water, pushing it across the surface until it reached the bat, now butting desperately against the side of the pool. He scooped it up and the animal shrieked manically, flapping its leathery wings.

'Where will I put it?'

'Under a tree. Then it can climb up and go to sleep.'

Swiftly, Eliot took it to a gum tree near the rockery and carefully tipped it out. The bat's mews softened. It shivered and shook off the water, blinking piteously.

It stayed there for a few hours. Eliot, anxious, wandered out to check on it. Eventually, it laboriously clawed up the trunk and suspended itself from the first limb it reached.

'It went to sleep,' Eliot said with satisfaction, coming into her room. Cate looked up, untangling herself from an algebra problem.

'Tonight it can fly back to the fruit trees,' he added.

'That's great, El.' She returned to her *x* and *y*. Eliot stood by the door, watching, then wandered back out again.

Now Cate took her sandwich to the table. Leonora peeled green spines from the beans and made a pile of curlicues on the table. She dropped the beans into a chipped, enamel bowl.

'You're very thin, darling,' she said.

'Don't start, Mum.'

Leonora split green flesh with her thumbnail. 'Did you have a good run this morning?'

Cate shrugged. 'I saw Mellor on the road yesterday.'

'How was he?'

'What's going to happen to him and the aunties if you sell?'

Leonora spoke carefully. 'We'll try and find someone who's willing to take him on.'

'Dad won't do that. He doesn't give a shit about Mellor. I doubt Charlie does, either.'

Leonora shredded roughly.

IO

The aunties sat on the couch, watching TV, a crocheted blanket over their laps, beers in their hands. The remains of their dinner of lamb chops and spuds lay on chipped plates at their feet. Kath, the eldest at seventy-seven, wore her favourite red cardigan that was unravelling at the sleeves, with a dark-blue house dress she'd found at the Salvos store in Tumbin. May, a year younger, grew her grey hair long and kept it in a plait. She had the same round figure as her sister, hidden in a loose brown sweater and a baggy black skirt that used to belong to Mellor's mum. Sparks slept close to the TV.

Mellor appeared in the doorway. 'You two orright? I'm going to do some reading.'

They nodded, but didn't move their eyes from the screen.

Mellor picked up the plates.

'Dog'll get these,' he muttered, taking them to the kitchen.

Sparks lifted an eyebrow when Mellor left, then jumped onto the couch between the aunties.

'Fleabag,' May said affectionately, pulling his ears.

Kath stared, unseeing, at the TV. Her head was full of stories that she couldn't tell. Sometimes she got so desperate she wanted to talk to Mrs McConville, but her bad eye made her unsteady and Mellor would never drive her there.

That afternoon he'd come home with his hand torn by fencing wire. As May cooked dinner, Kath swabbed the cut with Mercurochrome.

'How old is this stuff?' Mellor held the bottle close to his eyes, reading the peeling label.

''Bout as old as Rachel, bit less.'

She used to dab it on the kids' scraped knees when they came crying. It would stain Cate and Eliot's skin an ugly orange red, but on Rachel's it came up a deep crimson. Once, she came across them using it to paint patterns on Rachel's legs.

'Does it still work?'

'Dunno.'

She cut a strip of paster and placed it over the cut.

'Do you remember Dad's cousin Carol?' Mellor asked suddenly.

Kath carefully folded the leftover plaster back into the shoebox. 'Whose kid was taken?'

'Yeah.'

'She was never right in the head after. Why'd you ask?'

'I was thinking about it today. What might have happened to her little girl.' Mellor smoothed down the plaster. 'Thanks,' he added.

May was elbowing Kath.

'Shhh!' Kath hissed, then realised she was in front of the television and Sparks was farting beside her.

'You bin dreaming again?' May asked.

Kath rubbed her eyes. 'That dog stinks. What did you feed him?'

'Changing the subject again, Kathy.'

Kath shrugged and picked up the remote.

II

Charlie sat on Sally's dressing-table stool, rolling one of her perfume bottles between his palms, watching as she dressed for a County Women's Association lunch in Tumbin.

'Have you seen Cate yet?' he asked.

'No, she hasn't come up here. Nora says she's been out running at all hours.'

'Strange. I would've thought she'd come for the horses first thing.'

'Yeah.' Sally, in her bra and slacks, selected a lilac blouse from her wardrobe.

'Do you remember why she left?'

'She didn't want to be reminded of Eliot.'

'I thought it was the fight with Blake.'

'Don't know.' Sally took the perfume bottle from him and sprayed scent onto her wrists. She brushed her blonde hair with three quick strokes, then bent to the mirror and smoothed bright pink lipstick over her lips. 'I don't think you should get caught up in all that again, Charlie.'

'I never was caught up in it.' Charlie, scratching his beard, opened the drawer that kept his socks and fished out his tobacco tin.

'What're you doing?'

'It's just one,' he said, irritated, sliding open the door to the verandah. He sank into a director's chair that faced the hills, pressing a cushion behind his back.

A sense of guilt blew about Charlie like a bad smell. He'd intended to fix the windmill pump, but he never quite got around to it. Then Blake fixed it and he felt ashamed. He ordered lucerne for the cattle, but it was a few weeks too late and they had to move the cows from paddock to paddock to make sure they got enough feed. He couldn't be bothered with finding a wife until Sally, a divorcee, hassled him into marriage, and then it was too late for them to have children. She constantly harangued him about getting a financial planner.

'I'll call Jackson tomorrow,' he said.

'You idiot. Tomorrow never comes.'

What Charlie liked to do best was sit on the verandah and smoke, read the newspaper and dream about going to the Caribbean to watch Australia play cricket against the West Indies.

Lately, his cough had worsened and the doctor said to give up smoking. Sally, having watched Blake's hips crumble, didn't want her husband's lungs to go the same way. She hadn't confiscated his tobacco pouch yet but Charlie knew it wasn't far off. In the meantime, he had every intention of giving up.

He pinched the tobacco from its plastic pouch, lined it on the paper and nudged in a filter. Crows flew overhead and a breeze ruffled the eucalypts lining the driveway. If Sally didn't have the radio going he'd be able to hear the horses whickering in the noonday heat.

Sally wanted a house by the river. He knew which one; she mentioned it every time they drove past. It was encased by a wide verandah with a lawn bordered by twining roses. He supposed if they bought it they'd need an irrigation licence for the roses. Sally was full of wants.

As nicotine unfurled in his bloodstream, Charlie remembered sweeping down the floor of the shearing shed when he heard a motorbike engine. It was revved so loud he thought it was one of the neighbour's boys, who rode like hoons. It must have been late winter, for they were tending to the shears and wool press in preparation for shearing.

He went outside, surprised to see Cate on the bike, skidding as she braked.

'What's the rush, love?' he asked with good humour. 'Got a baby to deliver?'

'Where's Blake?' she demanded. He couldn't recall her ever having called her father by his Christian name before. It had always been 'Dad'. His smile died.

'With the shears.'

She strode up the stairs to the shearing floor, Charlie following cautiously. Light filtered through a grimy skylight, baskets of old wool sat in the corners and the wooden pens were smooth and waxy from years of sheep rubbing against them. The air was sharp with the smell of old sheep shit pushed between the floorboards.

His brother sat on an upturned petrol can, squirting lubricant into the joints of the shearing handpiece.

Cate thrust a sheaf of papers beneath his nose and demanded, 'What's this?'

Blake stared blankly at the papers.

'Paul Finley Agricultural College.' Cate was abrupt. 'Filled out in your hand, awaiting Eliot's signature.'

'I don't see what the problem is.'

'The *problem*, Blake, is that you expected him to go.'

'He wanted to go.'

'How do you know that?' she screamed, the suddenness of it more shocking than the sound. 'None of you ever let him be. You, Mum, the music teacher. You expected him to be a farmer – that's why you made us part of the partnership. Did anyone ever ask Eliot what he wanted?'

'What's there to be so angry about?'

'Maybe Eliot left because of this. Maybe you made him disappear.'

Charlie watched his brother's heckles rise, the way they did when he was threatened. He wondered if he should intervene.

'You think it's my fault that he left?' Blake put down the bottle of lubricant and stood. Next to his tiny daughter, he looked huge.

'He never wanted to go to fucking Ag school. You were always imposing on him —'

'Cate, I'm warning you.'

Charlie relished the soothing effect of the tobacco. He should have stepped forward, taken Cate's arm, and led her outside. Instead Cate continued to fire accusations, until Blake slapped her cheek so hard it was like a punch.

His daughter looked at him in disbelief, then walked out of the dim shed into the blinding day. By evening, she had packed and gone and Leonora was hysterical. As far as Charlie knew, Cate hadn't spoken to her father since.

Charlie crushed his cigarette out on his boot cap, as Sally had confiscated the ashtrays. His brother was so stupidly proud and his insecurities so many that he constantly wanted to assert himself. And Leonora, with her pervasive brightness, hadn't been able to see it all. It was only Charlie, having known Blake for more than half a century and standing outside their unit, who could see the depression that his brother kept tightly to himself.

12

Though she knew she'd be lucky to find anyone in Tumbin connected to the web, Cate drove into town to find internet access. Every night, when she was in Sydney, she checked and sent emails, placed missing-person advertisements and searched national and international newspapers for Eliot's name. Without that routine on the property, she was starting to get agitated.

Closer to town and the river were irrigated paddocks planted with rows of cotton bushes. It was the same road they once took to violin lessons. Cate heard Eliot singing in the back of the car.

'Jump down, turn around, pick a bale o' cotton.'

'Mum?'

'Gotta jump down —'

'Yes, Cate?'

'— turn around —'

'Did they make the Aborigines pick cotton?'

'— pick a bale o' cotton —'

'No, Cate.'

'Oh, Lordy —'

'Why, Mum? They did in America.'

'— gotta pick a bale a day —'

'Irrigation came here in the eighties. The Aborigines had rights by then.'

'Gotta jump down —'

'Shut *up*, Eliot!' Cate hissed.

He stopped.

'But they don't have rights,' she continued.

'They have more than they used to.'

'That doesn't mean they have the same rights as us, Mum.'

Her mother ignored this. 'Sing us another song, El.'

'Swing low, sweet chariot —'

'Not that one. How about the theme song to *Secret Valley*?'

Their violin teacher's name was Esmeralda Dickinson. They could never cram all the syllables of her name into their mouths so they just called her Mrs Emerald. She lived in a big house with a verandah dotted with pot plants that smelled of urine. Her mongrel did a circuit of them each morning, lifting his leg against the pots.

While they had their lessons, their mother went into town to buy groceries. Cate played first, and as she waited for Eliot to have his turn she explored the gardens, chased the mongrel and climbed trees. When Eliot came out, Mrs Emerald gave them a glass of milk and a piece of orange cake. Sometimes Cate asked, 'Do you have any chocolate cake?' but there was only ever orange. Then they went off to build fortresses in the stand of she-oaks out the back until their mother returned.

Before they were allowed to play outside, however, there were the duets.

It was Cate who asked if they could perform together. They were seven and eight, learning Grade One. Mrs Emerald dug out a simple version of 'Jack and Jill' and, to her astonishment, found that the children listened to each other's melodies so clearly, and played so empathetically, it seemed they were the same person.

When their mother arrived, ready for a cuppa and chat with Mrs Emerald, she was surprised to find the music teacher flushed and beaming.

'It's wonderful, Leonora! Come and listen.'

Leonora followed Mrs Emerald into the music room. Cate and Eliot turned their heads, waiting expectantly.

Mrs Emerald clapped her hands. 'Play it again, children.'

They looked at the music and, with the same unearthly intuition, wove the tune.

'Very nice, kids,' Leonora said, when they finished with an identical draw of their bows.

Mrs Emerald was red and pulling at the hem of her blouse. 'We must put you in the eisteddfod this year! It's magical.'

'Can we go in the pool now?' Eliot asked.

'Yes, off you go.'

After that, Leonora wrote a cheque for another hour of weekly tuition and her children began to blitz every eisteddfod in the district. Leonora's clippings book grew fat.

Eventually, Mrs Emerald wanted them to play in Sydney. Leonora refused.

'Why not?' Mrs Emerald protested. 'There could be a career for them. Eliot, especially.'

'They're too young for that kind of thing, and I don't want them to get ideas.'

'But that's how they grow, by stretching —'

'No, Mrs Dickinson.' Her tone shut the door on the conversation.

To Cate's surprise, the Tumbin Hotel had internet access. She sat before an ancient computer in the gloomy interior, a poker machine glowing luridly against the wall beside her.

She checked her emails for messages from the Red Cross and Salvation Army tracing services. As usual, there was nothing. She logged into the State Library and began her searches of the newspapers. Waiting for the results to appear, she glanced to her left, and saw the table at which she used to sit with Eliot and Russell. She saw the three of them around it after her final school exams.

Cate hadn't wanted to go to the pub that afternoon. She wanted to sleep, but Eliot had wagged school and was so cheerful she couldn't bear to disappoint him. As she downed her beer she was glad of the fuzziness it created. She didn't know what else to think about now that King Lear and his daughters were no longer there.

She leaned her back against the wall and closed her eyes. Eliot and Russell joked about some rugby player and laughed like they were twelve-year-olds.

'Another beer, Cate?' Eliot asked.

She opened her eyes, studying him. They'd always been skinny, with the same fine-boned features but, on the cusp of seventeen, Eliot was starting to fill out, his jaw and shoulders becoming broader. 'How many've you had?'

'Four. The coppers went to Kynidia so they won't come to check if I'm underage. Paddy knows, and he's friends with Dad.' He gestured to the barman.

'I meant, who's driving home?'

Eliot looked guilty.

'So this celebration isn't really about the fact that I no longer have to sit on my arse and cram for fourteen hours a day.'

'I'm sorry, Cate. I forgot to count.' He was stricken.

'Forget it.' Cate slumped against the wall. 'Just bring me a glass of water.'

Eliot went to the bar.

'You boss him around a bit.'

Cate focussed on Russell, irritated. 'What, and you don't do the same to your brother?'

She rubbed her sore eyes. Eliot arrived with the drinks. She had killed their humour but was too tired to care.

After Eliot had finished his beer, he gripped Russell's shoulder. 'I'll see you on the weekend, Russ?'

'Yeah.'

As they walked out, Cate sensed Russell's gaze still on them. She glanced back and was startled by its intensity.

On the computer, the clock icon finally stopped whirring. There were no results. Cate logged off and went to the bar to pay.

The publican came out of the kitchen. 'You McConville's daughter?'

'Yes.'

'Did you ever have news?'

'No. I'm still looking, though.'

'Shame. That'll be two bucks, thanks.'

Cate gave him a coin and nodded toward the computer. 'I'll probably come every couple of days to use it.'

'No worries. Probably the most action it's had in a while. Harry's the name, by the way.'

She shook his hand then stepped outside, the light so harsh it hurt her eyes.

13

As the sun struggled above the Moreton Bay figs, Finch jogged around Centennial Park. It was a damp morning and sweat mingled with drizzle on his forehead. There weren't many runners at that hour, so it was easy to recognise the doctor's small figure, even from a distance.

He sprinted until he was close to her and called, 'Doctor McConville!'

She whipped around. 'Do I know you?'

'Sort of. I'm Finchley Accorso. I visited you in the surgery. Three weeks ago. Pneumonia.'

Her calves were spattered with mud, her nipples erect from exertion.

'Clearly, you're better,' she said brusquely.

His eyes snapped to her face. 'I took the antibiotics.'

'They tend to have that effect.'

She turned to go, but he stepped towards her. 'Would you like to go out for a drink?'

The doctor's gaze slid away from his face and past his shoulder. Drops of moisture had beaded on her fringe. She wasn't wearing foundation and her nose was scattered with freckles.

'Only on one condition.'

'Sure.'

'Could you ring your aunt and uncle for me, and ask if they've heard anything about Eliot McConville or Russell Wakeley?'

'Yeah, I'll do that.'

'Meet me at the entrance of St Vincent's, eight o'clock on Thursday night.'

As she ran off, the cheeks of her buttocks bounced and her calf muscles flexed. Jack would have resented her archness, but Finch liked it. He headed back to the Paddington gates, deciding he'd put the coffee on for Jack when he woke.

As soon as he was home he picked up his address book beside the phone. The back had fallen away and the front, once covered in tartan cloth, was grey and shiny with grime. He pulled off the rubber band that held it together and opened the pages at 'N'. Here was Carlotta Nelson, his mother's youngest sister, an accident who popped out long after Grandma thought she couldn't have any more kids. There was fourteen years between his mother and her sister.

They'd sometimes visited Grandma while Carlotta was still living at home with her. To a nine-year-old boy, his aunt was frighteningly sophisticated with her soft brown hair, floaty kaftans and bubblegum.

'She won't stop chewing that effing gum,' Grandma complained. "No one's looking at you," I say to her. "We're in the middle of the frigging outback." "That's not the *point,* Mum," she says, and I say, "What is the bloody point?" And she goes off in a huff. Bloody teenagers.'

A few years later, Carlotta dyed her hair purple and cut it into a mullet.

'What do you think?' she asked when they met her at the front door in hot pink leotards and white legwarmers, still chewing gum.

'Um.' Finch was shocked by its spikiness.

'Don't ask him,' his mother intervened, 'he's just a boy. It's awful, Carlotta. You had such lovely thick hair. Now it's all gone.'

'I didn't ask your opinion. I knew what it would be.'

It was too early to call Carlotta, so Finch made coffee and put some aside for Jack, then sat on the verandah outside his bedroom, which overlooked the street. He figured Cate would have showered and would be on her way to the surgery.

Rain drifted, coating the tin rooves and slicking the leaves of the eucalyptus tree that had grown through the footpath, buckling the cement around it.

His mother, Sylvia, and Carlotta stopped speaking decades ago, after too many arguments. Sylvia, who was already pretty much estranged from the family, could never understand why, if she'd been able to bring up a son on her own in the sixties and send him to a private boarding school in Sydney, Carlotta couldn't divorce her coalminer husband and raise herself from the mire of Tum bin. It never seemed to occur to her that love might be the reason, although Finch did share his mother's dismay that the bright, sparkling young woman, with her pink plastic headbands and bracelets, had settled into such dullness.

At 9 a.m. he dialled Carlotta's number. After six rings, she picked up the phone.

'Hello?' She still had her father's Italian inflection.

'Carlotta? It's Finchley.'

There was silence.

'Sylvia's son,' he added.

'Finchley! It's been years!'

'I know, Carly, I know.'

Her questions tumbled out: what was he doing, was he married, how was his mother?

Finch's answers were broken by the interjection of the next question, and then Carlotta began a litany of the births, deaths and marriages of people he pretended to remember. It was forty minutes before he could ask about Eliot McConville.

'The McConvilles? You know Dad worked on their property for a couple of years?'

'When?'

'During the war. That's how we ended up out here. He was interred for being Italian in Victoria, and the McConville's needed labour, so he was shipped to the farm. Met Mum in town and married her.'

'*That* was the property? I never knew. I thought it was way down south somewhere.'

'Well, Dad died young and your mother was always pretending not to know us, so she probably never talked about it.'

Finch couldn't really remember his grandfather. He'd disowned Sylvia when she got pregnant out of wedlock, so Finch rarely saw him. He recalled a thick accent, a pair of hairy legs, and the smell of ripe tomatoes, which his grandfather had liked growing.

'What about Eliot McConville, then?' Finch asked.

'Oh, no one could forget Eliot. He disappeared. Never came back. The cops were involved, everyone. Lucky they had a bit of money, the family, they could keep looking for years. But nothing came up, ever.'

'When was this?'

'It was after you'd left, otherwise you'd have heard of it. I guess it was about five years ago, maybe more. Eliot used to come and play with the Wakeleys next door, but not often. He didn't like coming into town. It was too boring, I remember him saying that. He was real close to his sister. Say, why do you want to know?'

'I just met the sister. She works in a surgery up the road. I had pneumonia. She recognised my surname.'

'She was real bright, always in the paper for things she'd won. She's still putting missing-persons ads up.'

'Where are the Wakeley boys now?'

'Russell drives trucks – we haven't seen him for years. He had a kid, Johnnie, and sometimes the mother drops him next door. Billy works on the docks in Melbourne.'

Finch interrupted before his aunt could carry on for another hour. 'Carlotta, I've got to go. I'll call you again soon, okay?'

'Yeah.' She sounded disappointed. 'Don't leave it so long next time.'

'I won't, I promise.'

Finch hung up and noticed the front door was wide open. Jack must have been late for work again and rushed out. Finch checked the kitchen. The coffee lay untouched beside the stove. He drank it himself.

14

Auntie Kath and Mellor, drinking their tea in the grey light before dawn, heard a rhythmic slap against the road coming from the base of the hill. Mellor had heard it most mornings when Cate was at secondary school, and when she was home from uni for the holidays. She would head to the Falls, turn around and be back in half an hour.

'Blake's not happy, then?' Kath asked. She wore a woollen beanie against the chill, and wrapped her red cardigan tightly around her.

Mellor shook his head. At the machinery shed the previous day when they were bagging wheat, Blake had stood by the bagging machine, shifting his weight because of his bad hip. Blake's brother Charlie had sat on an upturned oil drum a little distance away, smoking.

'Seriously, Charlie,' Blake called. 'Does a smoko have to go for half an hour?'

Charlie stared, cigarette in hand, then stamped it out and took Blake's place at the machine. The muscles around Charlie's mouth were tight. Mellor carried bags of wheat into the shed and kept away.

'He's been telling me to do more and more,' he told Kath. 'I'd ask if one of my boys could come down but he'd take everything out on them.' He splashed the dregs of his cup onto the soil. 'Gotta get going. You right for food?'

'Yeah, plenty of tins there.' She pulled a loose thread in her cardigan sleeve, unravelling another line of knitting.

'Orright. I'll go to the shops tomorrow.'

Mellor clapped a hat on his head and started the motorbike. Setting down the hill, the tall eucalypts thinning out to empty paddocks, he thought again of his father's cousin Carol, who became forgetful after her daughter Mary had been taken from her. Mellor would run through her house to play with his other cousins, and Carol would be staring out the window, a dishcloth in hand. Eventually, she couldn't remember that she needed to eat, and died one night in her sleep.

His own mother, Nance, became paranoid. She made sure Mellor went to school every day, that he owned a uniform, his hair was washed, his face scrubbed. If he went outside to play, she sat nearby with a cup of tea or some mending.

He lasted three years. When he was twelve, he walked home after school with his friend Lizzie, who lived a few doors down, his head ringing from a day of jeers from white kids and the teacher's mocking because he couldn't spell or put sentences together. A group of boys followed, throwing stones and laughing. Mellor usually ignored them, but when one grabbed Lizzie's bum, he spun around.

It was Mick, a pimply boy who slapped Mellor's calves with a ruler whenever he walked past his desk in the classroom.

'What's your problem?' Mick whined. 'Who says there's a law against touching a black bitch?'

Mellor was strong for his age. He punched Mick in the jaw and Mick dropped into the dirt, moaning.

'Go!' Mellor shouted to Lizzie as the rest of boys crowded around him, brutally hitting and kicking.

His mother, waiting for him when he got home, hurried him into the broom cupboard. She didn't have time to wash the blood from his lips and brow.

The cops knocked at the door.

'You the mother of Mellor Powell?' they asked.

'Have you seen 'im? He was supposed to come home with his cousin after school. I'm flat-out frantic.'

'He's assaulted another boy. He'll be put away when he's found.'

In the cupboard Mellor sweated, his breaths shallow. The smell of blood in that tiny space almost made him choke. When he heard his mother shut the door after the policemen, he began shivering.

15

'Cate!' her aunt shouted when she saw Cate's silhouette behind the gauze door. Sally flung it open. She was of medium height, with dry, blonde hair held back from her face with a black satin headband. Like Leonora, she wore jeans, a blouse and riding boots, her lips painted shell pink.

'Come through. I'm just getting a cake out of the oven for dinner.'

The kitchen was cluttered with books, empty mugs and a vase of browning roses, the sink full of unwashed dishes. On the fridge, magnetised letters held up photos, bills and a handwritten thank-you note. Two windows looked out to an unevenly mown lawn bordered by oleanders.

The oven opened and closed, releasing its warm breath that smelled of cinnamon. The cake tin clattered as Sally dropped it onto the bench.

'What's your place like in Sydney?' she asked, handing Cate a bottle of wine from the fridge and two glasses. 'Nothing like this, I hope!'

On Sally's verandah, they settled into old directors' chairs that creaked beneath their weight. The day's heat was settling into dusk. Cate loved the view of paddocks reaching out to low, purple hills

'It's pretty small. Spartan.'

Cate thought of the calm sterility of her place in Sydney, with its double-glazed windows that kept out the whirr of traffic and shutters that shaded the rooms. In the bedroom, the white counterpane was drawn tight, the cream carpet unblemished. The plain kitchen was bare, all implements and containers kept in the cupboards.

The only life that beat in the flat was in the study. There, the windows were barred against intruders and a woolly cactus sat on the sill. Shelves of folders lined the left wall, *Eliot* printed on the spines of each. They were crammed with names and addresses of people she'd contacted over the last eight years, transcripts of conversations with case officers, and copies of posters she'd distributed to bus and taxi drivers. On the desk, a photo of Eliot sat beside her laptop.

Sally swallowed a mouthful of wine. 'It can't be easy for you, coming back.'

'It isn't. I missed him in Sydney too, even for those two years that he was still here.'

Although in the city there were new people to meet, interesting lectures on valvular heart disease or atopic dermatitis, and cafes and the harbour to explore, at the end of each day when she sat at her desk to read, Cate ached for Eliot's company. Sometimes she wandered the lamplit streets, staring at her reflection in shop windows to find him looking back at her. If she was still sad when she got back, she picked up the phone.

Once, Blake answered. 'Eliot's started taking cattle to the stockyards for me. It's about time I got a rest after all the work I put into you two.'

'Why is it that I never hear Mum say that kind of thing?'

'Mum's different.'

'No she's not. She's put in just as much, if not more, "work" into us than you have.'

'So this is what happens: you go to uni and become a feminist —'

'Since when has pointing out the obvious made someone a feminist? By that logic, you could be one too.'

Her father made a strangled noise. There was a rattle at the end of the line.

'Cate.' It was Eliot.

'El.'

'Dad's annoyed.'

'So am I.'

'He said he was joking.'

'I'm so amused.' She heard him trying not to laugh, and smiled. 'Do you like going to the stockyards?'

'I don't mind. There's some all-right blokes.'

'You don't have to be a farmer, Eliot. You don't have to do what Dad tells you.'

'He doesn't tell me anything.'

'Suggests, tells – they amount to the same in his book.'

There was silence.

'Come and visit me, El. In Sydney.'

'Don't like big cities. You know that.'

'I'll be with you all the time. You might like it – you won't know until you come.'

He paused. 'I'll think about it.'

When she hung up, Cate tried to imagine him, tall and thin, directing cattle off the truck, the smell of dust whirling into odours from the sewage treatment plant down the road. It was a waste of talent when she thought how, when they played, their music was like watching richly coloured birds in flight.

~

Cate refocussed on her aunt on the verandah, whose face was almost in darkness.

'Do you want to leave, Sal?' Cate asked.

'Yes, I'm sick of it here. It's too far from town.'

'What about your horses?'

'Figure we're getting too old for them.'

She had almost finished her wine. Cate hadn't had more than a few sips.

'We've a lot weighing on you, Cate.'

'I know that, but Eliot needs a place to come back to.'

'So do we.'

'This is good enough, isn't it?'

'Not anymore.' Sally voice was hard.

'What if we don't sell?'

'That isn't an option,' Sally said briskly.

Cate refilled Sally's glass.

16

Blake lowered a piece of rope, weighted with a stone, into the well beneath the windmill. As it descended he gazed at his distant reflection in the black water. His children were nothing like him; they were their mother through and through, from their green eyes and dark hair to their quick walk. Even when their laughter had rippled from room to room, he couldn't tell if it was his wife's or his children's.

Blake's head pounded. He pulled the rope up, measuring the length before he reached the damp, frayed end, and left it in a bundle beside the windmill. Once he would have taken care to neatly coil it up, but now he limped to the quadrunner. It was a long ride back to the house and pain reached into the roots of his teeth, but the end of the day was always sweet, coming home to the house that smelled of Leonora.

Her lips had attracted him first, when he was introduced to her at a party in someone's shearing shed near Bromley. They made a small, neat bow as she listened to the friend explaining who he was, then stretched into a wide smile. He'd talked to her all evening amidst the increasing din, ignoring lewd gestures from his brother and mates.

It was this – her conversation – that he came to delight in, as well as her neat figure, trimmed by nights of social tennis, and the way she showed her affection so impulsively and openly. He flew into her dialogue, finding comfort in the sounds of her words.

Later that night he kissed her, and her mouth tasted of champagne and sugar.

After a year of country dances, picnics by rivers and a trip to the wineries where they'd slept in separate hotel rooms, Blake had said, 'I don't think I can offer you much.'

Leonora shrugged. 'I know it sounds like something out of Mum's novels, but if I'm with you, I'll be happy.'

He brought her back to the property and she began planting: the endlessly green lawn, the orchard, a rockery in which cacti nestled, the liquidambars whose leaves never turned well in autumn, but instead dried, half-brown, and fell.

Now, the green lawn rose before him. He drove into the garage and switched off the engine, enveloped by the silence. Once – it seemed not so long ago though it was surely a good twenty years – his kids would have rushed out, breaking the silence with their cries of delight.

Wincing, Blake lifted his leg over the quadrunner and thought about pouring his first brandy for the evening, its sharpness kicking the roof of his mouth.

17

Finch ran past the scaffolding for the Moonlight Cinema in Centennial Park, bare and desolate in the bright light of noon. He and Aubrey had often wandered down there with a picnic rug and plastic champagne glasses, striving to hear the film above the whine of cicadas, the air sharp with the scent of Aerogard. Aubrey would lean against him, her long hair out, silky from expensive hair products.

He'd been running around the park at different times every day, canvassing its perimeter and tarmac paths, but Cate never appeared beneath the Algerian oaks, nor among the paperbarks, as he willed. After running for an hour, he went home and sat on the balcony in a low-slung canvas chair, a bottle of beer in hand, the *Sydney Morning Herald* stretched across his lap. Absently, he scratched a callus on his toe against a nail that had popped up from the boards. The afternoon gathered up the city's heat and pressed it against his skin. Slow breezes drifted in from the harbour and half-heartedly rustled the overgrown gum tree. He concentrated on the article before him, but had to read the opening paragraph three times before he recognised what it was saying.

Jack turned on his CD player and *Metallica* blared. A magpie rustled out of the gum tree in fright.

'Jack!' Finch shouted.

His housemate lowered the volume. Finch finished his beer, folded up the paper and picked up the *Good Weekend*. Jack came into his bedroom, holding up two shirts.

'Which one?' he asked.

Finch peered through the door to his room. 'I can't see. Come into the light.'

Jack stepped onto the balcony in black jeans and a singlet. 'This one,' he proffered a plain white shirt. 'Or this one.' It was grey with purple stripes.

'They're both terrible. Get something out of my cupboard.'

When he realised Finch wasn't joking, Jack's face fell. He slid open the cupboard door. 'Why don't you come with us?'

'Thanks, but I'll be right.'

Jack flicked through the shirts. 'It's that woman, isn't it?'

Finch turned the page of his magazine, skipping over 'The Two of Us'.

'Wear the dark-blue one, Jack. It suits you.'

'Poofter.'

'I've just got good taste.'

'Yeah, in women too.' Jack found the shirt and pulled it out, surprised. 'It doesn't even need ironing.'

He tugged off his singlet and pulled on the shirt. 'Why do you bother? There are hundreds of women out there who'd want you. You do the vacuuming, and with a body like that —'

'Now who's the poof?' Finch said snidely.

'Seriously, Finch.'

'Yes, seriously, I don't want to talk about it.'

He lifted the magazine. Jack, dismissed, left the room and turned his music up again.

Once Jack had gone, having first returned to Finch's room to make liberal use of his cologne, Finch cooked a piece of snapper and opened a bottle of merlot. He turned on the telly to watch the rugby, but after a while he no longer heard the commentary, nor recognised the players running across the field. Instead he saw the doctor's yellow-green eyes, her hair falling down her back like Aubrey's.

He filled his glass again. The crowd was screaming; someone had scored a goal. Abruptly, he turned off the TV and went to the study. It was dark now but he didn't switch on the light. Instead he fired up the computer and stared at the garden.

The computer screen flickered to life and Finch, sinking into his chair, opened the most recent file of his boat. Although he owned a clapped-out yacht he'd bought cheaply from a friend's dad and fixed up, he dreamed of building his own. He zoomed in on the hull and copied the part into a new file. For a while he was occupied, shifting the angle of the bow as it fell away, but the way Cate's skirt brushed against her calves broke his concentration.

'Damn!' He saved the document and rubbed the frown lines from his forehead.

The Thursday after meeting Cate in the park, Finch waited for her at the entrance to St Vincent's hospital, his spine cold from leaning against a lamppost. As she walked into the over-bright reception room and waited for the automatic doors to open, he was taken aback by the strain on her face. At first he thought it was just that her dark hair was pulled back, and her white blouse sucked colour from her skin, but as they walked up to Betty's Soup Kitchen on Oxford Street he found that even her glimmers of humour from the surgery had disappeared.

'Where would you like to eat?' he asked.

'I don't care.'

This place was the closest and most comforting he could think of. She chose the first thing on the menu, a pumpkin soup, and drank the expensive sauvignon blanc he'd bought at the bottle shop as though it were cordial.

He piled sausage, mashed potato and peas onto his fork, and asked. 'What do you do on the weekends?'

'I run. Usually I work at the hospital. Sometimes I go to a gallery or to the shops. Not very often, though.'

'Do you read?'

'A little. Not much.'

'Friends, lovers, skeletons in the closet?'

'No. No knights in shining armour, either.'

Finch was reminded of slaters that crawled among the bark chips in his garden. When disturbed, they retracted their legs and curled up into a tiny, tight ball. Any other man would have had second thoughts, but each time Finch contemplated retreat, he remembered the loneliness of those bars with the girls sparkling like gems, too cold to touch. There was warmth in Cate; he could sense it, like sonar.

He tried again. 'Where do you like to go out?'

'I don't.'

'You don't do anything for kicks?'

'No.' She swirled the soup with her spoon.

'My aunt,' he ventured.

Cate looked up, alert. Her eyes had darkened to a deeper green in the dim light. 'Did she have any news about the Wakeleys?'

'Russell drives trucks and they haven't seen him for years. Billy's on the docks in Melbourne. Did you know them well?'

'I saw a bit of Russell,' Cate said quietly. 'He befriended us.'

'Your brother – it happened after I left the area. My aunt wanted to know if . . .'

'If I found him? No.' She returned her gaze to her soup.

Instinctively, Finch touched her hand, but she flinched. Carefully, he picked up his knife and fork again. In the silence he heard a waiter stacking plates. A man sat against the wall, smiling at a message on his mobile phone.

'And what do you do, Mr Finchley, on your two weeks off, aside from running each morning and the gym three nights a week?'

He looked up from his plate, triumphant. There was light in her eyes, her lips curled into a small smile.

'I have a yacht, so I sail when I can. Sometimes I go bushwalking.'

'Do you dance? Go out? You don't drink much.'

'No. I'm too old for that.'

'Thirty-six? I hardly think so.'

'How do you know my age?'

'It was in your medical record.' She bit her lip, showing her even teeth. Finch followed her mouth down her long neck to the smooth skin of her cleavage. Her hair was longer than since he saw her last, and she smelled of the rich, dense scent of roses.

Soon, though, the conversation limped and faltered. Eventually, Cate said, 'I'm exhausted. I have to go home.'

Outside, he flagged a taxi and kissed her cool cheek.

He walked back up Oxford Street, past the shops with their garishly lit mannequins, mute and alone.

'How'd it go, mate?' Jack called in his Queensland drawl when Finch switched on the hallway light, shutting the front door behind him. The house smelled of stale pizza, and from the living room came the excited pitch of a commentator. Finch put his keys beside the empty vase on the hallstand.

'C'mon, ya bastards!' Jack yelled.

Finch went into the lounge and sat heavily beside Jack on the couch.

'I told ya, she's a nutter. You need someone simple. Uncomplicated.' Jack passed him a beer and his pocketknife. 'Broncos are winning. Fifteen to nil.'

Finch prised the lid off the beer, listening to the bubbles hiss and flatten.

18

'My mind's not working,' Cate complained, as she sat the table with the crossword and a cup of tea.

'I'm not surprised.' Leonora, energetically filing her nails, was tart. 'What with all that exercise. It's not normal.'

Cate ignored this. 'What's "an encampment for the night"? Seven letters, third letter is "v"?'

'*Bivouac*', her mother replied promptly, dusting her fingers and reaching for the clear nail polish.

Cate studied the crossword grid. 'I'm not sure how to spell it. Can I have the dictionary?'

Leonora pushed the fat volume across the table. Cate found the word, arrested by its etymology. It came from the German word *Beinwache*, or 'watching or guarding', from *bei*, meaning 'near' and *wachen*, or 'watch'.

As she pencilled the word into the grid, she was pulled back to the recreation centre by the lake outside Kynidia.

Leonora kissed Cate and Eliot. 'Be good, kids. Play well. I'll see you at the concert in a week, okay?'

Left in the spring day with its deceptively hot sun, they sat on the edge of the verandah of the dorm, legs dangling, watching kids coming in with their instruments. Some of the cellos were bigger than the children themselves. A breeze brought the marshy smell of the lake.

Before dinner they lined up outside the mess hall to be divided into groups. They were eleven and twelve, and many of the kids seemed to be younger. An adult marked them off, ten at a time, and they shuffled along. The woman's hand stopped after Cate. Eliot stepped forward, about to follow, when the woman said, 'You don't want to go with all those girls, do you?'

He halted. Cate turned back, unsure whether to say anything. Eliot glanced from Cate to the woman. He didn't know who to please. He stepped back, and the woman continued counting.

It was the first time they had been apart. The mess hall was loud, and amid the reverberations Cate lost orientation. Her mashed potato and peas were inedible, the gravy congealing. Across the room, Eliot pushed food around his plate with a fork. Cate looked away.

Any reserves of courage they had left curled up like dead leaves when they saw girls were separated from boys in the dorms. Eliot picked up his bag and violin case, which he had left beside Cate's bed, and went to the boys' dorm.

Before lights out, a narrow-lipped woman showed the girls how to make and remake their beds so there were no ends of the sheets showing. If they weren't folded properly in the morning, they wouldn't go to breakfast.

The woman chose a small, round-faced girl to help her demonstrate how to fold, but the girl was so intimidated by the woman's abruptness that she went bright red and became too flustered to listen. Her mistakes made the woman even sharper.

When the lights were turned out, Cate lay awake in her perfectly-made bed in the long echoing room, listening to water birds crying out across the lake.

In the mornings they practised, learning to play in an orchestra, which few country kids had had the chance to do. Cate listened for the unbending lyricism of Eliot's violin but she couldn't find it.

A few days into their orchestral practice, a teacher finally noticed their physical similarity and how they gravitated towards one another after packing up their instruments. She placed them together. Soon they were leading the violins, their sound so sonorous that the conductor glanced their way, astonished.

In the afternoons they were given activities to do: abseiling, archery, sailing on the lake. Cate's equilibrium returned as she bounced down the rock face, the smell of gum blossoms hazy about her. Later, she laughed as a boy fell from their yacht into the muddy lake. Eliot, however, hung back, pale with shyness.

The night before the camp ended, there was a bivouac to another lake. They walked through the bush for more than an hour, sweating and thirsty. Although they wore hats, light reflected from the leaf litter beneath their feet, making them squint.

The sun was going down as they arrived and erected tents. They collected sticks for a fire and put a pot of water on to boil to make soup for dinner. A small boy with hair that fell into his eyes haphazardly chopped carrots. Cate, following orders from their leader Mr Martin, a friendly man with a lisp, tore open packets of minestrone flavouring and tipped them in. As the water bubbled and foamed, she heard a familiar pattern of sound. Her hearing, after years of listening to Eliot's violin, was acute.

She rose, brushing her knees. It was unmistakeably her brother's sobbing.

'Are there other groups here today?' she asked Mr Martin.

'Yes, two. A bit further down.'

'I think my brother's in one of them. Can I go to see?'

The man hesitated, then nodded. 'Be back here in ten minutes.'

Cate sprinted along the rim of the lake, the ground uneven from the dried imprints of cows' hooves.

Eliot was standing between two tents. An older girl, whom Cate recognised as a saxophonist, had her arm around him. She peered anxiously into his face.

'Eliot!' Cate called.

His head jolted up. He broke away from the girl and rushed to Cate. She grabbed him and held him tightly. His body shook as he cried.

'What happened?' she asked.

'Nothing.'

The saxophonist came up. Cate repeated the question to her and the girl shrugged. 'He just started crying.'

The leader of Eliot's group, a muscular, sunburnt man, approached.

'Who're you?' he asked.

'Eliot's sister. I'm in the next camp along. Why's he upset?'

'I don't know. First I've seen of it. Eliot, what's wrong?'

Eliot shook his head. The tears had stopped and he wiped his nose. They wouldn't get anything out of him now. When disturbed, he stuck to his rock like a mollusc.

'Could I please stay here tonight?' Cate asked the man.

He lifted his eyebrows in surprise, looking in the direction of Cate's camp.

'No, it's too difficult. We'd have to get you over there, explain to Mr Martin and come back with your gear, and it's getting dark. In fact you ought to go now or you won't be able to see your way.'

Cate stared. His eyes flickered under her hostility but there was nothing more that she could do. She was only twelve.

She rubbed Eliot's arm. 'It's just one more day, El, then we can go home.'

He nodded, staring at his feet.

'I'll look after him,' the saxophonist offered.

'Thanks.'

Cate ran off, her feet hitting the ground heavily.

They put out the fire and turned off the gas lamps at eight o'clock. Cate shared her tent with a stocky girl who played the trumpet. The girl fell asleep immediately, but Cate could only doze, waking each time she heard the water birds' cries.

Eventually she sat up and pressed the light on her pink Swatch watch. Eliot had one the same, in blue. It was 11.30 p.m. Silently, she pulled on a jumper and found her shoes. She carefully unzipped the tent and crept out to the eskies. There was a torch lying beside them for the kids who'd washed the dishes after dinner.

Cate crept along the edge of the lake. The moon was almost full, showering the ground in milky light. After a few metres she switched on the torch and moved more steadily.

She woke Eliot by unzipping his tent flap and tugging at his sleeping bag. When he rolled over she shone the torch beneath her chin so he knew who she was. She waited, and in a minute he was outside. She took his hand and led him out of the camp, further along the lake.

Cate hoped for a slab of rock to sit on but it wasn't the right sort of country. They found a smoother part of the shore where mud had dried. A breeze waved the smell of brackish water into their faces.

'What did you have for dinner?' Cate asked.

'Some kind of minestrone soup.'

'Same here. Except the boy put in too much Vegemite. It didn't taste very good.'

Eliot snorted.

Two herons flew past. Crickets jumped and whirred in the wiregrass behind them. The lips of fish touched the lake's surface, spreading circles. Cate and Eliot listened to each other's breathing, then curled into one another on the dry, cracked earth and fell asleep.

They were woken by shouting. 'Hey, you two, wake up!'

They blinked. The sunburnt man and Mr Martin, who no longer looked friendly, were standing over them, surrounded by a handful of kids.

'We've been looking all over for you!' the sunburnt man barked. 'If we hadn't found you I'd have lost my job.'

Cate stood, angrily rubbing sleep from her eyes. 'We would have made it back.'

'What, to the dorms?'

'Yes. You showed us how to read a map and use a compass, didn't you?'

Eliot scrambled up and took Cate's hand

'That's enough,' lisped Mr Martin, his speech thick with distress. 'We've wasted too much time looking for you. Let's get moving.'

Sullenly, Cate and Eliot followed the men and children back to their camps.

After the performance for parents that afternoon, there was a barbeque by the water. They met their mother, violin cases in hand. Leonora wore her straw hat with flowers and a dress in a noisy, blue print.

Eliot, tired and wan, had folded into himself. 'Mum, can we go home now? I don't want to stay for the barbecue.'

'Don't be silly. It was a lovely performance. We need to thank your teachers.'

'What for?' he returned. 'They were all horrible.'

'He's right, Mum. No one here likes children.'

Leonora looked from one child to the other, disconcerted.

'Nonsense,' she declared. 'You played so well, you couldn't possibly have found it so bad.'

She stalked off to the teachers.

'Mum doesn't know anything about music,' Eliot said.

Dejected, they lined up in the queue for their sausage sandwich.

19

'For God's sake, would you just take the bloody painkillers! If you sleep better at night, it gives your body a chance to rest.'

'Shut up, Leonora, I'm sick of it —'

'Not as much as I am, I can tell you.'

Cate sat on the verandah with a beer, listening. Her dinner of roast pork sat heavily in her stomach. If Eliot had been with her, they would have rolled their eyes at the bickering. Without him, Cate found it difficult to ignore.

One winter, they had sat before the TV with mugs of milky strawberry Quik heated in the microwave. Waiting for *Doctor Who* to come on, they tuned into the argument in the kitchen.

'I'm fed up with those blacks going to and from Mellor's. They're an eyesore,' Blake spat.

'What do you expect them to do? They're his rellies. How is it any different from us visiting Sally?'

'There's fifteen thousand of them buggering up the roads, that's how. I think Mellor should move.'

'But I *need* Jocelyn!'

'I didn't say "leave", I said "move".'

'Where to?'

'The bottom of the hills.'

'That's crown land. It's illegal.'

'Not quite, Leonora.' Blake was patronising. 'Up to the fence, the land is ours. Mellor can live there and his rellies can take the back road on the other side of the fence. If they wreck that road, it's the council's job to fix it.'

Eliot picked the skin from the surface of his Quik and draped it over the side of his mug.

'That's disgusting, Eliot,' Cate said.

'It's better than drinking it.'

Cate contemplated her pink milk, then did the same.

'Dad's not very nice sometimes, is he?'

'That's an understatement.'

'Especially when Mellor's mob are good to us.'

The theme music for *Doctor Who* came on and Eliot became fixated by the telly.

Mellor took Blake's orders to decamp without demur. There was a cottage already half built at the new site and Leonora, feeling guilty, helped Jocelyn transplant her vegetables.

Two years later, Jocelyn asked, on Mellor's behalf, if his two elderly aunts could live with him.

'Not more bloody boongs!' Blake shouted to Leonora.

'You can't leave two old ladies in town with no one to look after them. That's just wrong.'

'You watch,' Blake ended the argument, 'more of them will come and it'll be your fault.'

Somehow, however, Leonora convinced him to build another shack beside Mellor's, and the aunties moved out.

~

The screen door to the verandah banged. Leonora came out with a shandy.

'Your useless father,' she complained, dropping into the chair next to Cate, 'never listens to me.'

'He doesn't listen to anyone, Mum.'

'The pain makes him irrational. I used to be able to talk sense into him. Now it's hopeless.'

Cate looked at her mother's lined face, the creases around her mouth. 'Do you ever hear how the aunties are getting on?'

'Who? Sally?'

'Kath and May. Mellor's aunties.'

'No. Sometimes he takes Kath into town, though she can't get out of the ute. She might have cataracts. I know one of them can't see well.'

'I should go and visit them.'

'That sounds lovely, dear.'

Cate bit back a retort to her mother's saccharine adjectives, and drank her beer. Moths circled the outside lamp and the still air was sweet with the dusky smell of Leonora's Balmoral roses.

'The garden's flourishing, Mum,' Cate ventured again.

'Thank you, darling.'

This time, Cate smiled.

20

Cantering through the paddocks, Cate was invigorated by the rhythmic thumping of Biscuit's hooves, the lurch and soar as they leapt fences, the wind cooling sweat on her forehead. When the paddocks ended at the creek, she dismounted. She let Biscuit crop the fine grass beneath the ti-trees and, after checking it for sticks and ants, lay down in it.

She closed her eyes and she was thirteen again, Eliot lying next to her, brushing the back of his hand over the moist grass. He pulled a Kit Kat from the backpack and offered it to Cate. She shook her head and reached for an apple. She watched the clouds and listened to the wrapping crinkle and Eliot crunching through the wafer.

When their clothes became damp, they stood and brushed themselves down. Eliot took the pack and they walked along the gravel floor of the dry creek bed, pulling up their socks to protect their legs from nettles. They passed the place they'd found Sally's dead dachshund, black and bloated, then they discovered a rusty tap, which meant there must have been a house once beside the creek. When they twisted it on, orange water jerked out. They climbed over barbed-wire fences in which logs had been trapped by the spring floods, checking for brown or black snakes coiled loosely in the sun.

Eliot, who'd given up singing when his voice began to swerve unreliably, whistled as they walked. Cate picked up a stick and trailed it through the fine grass behind her. Sometimes she whacked the ti-tree's branches so she was showered in their tiny leaves.

The paddocks on either side gave way to dry soil punctured by stubbly wiregrass and rocky outcrops, which smelled of trapped sunlight. They moved away from the shady banks, neither one leading but, like a pair of swallows in flight, only responding to the other's movements.

The house was on Harper's land. Harper had disappeared two decades before, after Mrs Harper had upped sticks and gone to the coast. No one knew why, though rumours blew about the town like grass seeds that took root, growing into a tangle of stories: she had a coastal lover; she had cancer and wanted to live her last years by the sea; Mr Harper was seeing a prostitute. Whatever the reason, Mr Harper was left on his own, and he too moved away after a few years.

The house was on the other side of a gully. It was a stupid place to put it, their father always said, because the Harpers wouldn't be able to get out if it flooded.

'Didn't they have a rowboat?' Eliot asked.

Their father snorted. 'Harper wouldn't have had enough sense for that.'

Cool air brushed their necks as they crossed the gully. From the sagging fence, they viewed Harper's want of sense. The house's paint had almost worn away, leaving weatherboard flecked with pink undercoat. In a corner of the verandah was a rusty petrol can.

The front steps had fallen in and windowpanes were missing.

Eliot stepped over the limp fence. Cate followed, catching her shorts on the barbed wire. She unhooked the fabric and brushed off the rust. Three stunted rosebushes lined what once had been the front path. Cate snapped a twig off and examined it for green; it was completely dead.

Inside, floors were smothered with old sheets and clothes stained by rain. Cate picked up a floral dress stiff with dirt. Wasp nests sprouted in the corners of the ceiling and some of the corrugated-iron roof had lifted away. In the kitchen, the lino was cracked and covered in soil. Eliot opened a cupboard and a lizard scuttled out. Cracked bowls and plates were still stacked there, along with a chipped enamel mug.

The back door had come off its hinges and lay on the ground. Beyond it was an orchard of gnarled apricot and peach trees. Further back were citrus trees, oranges, lemons and mandarins lying at their base.

Cate tossed the backpack beneath a peach tree. She handed Eliot a sandwich and the water bottle, which she had filled with cordial and frozen overnight. He drank and passed it back, an orange moustache on his upper lip. They sat on the backpack. Salty Vegemite stung Cate's mouth as she bit into her sandwich. The sickly smell of overripe fruit hung in the hot air. Flies buzzed closer, attracted by the scent of butter.

Cate took a slug of cordial. It was still icy and pain sprang in her forehead. She closed her eyes.

'Look, Catie.'

Her eyes flashed open, startled by the sound of Eliot's voice after hours of silence. He was digging soil away from a black stone that jutted from the ground.

He wriggled it free and brushed off the dirt. It was a smooth hemisphere, dark grey in colour, with two edges making a sharp ridge.

Cate ran her fingers over the ridge. 'It must be Aboriginal. Maybe they used it to cut things.'

'Or it was part of a spear.'

'Dad would know.'

'We can take it to Mellor.'

'Yeah.'

Eliot turned the stone over in his hand. Cate waved flies away. Ants appeared and carried off crumbs from their sandwiches.

'Should we pick some fruit for Mum?' Eliot asked.

'They'll all have fruit flies.'

'She can stew them.'

'You'll be cutting the bad bits out, then.'

'Lazy cow.'

Cate smirked. 'C'mon, then.'

Most of the apricots were rotting, but the peaches, despite the brown holes where fruit flies had burrowed into the flesh, could be salvaged.

'Will you make me peach cobbler, Cate?'

'If you carry them back. Let's look at the mandarins.'

The citrus were disappointing, either hard and tart on the tree or mouldering into grey spheres in the soil.

'Let's go,' Cate suggested, kicking a mandarin and watching it thump. 'It's too hot. I'm getting tired.'

Eliot shouldered the bag of fruit.

They were halfway across the land between the house and the creek when the horses appeared, trotting towards them. Cate stopped with an intake of breath. Horses made her nervous, and these ones were tall, almost a head higher than herself. They slowed as they approached, but Cate stepped back with a noise of protest. Instinctively, Eliot moved in front of her.

'Maybe they can smell the fruit,' Cate said.

'Get a peach.'

Cate dug into the bag, passing the fruit over Eliot's shoulder. He twisted it open and pulled out the stone, then laughed as the horse's lips tickled his palm.

'There. It's friendly, Cate.'

'They're too big.'

'His friend wants one too.'

Cate found another peach. The second horse nuzzled Eliot. He rubbed its nose. As the horse crunched the peach in its yellow teeth, Eliot said, 'All right, let's go.'

'They're following!' Cate cried as they set off.

'They just want the fruit. Walk faster.'

They reached the creek and the horses stopped, looking at them impassively. Cate thrashed down the bank but Eliot stayed to watch.

That evening Cate sat with a plastic ice-cream container at her feet, paring away bruised parts of the peaches and scraping out maggots. Then she cut the fruit into segments and melted it with butter and sugar on the stove, watching the juice bubble and turn golden. As she stirred, she gazed at Eliot at the dining-room table, studying his music theory. The kitchen filled with the aroma of sweet, oozing fruit, the smell of Eliot's protection.

Biscuit snorted and Cate opened her eyes, her vision darkening as it adjusted to the light. Slowly, she stood and led Biscuit through the paddock to the gate.

Back at the house, after she'd unsaddled and brushed the horse at Sally's stables, Cate entered Eliot's room and opened his drawer. There, among his socks and undies, was the stone. Cate slid her fingers over its smooth surface and fingered the ridge. It was still sharp.

21

Kath shook out the crocheted rug over the verandah, releasing cake crumbs that May had dropped into it. She spoke to the currawongs in the trees, complaining of May's messiness, and thought, with a pang, of how they might have to leave those birds and the stories they sang, and return to town.

Inside, May had the TV on again.

'You're cooking your brain, woman,' Kath told her.

'It's already cooked. Besides, I don't need it no more.'

'Always need your brain, darling.'

In the kitchen, she dried and put away the dishes in the dish rack.

'Stop being such a white woman!' May yelled. 'Leave the dishes. You ain't a servant anymore.'

'I like doing the dishes.'

Their mother's country had been up north. When it was clear that, as the girls grew older, the McConvilles didn't have enough work for them and that only their brother Stanley could stay on the property with his wife, Nance, and baby Mellor, they found places as domestics on a station not far from the reserves where their mother once lived. The owner's wife, Mrs Musgrove, never gave them enough food or blankets in winter, and they were frightened of the shearers and drovers who passed through each season, dragging girls from their tin shacks at night. Kath and May kept their wits, though, and when they felt the drumming of hooves in the distance, they hurried down to the creek and hid among long grass. They never noticed their ant bites until they were back in their huts, but stings and itching were nothing against a man's grip on the back of their neck. On the weekends the girls went to their grandmother's and aunties' camp, where they were fed properly on yams and possum, and told stories about their mother and her country.

They stayed at the station more than a decade. May fell for a black stockman, Freddy Lancaster, and married him. They had a couple of kids, but they were taken away. Freddy turned to drink, then, and beat May when he was on the bottle. They were glad when he got booted off the station. As for Kath, she liked working in the house, pushing beeswax into the fine wooden furniture, scaring the daylights out of Mrs Musgrove's kids when, hanging out the washing, she wrapped herself in a sheet and pretended to be a ghost, and the excitement of a fridge turning up to replace the icebox. Mrs Musgrove taught her to cook and to wait on the table, and sometimes they had a joke or two together.

Mrs Musgrove also noticed, when her brother-in-law came to stay, that Kath lingered over the washing up, scrubbed the floor late into the night, and flinched when her brother-in-law, after several glasses of red wine, stroked her back with his hand.

One evening, as Kath poured hot water into the porcelain washing basin to wash Mrs Musgrove's hair, her boss noticed bruises exposed by her rolled-up sleeves.

'What did you do?' she asked.

'It's nothing, Miss.'

'Are they anywhere else?'

Kath had looked at Mrs Musgrove's grey eyes, and glanced away.

'How often does it happen?'

'I lost count, Miss.'

The next day, the brother-in-law's bags were packed. Kath never had much to do with men after that.

When a young man the image of Stanley appeared at the reserve one day, looking ready to drop, they could hardly believe it.

'It's Mellor!' they shouted, wrapping him in a moth-eaten blanket. They gave him strips of kangaroo meat and a hunk of damper cooked from precious rations, then boiled up a billy of sweet tea. In between mouthfuls, he told them of hitting another boy, and of a friend driving him a hundred miles north. After that he hitched and walked inland until he found the station.

They kept him there for a few days, then took him to the station's manager, who grumbled about extra rations.

'He's one of our mob,' May said firmly, staring him down until he agreed to take the boy on, and put him with the horses.

'Come here, Kath!'

May called her back, and Kath returned to the living room, damp tea towel in her hands.

'Look at this woman – the silly bitch's boob job.'

'I'm half-blind, how am I supposed to see her tits?'

'Her top can't even hold them in, Kathy,' May said, gleeful.

Kath lowered herself into the couch with its broken springs, feeling her sister's body jiggle with laughter.

22

Cate, red-faced and sweaty, ran past her father as he wheeled the motorbike from the shed. She intended to ignore him, but he demanded, 'Where've you been?'

Cate stopped, hands on hips, breathing heavily. 'In case you hadn't noticed, I'm twenty-nine. I don't need to explain every move I make.'

'Unless you want to give your mother a heart attack, I suggest you leave a note.'

'Bugger off, would you?'

'I won't have you using that kind of language here.'

'Fine. I'll fly back to the city tomorrow and we won't sell the bloody property.'

They were back where they had been when she was fifteen, the same clash between his close-mindedness and her longing to escape. Only she'd got as far as Sydney and she was trapped again.

Her father shook his head and pushed the bike down the drive. Cate watched his antalgic gait; he walked as though there were a burr in his foot. He kicked the bike's motor into life with his good leg, the left, and when the bike was finally going he lifted his right leg over the seat. Cate unlaced her sneakers, refusing to feel remorse, and left them outside the back door.

In the kitchen, her mother rattled bowls then switched on the mixmaster, filling the room with a mechanical whirr.

Cate's feet were cool upon the slate floor. She was fetching eggs from the fridge for Eliot, who'd taken to baking. He'd mastered Anzac biscuits and now he was trying pavlova.

'Six eggs, Cate,' he said.

She lined them in the crook of her arm. Eliot had the *Australian and New Zealand Cookbook* open on the bench, stained with the albumen of previous attempts.

He took each egg from her arm and cracked it into the bowl, stacking the shells on the sink. When the yolk from the sixth egg spilled out, he gave a gnarled cry.

'What's wrong?' Cate asked.

'There's a baby bird in there.'

Together they bent over the bowl, ears touching, observing the bundle of yellow slime and slick feathers, an eye and a beak poking forth.

Leonora, noticing their silence, came over.

'Mum, the egg had a bird in it,' Cate said.

'Why did you crack it? You know your father's obsessed with hatching chickens.'

'We didn't know it was in there!' Eliot cried. 'I wouldn't have cracked it if I'd known there was a baby.'

'Shush,' Leonora soothed. 'It's okay, El. I'll get it out.'

Leonora grabbed a measuring cup, scooped the bird out and flung it over the back fence. The next day it was gone, probably eaten by Tank.

The mixmaster stopped.

'Nice to see you back,' Leonora said brightly. 'You know, you don't have to leave your shoes outside. I don't mind about the grass seeds.'

'Whatever, Mum,' Cate replied numbly, filling a glass with rainwater from the tap.

23

Wind brushed the hair of Finch's forearms as his old yacht bumped over small waves. Once he was past the headland, where there were fewer boats, he knotted the ropes, smeared more sunscreen over his face and lay on the deck with an engineering magazine. He read for half an hour, then pulled his hat low over his face.

After Aubrey had left two winters before, it had taken a long time to get used to being on the boat without her body stretched out next to him, her skin shining with sweat, a textbook on railway tracks open on her stomach. He would watch her as she dozed, his erection growing, torn between waking her to do something about it, and the delight of watching her sleep.

Once she'd woken and found him looking at her, and smiled languidly.

'What're you thinking about?' he asked.

'Tribology.'

'Come again?'

'The study of friction, lubrication and wear.'

He'd laughed, tossing the textbook aside.

Since the clandestine afternoons with Miss Morton, the geography teacher, in the stationery storeroom, pleasure had been about conversations mingled with the smell of a woman's skin; the way she looked just after she woke, only half alert but her mind already working; or heated debates in which her cheeks flushed and pupils dilated. This was something that Jack, appreciative of women for their tits and flattery, could never understand.

But then Aubrey had fallen in love with her work and left, and the affair with Miss Morton hadn't ended well. The only evidence of their fucking had been a few disarranged sheets of paper, until he was careless and a staff member found a torn condom packet peeking out beneath the shelves. They'd had their suspicions and confronted him, but there was little they could do. He was going to bring the school top marks and the principal had always been sympathetic to his mother.

Sylvia Accorso was a tall, striking woman. When she put down the phone after talking to the principal of her son's results, she was frightening.

'Finchley, that was Mr Stevenson.' Her hands were folded so tightly that their veins stood out.

'Yeah.' Finch dried the dishes, wiping suds from cheap white china plates.

'He said you came second in the state.'

'That's pretty good.'

'If you hadn't been carrying on with that woman you would have come first.'

'On the contrary, Mother,' Finch placed a bowl onto the stack on the bench. 'If I'd been allowed to keep seeing her I would have come first.'

'It was only because of me that you weren't expelled!'

'What, because the principal liked you?'

'You selfish boy! I worked my fingers to the bone so you could go to that private school! Day in, day out, nothing but work. One dress a year for myself, one pair of shoes, and that was it. Everything else I gave to you.'

'Did I ask you to, Mother?'

Sylvia grabbed the bowls and threw them at his feet. The noise hurt his ears. He stepped past her, into the claustrophobic streets of Kynidia, followed by the sound of her sobbing.

After walking to the river to skim rocks and lie beneath the shady gums, he returned to the house and found her sitting at the kitchen table. She faced the wall, a half-drunk cup of tea before her.

'I'm sorry, Mum,' he said, kissing her temple and dropping into the seat beside her. He took her hand, worn and dry from years of tending to sickness. 'Of course I appreciate all that you've done, but I got the marks I needed for the course and that's all that matters.'

She nodded, but a tiny gust had entered their formerly airtight relationship, and he was never able to close it out. Her father, who had worked on the McConville's farm, had never forgiven her for falling pregnant. He wanted her to give up the child to a hospice in Sydney, but she refused. He gave her a stipend to move out of the house and rent on her own, and rarely spoke to her. He died when Finch was five, and left her enough money to start putting him through boarding school. When the fees became more expensive as he grew older, she started doing double shifts at the hospital.

Later, Finch realised the stupidity of what he'd done. If he'd got Miss Morton pregnant, her teaching career would have been finished. They met only once more after his exams, in a hotel room she'd arranged. In the blatant afternoon sun, the magic and surreptitiousness disappeared and their intercourse, though enjoyable, was routine. It went unsaid that they needn't meet again.

When Aubrey came along, Finch's mother cheered up. She loved Aubrey's class, porcelain skin and intelligence. Often they would lunch together, drinking champagne by the sparkling water of Double Bay, or shop in Paddington's boutiques in the afternoons when crowds were light, returning to Finch's in the evening to cook dinner.

'When are you going to propose?' Sylvia harassed him, almost continually in the weeks before Aubrey left. He wondered if Aubrey had said something, or rather, wasn't saying something. He went as far as stepping into a jeweller's to order stones, but left with the proprietor's business card and a promise that he would call again.

It was only later that he recalled the way she had waited for the mail, the phone, or emails for notification of her scholarship application, and realised she hadn't listened for his step in the hall with anything like that keenness.

The day she boarded the plane for England, his mother called him, almost incoherent through her tears. 'What did you do to make her go? Why didn't you propose?'

'There wasn't anything I could do, Mum. She wanted her PhD. Even if we were engaged, she'd have broken it off.'

'Finchley, you should have tried harder.' Sylvia hung up, leaving the dial tone beeping in his ear.

24

'Shuddup!' Blake shouted at the yelping dogs, as he pulled skin from the kangaroo's legs. They were only silenced when he threw them the shanks, lolloping with them into the evening.

Blake stepped into the bathroom to wash his hands. Cate leapt off the verandah and stood beside the tank stand where Blake had leant the rifle. Tentatively, she lifted it and stroked the metal barrel. It was an alien feeling.

It was as their mother served lamb chops and spuds one evening that Eliot announced, 'Russell's gonna teach me to shoot.'

'You know how to shoot,' Blake replied.

'This is proper shooting, marksman shooting.'

'What does Russell know about shooting?'

'He was in the army for a year.'

'Why'd he only last a year?' Blake demanded.

'I dunno.'

Leonora laid down the plates of food. 'I think it's lovely you've got a new friend.'

'Why does everything always have to be "lovely" and "nice", Mum? Can't you have some new adjectives?'

'That's enough, Cate,' Blake said sharply.

'So can I have the ute on Wednesday?'

'All right,' Blake grunted.

When Eliot came back after the shooting lesson, their father pecked at him.

'What does Russell do for a job?'

'Not much. Bit of farm labouring. He just got back from mustering down south.'

'Why'd he come back?'

'I dunno.'

'Have you asked?'

'I thought you told us to always mind our own business?'

Cate put the rifle back and rested against the tank stand. The warm, sickly smell of roo blood was the same that Eliot carried home after his nights of shooting with Russell. Sometimes, even after he'd showered, Cate couldn't get it out of her nose.

The last of the sunset – a thin strip of orange – burnt out. In the darkness, Cate wished yet again that she had answered 'No' to Sarah's question.

'Are you coming to the B and S?'

Cate looked up from her maths textbook, squinting. Tall, skinny Sarah hung over her like a sapling.

'I haven't really thought about it.'

'C'mon, it'll be fun! You can bring Eliot.'

'He's too young.'

'Sixteen is too young?' Sarah was scathing.

Cate looked at the textbook. 'I've got better things to do than get pissed in a paddock.'

'When was the last time you came out with us?'

Cate waded through the net of calculus in her mind and retrieved the memory of Maxine's birthday party. Murray had pushed her up against a wall and shoved a knee into her crotch, as if this was something that would excite her.

'When I discovered Murray was the worst kisser in history.'

Sarah snorted and folded her long limbs to sit on the bench. 'He wasn't very happy that you told the whole school.'

'I didn't. I only told Emily.'

'Which is the same thing.'

Cate smirked. 'Will he be at the ball?'

'Probably. But don't worry, there'll be plenty of other boys around.' Her mouth curved into a knowing smile.

Eliot had grudgingly agreed to come, only on the proviso that Cate didn't leave him with some slag. Leonora wasn't enthusiastic either, but Blake clapped his son on the back.

'You'll have a great time, mate.'

It meant a suit for Eliot, but Sarah told them it would get trashed, so they pulled out the dress-up box and discovered their father's blue velvet bellbottoms. Cate laughed when Eliot put them on and mimicked their father's swagger. They dug further into the clothes, releasing the scent of camphor. Eliot found his old grey plastic sword and shield, and Cate unfolded their mother's Prue Acton mini-dresses.

'These are almost fashionable again! Do you think I can wear this one?' Cate turned from side to side in the short, red-and-purple frock.

'You'd look a bit weird, Cate.'

'I don't care. I'll wear it with my riding boots.'

Eliot didn't reply, and substituted jeans for the bellbottoms.

Boys hovered around Cate, attracted by her confidence, but when they saw she wouldn't leave Eliot, they wandered to the girls with fob chains and silk ball gowns. They'd been given styrofoam cups attached to a string to hang around their necks. Spirits were poured into the cups from a sheep-drenching hose attached to a 44-gallon drum.

When their mother had dropped them off at Sarah's house in town, Sarah surveyed Cate in despair.

'When are you ever going to be normal?' she asked.

'When I become boring,' Cate snapped.

Now Sarah left them, a tall tree moving through the crowd towards the loos outside. When they saw her again, she was glued to a man in an Akubra, his huge hand wrapped about her bony arse.

Cate turned to Sarah's friends Paula and Emily, but they were laughing hysterically, drawing faces on the cups with lipstick.

Men roared, sloshing their drinks. They pulled out capsules of food dye, tipped them into their mouths and spat, spraying their mates' white shirts. Others lifted the catches of water pistols, tipped in the dye with their beer and squirted. Women shrieked and swore when it stained their gowns.

'Remind me again why we're here?' Eliot muttered.

Cate ignored him, thinking of the simplicity of the algebra she could have been doing instead of watching couples gyrate on the dirt dance floor, compacted that afternoon by a steamroller. Their shuffling boots transformed it back into soft runnels of dust. Someone tried to organise a row of linedancing, but the participants lurched in anything but a line. In the dark corners of the shed there were men with their pants around their knees, banging into girls who gripped their shoulders to balance their short pleasure. Cate wouldn't look in that direction, but still heard their cries and grunts through the raging music, their heads thudding against the corrugated-iron wall.

Then Murray was before her with three of his mates, a bottle of Bundy in hand, his pale-blue shirt spattered with pink and green.

'Look who it is, boys, it's Lady Muck herself.' His gaze shifted to Eliot. 'And her Prince Regent. Please, allow me.' He gave a mocking bow, staggering, and his friends giggled.

'Go away, Murray. You're not being funny.'

'Not funny? How about we practise kissing – that might make you smile, Catie.'

Abruptly, he grabbed the back of her neck and pressed his lips against hers. His teeth broke their skin and, without thinking, Cate kneed him in the groin. He fell to the dusty earth, curling up like a spider.

A pool of silence widened about them. Eliot put his arm around Cate. She wiped her mouth with the back of her hand and it came away bloodied.

Murray's mates looked at each other, then one leaned over and pulled him up.

'You *bitch*,' Murray spat, shaking off his mate's hold. 'You fucking little *cunt* —'

'Don't speak to her like that.' Eliot's voice was reedy.

'Oh! Little brother is standing up for big sister!'

An excited whisper ran through the crowd, feeding off alcohol and pheromones.

'C'mon, c'mon,' Murray wheedled. 'Throw us a punch, love. Don't let your sister start something she can't finish.'

Cate's heartbeat skittered. Her brother, who baulked each time their father asked him to kill a sheep, was raising his fists.

'Now, boys, I don't think we need any of this, do we?'

Cate turned to see a man step into their circle. She recognised his voice and muscular frame, a good head higher than Murray's, but couldn't place who he was.

'Who're you?' Murray frowned with irritation.

'Mate of Cate and Eliot's.' He peered down at Murray. 'Any problems here that I can help you with?'

Slowly, Murray processed the logistics of a new fight. 'Uh, no mate. Everything's good.'

'Glad to hear it.' The man smiled broadly.

Murray turned away, muttering.

Cate, unable to resist, winked at his mates in victory before they, too, slouched off.

The man smiled easily at her, and Cate recognised him as the brother of Billy Wakeley, a boy in Eliot's year at school.

'Russell!' she exclaimed. 'We haven't seen you for years. Where've you been?'

'Up north, mustering. Gave up on school.'

Eliot blinked, as though in shock. Russell glanced at him.

'Here, fill up your cups. Let's get away from these losers.'

They followed Russell through rows of utes and past couples groaning in swags or on ute trays.

Russell had parked beneath a peppercorn tree. He unlatched the back tray and they hauled themselves up, legs dangling over the edge.

They sipped Bacardi from their cups, wincing at the taste. Eliot tipped his onto the ground. Russell pulled out a six-pack of beer, flicked the bottle top off one with his pocketknife, and handed it to him.

Slowly, Eliot's spine relaxed. They listened to Russell's stories of jackarooing, the bitterly cold nights under stars, of having to kill snakes and shoot roos for dinner. There was an expansiveness to his tone that Cate liked.

'Why'd you come home, Russell?' she asked.

'A woman,' he answered after a while. 'Got a baby on the way.'

'Oh, that's exciting!'

'Yeah,' he replied, without enthusiasm.

'Do they pay you good money, up north?' Eliot asked.

'Yeah, yeah.' They chatted about wages, accommodation and free meals, and the colour returned to Russell's voice.

Later, they slept in Russell's ute tray, unwilling to walk forever to find their own vehicle while blokes in their built-up utes spotlighted bare bums in the paddocks. Russell dug out a spare swag for Cate and gave his own to Eliot, who protested.

'Don't worry, mate, I'll stretch out in the cabin,' he said.

They fell asleep to the screeching of men doing circle work with their utes, and the squealing of women.

They left early the next morning, when the sky was the colour of slate. Smoke from burnt-out campfires unravelled in the air. A few figures staggered about, weakly shooting empty water pistols.

'I'm sorry I subjected you to that,' Cate said, as they rumbled over the cattle grid and turned onto the main road. 'I knew it would be bad, but not that bad.'

The sun began to split the horizon with gold streaks.

'It's okay. Russell was a nice bloke. He knows about shooting. We might go out and about together. Get some pigs. They bugger up the land.'

'I see.' Cate had been unnerved by Russell's covetous gaze. 'How come you've never been interested in this before?'

'First time for everything, isn't there?'

'I guess so,' she replied.

The night was dispelled as sunlight lit insects on the windscreen.

By the tank stand, the dogs returned and nuzzled Cate's legs, hoping for more food.

She showed them her empty hands. 'It's time for my dinner, now.'

As she wandered back up the verandah, a breeze carried the sickly sweet smell of rotting figs from the tree in the paddock before the house. Cate, feeling sullied, went quickly indoors.

25

They got as far as mid-afternoon until Leonora, making a loaf of bread, erupted.

'Why do you hate us, Cate?' she demanded, hands bathed in flour.

'I don't, Mum,' Cate replied, turning the pages of the local newspaper.

'What is it, then?'

'I'd rather not talk about it.'

'That's what you always say.'

'Maybe I mean it, Mum. Talking about it just makes it worse.'

'You're not the only one who's suffering.'

Cate became terse. 'Different people deal with it in different ways. Why can't you see that?'

'It's been eight years, Cate. He's gone!'

'He hasn't! How can he be "gone" when his stars are still stuck on the roof, his clothes are in the wardrobe and his textbooks are still on the bookshelf? Why are you so obsessed with cleaning? This place is like a museum! You haven't moved on —'

'We're trying, Cate. That's why we need you to sign. We need to get on with our lives, what's left of them.'

Cate shook her head. 'What if he returns? And doesn't have a home to come back to?'

'He *won't*!' Leonora threw the glass measuring jug onto the floor. It shattered against the slate, pieces smacking against the cupboards.

To her surprise, Cate picked up the thick shards and stacked them neatly in a pile on the bench. She took the dustpan and brush from beneath the sink and swept up the smaller fragments. When she'd shaken them into the bin, she said, 'I'm sorry, Leonora, but I'm not going to sell. He hasn't gone.'

She left the room. A few minutes later Leonora heard the bang of the screen door.

Leonora stared blankly out the window, then made herself a shandy.

A while later, she heard Blake's motorbike coming up the hill and topped up her shandy with more lemonade. The rolled dough remained in its bed of flour.

When Blake entered the kitchen, he noticed the broken glass stacked on the bench. 'What happened?'

'We had an argument. She ran off.'

'Did you tell her about Rickett?'

'No. Not yet.' Leonora put down her drink. 'Sometimes I wonder if I caused all these problems.'

'Of course you didn't.' He bent and kissed her forehead. 'It wasn't anyone's fault.'

'I doubt she'd agree with you, and she'd have a thousand scientific explanations to prove you wrong.'

'I don't care what she thinks.' He washed his hands, suds collecting the grime and washing it down the sink.

'Don't pick a fight with her, Blake.'

He dried his hands on the tea towel. 'It sounds like you just did.'

'Yes, and it was a mistake. We'd shoot ourselves in the foot. I'll tell her about Rickett, I'm just waiting for the right moment.'

Blake poured himself a brandy. 'Don't leave it too long.'

Leonora pummelled the dough.

'Forget about cooking,' Blake said. 'Come and sit with me on the verandah.'

Leonora dusted flour from her hands, took her drink and settled in the wicker chair among the sound of crickets.

'I heard on the radio today,' Blake said, 'that at two-thirty it's time to go to the dentist.'

'What?'

'Tooth-hurty.'

Leonora laughed. 'That's dreadful, Blake!'

'But you're smiling.'

She placed her hand on Blake's forearm, reassured by his smell of perspiration and machinery oil.

'You were at the shed today?' she asked.

'Yeah. Tractor needed the oil changed.'

As she stroked the hard muscle of his arm, Leonora's resentment over their daughter dissolved.

There'd been shandies on those Friday nights with her best friend Jane in the Bromley RSL. She'd carefully applied eyeliner and smoky eye shadow, swept her teased hair into a beehive and dressed herself neatly in a lemon mini-dress with white stockings and navy platforms.

In the dreary interior, with its brown and orange swirling carpet, they spoke to the same boys in bell-bottoms and white shirts they'd spoken to the week before, laughing politely at the same jokes. Jane flirted with the same farmer who travelled every week to see her, so Leonora was often left alone, resentful because she knew Jane had no intention of marrying him.

She was home by 10.00 p.m. Sitting at her dressing table, removing her make-up with Pond's Cold Cream, she wondered if there would ever be a man who had new jokes for her every week.

She'd met Blake not in the smoke-filled RSL, but at a neighbour's party in a shearing shed. He was gruff and burly, with blue eyes and sideburns stretching the length of his cheeks. At first she thought him rough, but soon he had her smiling, then laughing, with quips and jokes. The other young men glanced around uncertainly as Leonora Carrington's laughter bounced off the corrugated-iron walls.

When Leonora took her make-up off that night, the face in the mirror was smiling.

'It's that funny?' Blake asked.

'What? Oh, the joke. No, I was just thinking.' Her smile faded. 'Cate's adamant she won't sell. She imagines he'll still come back.'

'I can't stay here, Nora. It's all well and good for her to want to keep the property, but who's going to look after it?'

'She mentioned something about paying an overseer herself. Maybe we haven't exhausted every option yet.'

Blake shook his head. 'We have to sell. Sally and Charlie don't want to be here for much longer either. She's the only one who wants it.'

The crickets dropped off, until there was only one singing by itself.

Jane was still one of Leonora's closest friends. She eventually married the farmer's cousin, and moved into Tumbin. Leonora visited her each time she went there for groceries.

'So Rickett's still interested?' Jane asked the week before, pouring hot water into the coffee plunger.

'Yes, if we can get Cate to agree.'

'Do you want to go?'

She avoided Jane's eyes, watching swirling coffee grains in the water. 'For Blake's sake, yes. Even though he doesn't want to.'

'And you?'

Leonora looked down at her plate, patterned with the long tail of a peacock, and pushed around crumbs of lemon cake.

'Not really. I have you and my friends. I love my garden, and the house is all I have left of Eliot and Cate. And, you know, my son might come back. But "might" isn't a very strong word when you put it next to Blake's pain.'

Jane watched her sadly. 'Whenever you talk about your kids, it's like a tide going out.'

Leonora hadn't replied to that.

Blake rattled the ice cubes in his glass. 'We should wait for Natalie. Maybe she can change Cate's mind.'

'Nat says she won't be the one to tell her about Rickett. But then again, Cate will be less volatile when Natalie's here.'

Blake tipped back the brandy. 'God knows what we were thinking when we made the kids part of the partnership.'

'It was your idea, remember, to encourage Eliot to stay on the farm.'

'And if you hadn't let that bloody music teacher put ideas in his head, we'd have been fine.'

'I told her they would never play in Sydney, Blake.' Leonora rose. 'I'm going to finish that dough before it dries out.'

In the kitchen, she dashed drops of water onto the drying dough and continued kneading until it was elastic and malleable beneath her hands.

26

They were playing at the community hall in Tumbin for the residents of the nursing home. Three old men sat in the sun pouring through the window, one with his eyes closed. Two ladies smiled and nodded to the music. Mrs Jones, the Country Women's Association lady who organised outings for the residents, manned the stainless-steel tea urn in her floral blouse and grey skirt, a tray of biscuits and scones on the table before her. Leonora sat near the door, smiling, her Indian cotton skirt rippling in the breeze.

The children finished their piece to disjointed applause. They shuffled their music.

'This next piece is Bach's *Minuet in D Minor*,' Eliot explained in his clear voice. They lifted their violins and the music was like a blue wren and its jenny chasing one another about the room, dipping in and out of the teacups and lifting pieces of the old people's hair to make their nests. Leonora smiled on and on, gratified.

Cate sat up, sweating. She couldn't tell if she'd been awake or asleep, if it had been a memory or a dream. She checked her watch: 4.20 a.m. Four hours of sleep. She stared at the clock, vaguely watching the digitals flick over, then went to the bathroom.

Sitting on the bath's edge, she waited for hot water to run from the old showerhead. Her body was lean and hard, calves firm with muscle, buttocks taut. Running had taken its toll on her breasts, stretching and softening them. She was almost thirty, and her body hadn't been caressed in any meaningful way for the last ten years.

The first six months of university had been an obligatory haze of alcohol and late-night fumblings with beery boys barely out of adolescence. In frustration, Cate had tried sleeping with a girl, but found herself unmoved. There was something delicious about the velvety feel of a cock in her mouth, or pressing firmly against her clit.

She quickly gave up on the flirting game; it wasn't worth waking and discovering she'd given herself to someone who couldn't be bothered to make her laugh. Then Eliot disappeared, and in the flurry of finding him she got out of the habit of looking for men for sex and affection. She searched for their lope and freckles instead.

She stepped into the shower, sliding her hand between her legs. Even masturbation had become perfunctory, a brusque crescendo that halted in a few minutes.

For the duration of that spasm in which she lost herself, she remembered overripe figs slipping onto the dry grass beneath the tree, and the clouds of fruit flies that hovered there in the heat of the day. When the sensation faded, she rubbed her fingers into the soap, washing away their sour smell, and stood beneath the pouring water.

Initially, she couldn't see what Eliot liked about Russell. He'd left school after Year Ten and didn't seem to do anything except work casually as a farm labourer, shoot pigs and occasionally check in on his new son. But as she sat with them in the evenings drinking beer before they went shooting, she came to appreciate his humour and easy charm, and the way he smiled so readily. He brought out Eliot's boyishness, which had slipped away in the past few years, replaced with a quietness that was sometimes sullen.

In the months leading up to her exams, she used to think that Russell couldn't have come at a better time. As she stuffed her mind full of quotes from *King Lear* and *To Kill a Mockingbird*, the timeline for war in 1914 and the equations of *sine* and *cos*, she was relieved she didn't also have to contend with her anxiety over her brother, who had no friends other than herself.

Russell was lean, his face angular and often unshaven, his teeth uneven. The palms of his broad hands, Cate came to find, were surprisingly soft. At first his caresses were imperceptible: his hand dropping on the back of her neck, his leg brushing against hers beneath the table at the pub. Cate thought nothing of it until, one night not long after she'd finished her exams, Russell and Eliot trudged over the lawn, bringing the smells of kangaroo blood and beer.

Cate always waited up for Eliot, reading on the verandah. Insects clustered around the light, sometimes landing on the pages of her novel. When she brushed them off, they released an acrid smell.

'Hi, guys,' she said.

'Hi, Cate,' Eliot replied tiredly, going indoors to shower. He was religious about cleaning the blood off after he'd been shooting.

Russell paused beside her. When Cate looked up, questioning, he bent and kissed her long and lusciously, his tongue touching the edge of her teeth. Then he followed Eliot indoors.

Cate stared at the dark garden, her skin burning. She went to her room so she wouldn't have to face him again.

'Cate!' Blake was banging on the bathroom door. 'Stop wasting the bloody water!'

'We're not in a drought,' she shouted.

'At this rate we will be!'

Fuming, Cate twisted off the taps. As she dried herself off, she noticed contusions forming on her thighs. She lifted her arms and found more by her armpits. They had appeared after Eliot went missing. She knew it was a lack of vitamins and that she was underweight. She knew, too, that she should eat more, but food had lost its appeal. She glanced at the scales resting beside the bath, then pulled on her clothes.

27

On his way to the shed, just after the sun had risen, Mellor passed Cate galloping along the creek on Biscuit. He almost expected Rachel and Eliot to appear soon after, the way they always had when they were kids. Blake never liked the comments about the kids being seen halfway to town on their horses and the jokes that they'd need Mellor's girl to track them back, but Mellor ignored the jibing. In the company of those kids, Rachel became spirited and talkative.

Sometimes he'd be working in a paddock and his daughter's laughter would reach him. He'd straighten, listening, and she'd appear from the bend in the creek.

'Hi, Dad!' she called gaily as the three of them rode past, waving.

Mellor, gladdened, waved back, and returned to fixing the windmill pump, or hoeing the Bathurst burrs. Sometimes he watched after her, marvelling at her lightness on the horse. She would bend over its neck, talking to it just as he had when he was up north.

There, he still carried his longing for country like a bag of stones, but it was easier to bear on horseback with the long plains stretching on either side of him. He'd gallop across the earth, chasing a herd of cattle, thrilled by whirling dust, beating hooves and the men hollering and whistling. Camping and riding for days on end, until they reached the outskirts of the station and corralled the half-wild beasts, reminded him of nights with his father in their country.

He'd only ever had one fall, in early spring when his horse shied at a snake curled in the road, warming itself after hibernation. The horse bolted, leaving Mellor writhing in the road, while the snake struggled to uncoil itself and make its way to safety in the grass. Mellor passed out and found himself in hospital, his arm pinned to his body with bandages. He'd broken his shoulder, they told him.

He was in that bare ward for a long time, watching clouds pass by the windows. One of the black girls who emptied bedpans and pushed a wet mop over the lino sometimes stopped for a few words. Her father was a Scottish shearer who'd loved her mother for a season, then left.

Mellor watched her as she moved about the wards, carrying cloths and pans, her sandshoes squeaking on the floors. He admired her large brown eyes and the way her hair crinkled about her face. She had a narrow figure, spindly ankles and a sway to her walk. Her name was Jocelyn.

When he came out of hospital and was back on his horse, he hitched a ride into town and waited under a solitary pine opposite the hospital entrance. When she saw him, she couldn't stop her shy smile.

'Want to go for a walk, Joss?' he asked as she approached.

'Where?'

'The river.'

They wandered through the wide streets of the town, which was hushed in the evening. At the path to the river, Joss took off her sandshoes and stepped through the long grass.

The river moved slowly, circled by clouds of midges. Willows, dipping their branches into the water, were tugged by the slow current. A pelican appeared, skimming the surface, then flapped its strong wings and bore away. Cicadas wove their insistent songs in the trees.

They didn't say much, but Mellor was aware of the hairs on Joss's arms brushing his, the arches of her feet printed with soil, her narrow ankles. He wanted to turn to her, push her back onto the earth and bring her knees up, opening her musky smell. Yet she was a self-contained girl, unlike his teasing rellies, and he didn't want to disturb her stillness. He locked his hands together beneath his legs.

'I can't leave my family,' Joss said softly. 'I was lucky. Mum hid me in an old tree trunk every time they came. I squeezed myself right up, so they couldn't see my feet. If I went, I'd break Mum's heart.'

Mellor nodded. Joss took his hand and laced her fingers through his. The pelican swerved back over the river again, braking downstream with its large, webbed feet.

A few days later, when the men thundered past on their horses, driving dusty cattle with hoots and shouts, Mellor noticed Joss was standing beneath a tree. He pulled his horse around to check it was really her, waved his hat, then re-joined the riders.

Afterwards, he came to the servants' shack, dust and sweat sluiced from his skin by a bucket of water from the tank. Joss met him at the door.

His teeth were white in the darkness as he smiled. 'How'd you get here?'

'Got a ride with Annie. She works in the kitchen.'

'How you gettin' back?'

'Dunno.'

'C'mon.' He took her hand, leading her to the stables. Among the smell of horseshit and old hay, Mellor kissed her, pressing her against the stable wall. The rough wood scratched her back.

'Not here,' she whispered.

So he saddled the horse, lifted her into the seat and leapt up behind her.

The horse walked slowly. Joss told stories of the constellations. Mellor kissed the nape of her neck, his arms holding the reins and touching the sides of her breasts, his erection hard against her back.

He turned off the road, down to a creek that fed into the river. With the water trickling nearby and the smell of wet earth, he unfolded the blanket that had lain beneath the horse's saddle, lifted off her dress and touched her so gently she couldn't stop trembling.

28

Even though it was early January, the Christmas tree still perched gaudily in the living room, its needles browning and dripping onto the floor. Blake and Leonora had cut it from the stand of native pines at the base of the hills, as they did every year. Cate, wondering if Leonora had left it there as a reproach for not coming home for the previous eight Christmases, pulled off small felt reindeer and glass baubles, their patterns worn away. She wound up fluffy silver tinsel, packed the gold angels standing on the mantelpiece and folded the cardboard nativity scene that rested before the empty fireplace.

In the summer holidays, when she and Eliot were bored with playing with the cut-outs of Mary and Joseph, they pulled on hats and shoes and visited Mellor's camp.

They were seven and six when they first wandered in, holding hands. The clearing among the trees held two shacks, with the tin humpies beneath a stand of gums further back. The largest house was an old worker's cottage, propped up on stumps and surrounded by the framework of an unfinished verandah. It still had the original sash windows, but their sash cords had broken and Mellor kept them propped open with narrow pieces of wood. Close to the house was a rainwater tank surrounded by green tufts of grass, but the rest of the soil was flat and bare. Pieces of rusting machinery and a tipped-up trailer lay beside the humpies. A strand of wire strung between the side of the house and a tilting post served for a clothesline; pegged onto it were a tea towel, two grey singlets and several shirts. Across a small yard from the house was a fibro hut, with a verandah tacked onto the front.

A knot of children played with a yo-yo in the shade of the middle house. They stopped when the McConvilles appeared, and watched them silently. Suddenly Rachel broke away from the kids and dashed towards Cate and Eliot, swinging her small arms around them.

Rachel's brothers had left the primary school by the time she entered it. She walked to Cate and Eliot's place in the morning, then they went to the bus stop together, making sure they arrived at the piece of granite in the long grass with enough time to spare for a game of hopscotch or handball. On the bus Cate and Eliot protected her from bullies, tangled their fingers together in cat's cradle and told jokes to make one another laugh. It was always Rachel who reduced Eliot to tears with the ones Mellor had told her. She and Cate looked at one another with bemusement as Eliot clasped his stomach, wheezing with laughter.

'It's not that funny, El,' Cate would say blankly.

'Yes it is. It is.'

She and Eliot loved Mellor's aunties, and the aunties loved them. The old women listened eagerly as Cate and Eliot ate their cakes and solemnly answered questions about books they'd read, games they played, and what their mother was doing that day.

Gradually, Cate worked out that Mellor lived in one house, the aunties in another, and that the humpies were for rellies, whose visits seemed to go on for months.

'Does your mum know you're here?' Auntie May once asked.

'Yes.'

'Does your dad?'

'No.'

'What would happen if he found out?'

Cate shrugged. 'Mum would sort it out.'

Rachel's cousin Robbie, a little boy of four with thick hair curling around his eyes, ran and knocked into May's knees. 'Auntie May, can I have a biscuit?'

'You fat little grub.' She scooped him up, peppering his cheeks with kisses until he squealed.

Auntie Kath must have seen the hunger in Cate's face. When they sat around the fire on a dirty tartan rug, she gathered the girl into her lap. Though Auntie Kath was hot and sticky from summer and the fire, Cate nestled in her arms, feeling the woman's voice vibrate through her back as she told them stories.

Rachel had been with Cate and Eliot one year when they cut down a pine tree, when they were in their teens. They had picked up sticks and whacked away spiders' webs strung between the pines while Blake sawed down a small tree. Back at the house, the three of them decorated it, laughing when Eliot hung baubles around his ears.

Afterwards, Rachel and Cate sprawled on Cate's bed, reading *Sweet Valley High* while the fan whirred. Eliot came into the room, watched them for a moment, then left. A few minutes later they heard the sound of wood chopping.

Rachel rolled onto her stomach, listening. 'He feels left out.'

Cate sighed, marking her place in her book. 'We'd better go and get him.'

A few minutes later, Rachel was standing on Eliot's shoulders in the pool, diving into the water, while Cate floated on her back, watching a wedge-tailed eagle in the sky.

~

Leonora came into the room and Cate tugged off the last tree ornament, a wooden star.

'It's nice that you're helping around the house, darling,' she said, dusting the mantelpiece.

'I didn't want to look at the dead tree anymore.' Cate turned the star over in her hands, and placed it in the box.

'Look at all those needles! I'd better get the vacuum out.'

'Whatever makes you happy, Mum,' Cate said dryly, lifting the tree out of the bucket of sand.

29

Blake stepped down the tractor steps and carefully placed his left leg on the soil to take the weight off his hip. That morning he'd swung his legs over the side of the bed, wincing as the pain, like a tree root, stretched from his thigh, up his groin and through his stomach. He began the agonising process of pulling on his clothes, barred by branches. After breakfast he'd taken two Nurofen but the twigs kept growing into his chest and up his arm. Now it grew dully up his neck.

He walked towards the peppercorn where Cate and Leonora had unpacked the lunch things. When the kids came for lunch during harvest time when they were small, already as brown as Mellor's troops from half a summer in the sun, they swallowed the sandwiches in three bites then ran off to poke sticks into ants' nests. He always knew where they were from the constant patter of their conversation.

'Hello,' Cate said guardedly as he approached. He glanced at her briefly; her resemblance to Eliot struck him each time he looked at her. He eased himself onto the old camp stool Leonora had brought, and took the egg-and-lettuce sandwich she offered.

Cate poured tea into an aluminium mug, swearing as the metal conducted heat too quickly to her fingers, burning them.

'Dad, why don't you hire a manager to run the farm?' she asked him. 'Why do you have to sell it?'

'They cost money.'

'I can pay. It'll be less than I'm earning.'

'I'm tired. We're all tired.'

'So you're just going to give up.'

Blake clenched his jaw. 'Cate, you haven't been a teenager for years.'

'Stop it, both of you,' Leonora snapped.

Cate ignored her mother. 'I reckon that's the same as saying he's dead.'

The fights began when Cate was in her early teens, fuelled by a cocktail of adolescent hormones and intelligence. Once, she and Eliot had burst into the kitchen before dinner, hyperactive from a game of tag they'd played outside.

'Mum, can Rachel come with us to the races?' Cate asked.

Leonora paused in her vigorous stirring, her arm curved around the mixing bowl.

'Why?'

''Cos she's our friend.'

Leonora glanced at Blake and began whisking again. 'We'll talk about it. Go and get the cows in.'

Blake frowned as they dashed out again. 'They're getting too close to those Abos.'

'Does that matter? Rachel's still a kid, like ours.'

Blake poured himself a whiskey, amber liquid sloshing against the sides of the glass.

'They're hardly kids anymore. Cate's fourteen. She's getting taller. Eliot's voice is breaking.' He cracked ice from the tray into his glass.

Half an hour later, the children marched in, breathless and pink. They found the kitchen too hot from Leonora's oven and pulled off their jumpers.

Blake, reading the paper at the table, averted his eyes from his daughter's small breasts.

As they sat to eat, Mellor, his family and three dogs drove past in their battered ute. They stuck their hands up and waved. Cate and Eliot waved back.

'Useless dole bludgers,' Blake said. 'They're supposed to use the back roads.'

'Mellor works for us,' Eliot pointed out.

'Yeah, Mellor's all right, but what do his rellies do? Cash in their cheques on booze.'

'We live off you, Dad,' Cate said, waspish.

'That's because it's my job to look after you.'

'And it's Mellor's job to look after his mob.'

'That's enough, kids.'

Blake had clenched his teeth. In a few years more his daughter would move to a bigger town, a place where there was music and cafes and traffic, and he and Eliot would be left behind.

'So can Rachel come to the races with us?'

'I'm still thinking,' Blake replied.

'What's there to think about? If I'd invited Sarah from school, you wouldn't have to think about it.'

'Shush, Cate,' Eliot cautioned.

Cate sawed savagely through her steak, cutting away the rind of fat.

Blake mopped his broccoli in the steak's sauce. He glanced at Eliot. The boy's fringe flopped over his eyes and his huge hands, which waited for his body to catch up with them, curled around his knife and fork.

It was just one day. Blake's friends would snipe; it was only a few years ago that the council had allowed Aborigines to use the local swimming pool. Yet that wasn't much next to the brilliance in his son's eyes as he told them over dessert, 'Okay, but only for this year, all right?'

Even Cate gave him a wry smile as she said, 'Thanks, Dad.'

Those smiles had been rare. The girl had always reminded him of a half-tamed horse straining at the bit. She only had one or two friends at school. When he once asked why she didn't have more she replied that most of the girls were boring.

'How do you mean, "boring"?' he asked.

'They just talk about make-up and stuff.'

'What would you rather talk about?'

'Books. Things in the newspaper.'

'What about boys?'

She shrugged.

'You got a boyfriend?' he persisted.

'It's none of your business.'

Leonora could always forgive the fights, but for Blake, his daughter lay in his mind like a burr in a woollen jumper. He looked covertly at this prickly woman who had once been a little girl running furiously out the gate when she heard his motorbike coming home. She would stretch out her arms to be scooped up and placed before him on the bike, her head beneath his chin.

Blake broke off some fruit cake and fed it to the dogs, sitting by the edge of rug expectantly.

'Now they'll be farting all the way home,' Cate said dryly.

Leonora broke into a laugh. It caught Blake's heart by its corners and knotted them into a ball.

30

Though she couldn't get out of the ute and walk, Kath liked to go with Mellor into town. May waved goodbye to them, waiting until she heard Mellor changing gears and accelerating along the road. Then she pulled up a floorboard beneath the TV and dug out her packet of cigarettes.

Sitting on the steps to the small verandah, she took out a fag, stroking the smooth paper, and placed it between her lips. She lit a match, listening to it fizz and burn, and cupped her hand around the flame. Its warmth tickled her palm as she held it to the end of the cigarette, then she flicked out the match. As she exhaled, she dangled her legs down the steps.

Normally, this secret pleasure was like a clear morning before a heat haze, but today she was unsettled. Something was bothering Mellor. She didn't know if Kath could see it, but there was some kind of thinking going on.

Her thoughts drifted to her bloke Freddy, who had been silent, like Mellor. She liked watching him, his easy way of leaping on and off his horse. It took a lot to work out what was going on in his head. They'd had a little boy, then two girls, but Freddy's father had been white, and the kids were pale. May let them play in the sun all day to darken them, but it was no good and they were taken before the boy, Dan, reached five. Freddy turned nasty, then, and there were beatings every night. Even though she knew it was the drink, May was relieved when he was finally kicked off the station for rowdiness. Often, though, she missed waking with his long body curled around hers.

Like many other mothers, she travelled on the train to visit her kids at the mission, even though she could only spend a few hours with them. Kath came with her, packing food for the four days it took to get there and back.

Their spirits always sank at the sight of the weatherboard building and grounds of dry grass, and by the kids' blank stares as they stood in two rows, flanked by a brother at either end. When her eldest, Dan, recognised his mother and aunt, he dashed into their arms, chattering non-stop. He'd always been a talker, and it upset her to hear that sometimes he was shut in a tiny room without dinner for talking during church, or belted for asking questions about God. They tried to tell Dan news about their rellies, and stories of their country, but over the years he forgot who was who, and he couldn't work out if he was supposed to listen to May's stories, or to God's. It confused him so much that after a while they told him fewer of their stories.

Her two girls hardly knew her, but played with the dolls she brought. She was never allowed to leave the toys behind, though. They couldn't give their kids anything, except their words and food, and then the brothers taught the kids that their Aboriginal language was bad, so they forgot most of that, too. At the end of the day, when Kath and May picked up their handbags and the empty basket of food, and took the dolls from the girls, Dan's conversation stopped, his blankness returning.

As they walked out, the children ran after them, stopping at the gate that marked the start of the mission. Kath and May could hardly bear to look as they trudged out, but they always stayed and waved until the children, crying with confusion, were rounded up and hustled inside by the brothers in their shapeless black clothes.

Kath and May managed the trip twice a year for five years, but in the sixth year the kids were gone.

'Haven't you got an address?' May asked the brother who ran the mission, sitting on the edge of a hard chair in his office.

'They went to the city. Someone will pick them up as domestics.' He twisted the cross hanging around his neck.

'What about Dan?'

'He most likely got dropped off on a farm along the way.'

'Which city?'

'I don't know, Mrs Lancaster. Sydney, Brisbane, possibly Perth. I wouldn't worry – he's in God's hands, and God will provide.'

Still furious some forty years later, May stubbed out her cigarette and lit another.

31

In late afternoon, as the low sun gilded the mirror in Eliot's room, Cate opened her brother's violin case and stroked the curves of the wood.

It took a long time to tune, then she played some arpeggios and a scale in B minor. Once her arms were loose, she opened the piano stool and dug out a stack of music. She found the pages of Felix Mendelssohn's *Violin Concerto*. Cate was sixteen and Eliot fifteen when Mrs Emerald taught it to them, though not as part of their syllabus. That had been a year of Roxette, staying over at Sarah's on the weekends, wearing white lace gloves and ra-ra skirts to the Blue Light Disco, trying cigarettes and purple eye shadow and hating both, wanting to be back with Eliot, following the wild-goat tracks in the hills.

A year later they were studying for their Associate Diploma in Music, and in the scales book Cate shared with Eliot, she found pamphlets on the Conservatorium of Music in Sydney.

She took them into Eliot's room. He was lying on his bed reading *Dune*.

'What's this?' she asked.

'Don't tell Mum,' he said automatically, sitting up and glancing past her shoulder.

'Are you going? And where did they come from?'

'Mrs Emerald. And no, I'm not going.'

'Why not?'

He shrugged.

'Don't give me that. You've thought about it enough to decide not to go.'

'I'd rather not talk about it, Cate. And I don't want you to tell anyone, either.'

Cate hadn't pestered him; they never operated that way.

'Why don't you keep going, Catie?'

Cate whipped around. 'Eliot always played the second movement.'

Leonora folded her arms. She'd brought the smell of soil from the garden into the room. 'It's nice to hear music in the house again.'

'Did you know he was thinking of going to the Conservatorium?'

'When?'

'The year we were doing our Associate. Mrs Emerald gave him pamphlets.'

'That interfering woman!'

'What's there to be angry about?'

'I told her I never wanted you two to perform in Sydney.'

'Mum, that was when we were seven. I'm talking about when he was seventeen. What if he'd wanted to go and felt that he couldn't?'

'There's no point in talking about "what if?". He's gone, and that's that —'

'Maybe if he'd been with me in Sydney he wouldn't have disappeared.'

Leonora stood like a sentinel. 'I'm tired of fighting with you, Cate. I'm going to get dinner ready.'

Cate wondered if Mrs Emerald had been grooming Eliot for a violin career even then, for the piece was a requisite for any aspiring concert violinist. She folded up the music and played the second movement from memory.

32

Cate had become chummy with Harry, the publican of the Tumbin Hotel. Though his shirts were neatly ironed and clean, his face was usually dark with three days of growth, while sweat gathered at his temples and beneath his armpits.

'Can't believe it hasn't broken down yet,' he said of the internet. 'It was always going belly up before.'

'Touch wood,' Cate replied, stroking the smooth bar.

She looked towards the seat beneath the window. 'Did you ever see Russell Wakeley in the last ten years?'

Harry slowed his polishing of the brass beer taps. 'I've been waiting for that question. The answer's no. I asked me mates, too. I asked all round. No one's seen hide nor hair of him. Not even his own mother. I asked her, too.'

'Thanks, Harry.'

He tossed his cloth from hand to hand. 'You were his bird, right?'

'Only for a little while, before I went to uni.' She stroked the condensation on her glass. 'When I was too young to know better.'

A man in a cloth hat and khaki stubbies came to the bar.

'Got a customer,' Harry said.

Cate listened to him complaining about work on the eastern road out of Kynidia. She drained her beer and waved goodbye.

Slowly, she drove out of the town, stopped beside the bridge and wandered to the river. Beneath a tall gum tree, she found a piece of grass that wasn't infested with nettles. Carefully, she sat in it and watched the water moving sluggishly.

Even now, she remained perturbed by the way her teenage body had responded so violently to Russell's hand simply sliding down her arm. When she woke in the mornings, her first thought would be of him. On her run before breakfast, she was aware of the sun pushing through her skin in a way it never had before. The days lost the rounded shape of sunrise and sunset, instead elongating to the time when she would next feel his cheek grazing hers.

After he had kissed her on the verandah, she found herself re-reading the looks and touches they'd exchanged. When she thought of his full lips on hers, she began to glow.

The next time he and Eliot finished shooting, she lay awake in her bedroom, her bedside lamp on. When she heard Eliot say goodbye and head for the bathroom, she switched off the light and walked quickly across the lawn in her thin cotton nightie.

Russell was parked beneath the cedar tree. He was about to turn the key in the ignition when she appeared at his window.

Slowly, he opened the car door. He reached behind and pulled her closer, running his hands over her buttocks and up her thighs. When his fingers opened inside her, Cate gasped. His other hand reached beneath her nightie and slid up to her breasts. He licked her nipple through the fabric, then looked up, smiling at last.

Cate dipped her head and kissed him. His tongue was insistent, probing inside her mouth.

There was a sharp stabbing between her legs. Cate cried out and tried to pull away, but he held her close. His fingers kept on with their stroking until, moments later, a white light washed over her. Cate laid her forehead against Russell's shoulder.

'Next time, Cate,' his voice was almost inaudible, 'you'll be ready.'

When he took his hand away, it was impossible to tell what was her blood, or what was the blood of the animals he had shot.

Suddenly nauseous, Cate hung her head between her knees. The smell of the moist soil beneath the grass was too rich. She wanted to retch.

33

After weeks of waking from dreams of his hands on her hips, of unclasping her bra to hold her pale breasts, of the hint of humour in her smile, Finch picked up the phone and dialled Cate's surgery.

'Hi, uh, I'd liked to make an appointment with Doctor McConville, please.'

'I'm sorry, she's on leave. She'll be back at the beginning of February. I can make an appointment with Doctor Robertson if you like?'

'No, don't worry. It can wait.'

Finch carefully replaced the handset, the dispirited, gritty feeling the same as when his calls to Aubrey rang into emptiness.

Almost immediately, it rang again. It was his boss, Max. A tanker carrying zinc powder from the mines to the refinery was sinking as it headed across the Bight to Adelaide. While he waited for the office to send through the ship's plans, Finch held the phone against his shoulder, jotting down details on the draught, the cargo's weight, and the height and force of the waves.

When the plans appeared he printed them out and analysed information from the computer. The ship was carrying eight thousand tonnes of zinc powder and another four thousand tonnes of ship steel. It was raining hard and the waves were eight metres high. Water, both salty and fresh, had seeped in through the hatch doors on the deck, down into the hold. Over the course of a day and a night, it had drifted to the back of the ship, causing it to sink at that end. The waves, thrusting themselves onto the deck, pushed more water through the rear doors and vents and into the engine room. The engine was now failing.

Finch's eyes snapped from the plans to the data on the screen, his mind shaping options and discarding them.

At last he rang the office and said, 'It's stuffed. Once the power's gone the ship is condemned. Can someone start up the generator?'

'There is no generator,' Max said.

'What kind of ship doesn't have a generator?'

'One whose captain's going to court. Besides, six crew members are trapped at the other end of the ship in the bow. They've got a handheld radio.'

'What're they doing there?'

'Their living quarters were next to the engine room and they'd been evacuated for safety.'

'You'd better get a helicopter in so they don't go down with the ship.'

Finch went over the plans again to check there wasn't another way out, but it was hopeless without power. He imagined the crew huddled in a knot in the bow, water slamming and sucking at the walls next door, the sea thrashing above their heads. The air would be close with the smell of their sweat.

An hour later, the phone rang again.

'The helicopter can't get close. The weather's too bad.'

'That only leaves the life raft. They'll have to risk it. Thank Christ they have that radio – one of them was thinking right.'

The men would have to get from the small room at the bow to

the deck, which would be slippery, and listing dangerously. They'd be battered by wind and rain, and it would be hard to keep their footing.

In the kitchen he refilled his glass from the tap and wandered around the house, wishing for the distraction of Jack's seductions upstairs, but Jack had flown to Brisbane for the weekend to cheer on the Broncos. At times like this, Finch used to stand in the doorway of their bedroom watching Aubrey sleep.

The phone rang again.

'How's it going?' he asked Max.

'They're in the raft. We've got to save the ship now.'

The waves would be crashing into the life raft. The men would be soaked and terrified. Finch wiped sweat from his temples, gulped more water and continued his calculations.

By the time the ship was ballasted and the seepage blocked, a band of pain was tightening around Finch's forehead. He looked at his watch. He'd been at the computer for ten hours. Outside the French doors, night was lifting. He pulled off the headphones and stretched, his joints aching, and stumbled to the bathroom for a piss.

Washing his hands, he saw in the mirror above the basin that his skin was ashen. Once, after nights like this, he'd been able to work through and run off the adrenalin in Centennial Park. Now he pulled off his clothes, stretched out on the bed and slept.

He was woken by the phone at 4.00 p.m. They'd returned to the boat and found that, though cargo had been washed out, the ship had stayed afloat.

'That's good, then,' he said to Max.

'It's a pity about the zinc. I'll call again in a few hours.'

'Thanks, mate.'

Finch hung up and lay back, his eyes sore and dry, his throat parched. He noticed the red light of the answering machine blinking. Finch fumbled at it and pressed Play.

'Finch, lovey, this is Carlotta. I've just seen Cate McConville in the pub. Harry – he's the publican – says she's there a couple of days a week, checking her emails. The family want to sell the property – it's worth one and a half million. I just wanted to let you know, darl, because you asked before.'

Abruptly, Finch sat up. He went to the kitchen and switched on the coffee machine. As it whirred, he thought of Cate's taut figure, of the way her humour had escaped and lit up her face. He fetched his address book and dialled Carlotta's number.

34

Cate pulled a comb through her hair and stared at herself in the bedroom mirror. Her brother stared back at her. He was gaunt, with deep furrows in his neck. After days in the sun, his freckles stood out sharply. His hair was straggly and riddled with split-ends.

'Come back,' he said from the mirror, just as Cate had called that afternoon they'd celebrated Australia Day.

Her father's mother had died when her car rolled off the road and into a tree. She'd been playing cards with her friends in Tumbin; they guessed she must have fallen asleep at the wheel because she'd never been a drinker and there were no signs of swerving on the road. Cate, who was six when her grandmother died, couldn't remember much more than a soft cheek, the smell of lavender, and a portrait of the queen in a deep-blue velvet gown, with a tiara in her hair, hanging above the fireplace.

Aunt Natalie had once told Cate and Eliot how, on Coronation Day, their mother had taken her, Blake and Charlie and the portrait up to the trig station on the extinct volcano at the back of the property. They hung the portrait in a tree and unpacked a picnic lunch. At midday they sang 'God Save the Queen'.

'What's a trig station?' Eliot later asked Blake.

'It was used for measuring distances between landmarks and properties. Satellite does the trick now.'

At Eliot's insistence, on Australia Day when he was ten and Cate was eleven, they packed fresh rolls and a thermos, picked up Sally and Charlie, and drove to the base of the volcano.

Flies and mosquitoes plucked at their skin. The scents of the bush were drawn out by the heat and bundled together like a sweet, loosely woven shawl. Kangaroos bounded away in alarm as they made their way up the hill. Crickets whirred, rising from the long grass, and cockatoos screeched.

The kids scrambled up boulders, ignoring Blake and Leonora's cries to slow down. At the top they paused, surveying their property below: the smooth paddocks networked by fences and bisected by the creek's frothy vegetation.

The trig station was only a few metres away, a tall, pyramidal iron structure with an upright disc at the top. They tried to climb it but there were no footholds.

Their parents and aunt and uncle arrived, sweating, and laid down backpacks and baskets. They poured tea from the thermos and drank it while Cate and Eliot explored and pushed boulders down the hill to frighten the neighbours' cattle.

When the lunch was unpacked and sandwiches made, Blake whistled for the children. They pattered back, kneeling cautiously on the woollen rug that scratched their legs. As they ate ham-and-tomato sandwiches, Charlie mentioned that there was a second trig station, somewhere to the east.

Eliot wolfed down his sandwich and brushed his hands on his shorts.

'I'm going to find it. Coming, Cate?'

'No, I'm knackered.'

So was everyone else, it seemed, dozing in the shade of a gum tree.

'Okay, I won't be long.'

But he was a long time. Once they'd drained the thermos and their beers, and eaten Eliot's Anzac biscuits, Cate became restless.

'How far away is it?' she asked her father.

'Can't really remember. Maybe about five Ks, would you say, Charlie?'

'I dunno.'

Cate rose, frustrated with their stupefaction. 'I'm going to look for him.'

She walked for fifteen minutes, keeping the sun to her left. The scrub thickened, scratching her arms and calves. Against the rules of bush safety, she began to panic.

'Eliot, come back!' she called, over and over. Her heartbeat was like a bird trapped inside a house, bashing against windows. Sweat streamed from her forehead down her temples.

At last came his answering call, 'Cate! Cate!'

'Where the hell are you?'

'Coming!'

In a moment, his yellow Transformers T-shirt and grey shorts appeared through the trees.

'Why did you take so bloody long?' she yelled.

'I found something, Cate.'

'The trig station?'

'Yeah, that – but something else, too.'

She followed him through the wiregrass, which came up to their hips and scratched their legs. They passed the second trig station, rustier than the first, and an outcrop of boulders, then continued through the trees until they came to a clearing. The earth within it was raised and compacted, unlike the dusty soil from which the wiregrass grew.

'There's a path,' Cate said, following it a short distance until they reached another circle. It was similar to the first, but smaller. 'It joins them up.'

'Maybe it was aliens.' Eliot followed her.

'Don't be daft.'

When they ran back to the picnic, the adults were starting to pack up.

'We found these rings!' Eliot began excitedly, and launched into a description.

Charlie had frowned, running his hand over his beard. 'Sounds like something to do with the boongs. What are they called, Blake, is it bora rings?'

Blake shrugged.

'Don't you want to come and see?' Eliot pressed them.

'Not now, Eliot. The sun's going and we have to get home,' Leonora said.

Seeing his crestfallen face, Cate said, 'C'mon, I'll race ya!'

Soon the bush was ringing with their laughter and hollering as they ran headlong down the rocky hill.

35

Kath wiped dust from the television screen with the hem of her red cardigan then stopped, sniffing.

'You been at the fags again?' she asked May, who was finishing a bowl of ice-cream.

'Don't know what you're talking about.' May ran her finger around her empty bowl and licked off the last of the ice-cream.

'You silly bitch. What happens when you cark it? The doctor said emphysema.'

'I'll still be with you, Kathy.'

Kath pursed her lips and vigorously rubbed the screen again. Static lifted the hairs on her forearms.

'You finished with that bowl?' she demanded.

May handed it over. 'You're in the way. I can't see the TV.'

In the kitchen, Kath squirted too much dishwashing liquid into the sink and poured in hot water from the kettle. She loved the delicacy of suds, the way they built up like clouds.

'Can't you just take 'em down and rinse them under the tap?' Mellor would ask.

Kath ignored him. She used to stand like this in the kitchen with Nance, swirling her arms in the soapy water while they talked.

One of the happiest stories to which they returned again and again was of May standing at the door of their shack, watching the sun pass down behind the trees and dogs sniffing at the road, listening to squealing kids playing in the river. She was glad to have this moment to herself, before everyone crammed around the table, Rachel and the boys dripping river water, jostling and eyeing the food.

The silhouette of a tall man appeared at the end of the road. May leaned against the doorframe, wondering who it was and where he'd been that day; if it was work, or visiting a rellie.

When the figure began to run she stepped behind the threshold, but he shouted, 'Mu-um!' She paused, disbelieving.

'Mum!' This time she ran over the threshold. She threw her arms around him, surprised by the width of his shoulders, and cried for all the lost years of feeling him grow. Then she laughed, for her boy Dan had found his way back.

As he ate his way through two loaves of bread, he told them how, after the mission, he'd been put on a cattle train and sent to a shearer's in Victoria. He followed the shearing team along the south of Australia, along to Esperance, then they travelled up into Western Australia. When, after nine years, he figured he must have made enough to get home, he asked for his wages. The shearing boss gave a handful of notes.

'I'm owed more than this!' he'd protested.

'The rest was for feeding you, sonny. I wouldn't complain, if I was you.'

Dan, who'd been given mouldy bread and maggoty meat, and cast-off clothes from white station owners, figured this couldn't be right, but the shearing boss had a warning in his eye. Dan crumpled the notes in his fist and walked to the nearest town. It was enough to get him to Adelaide. After that, he walked and hitched the rest of the way. He was so hungry when he got to Tumbin he didn't stop eating that bread for two days.

Kath stacked the dripping plates on the draining board and took the bucket of dishwater outside. She threw it beneath a tree, startling Sparks, who was sleeping nearby.

Nance, in turn, described the tree beneath which Mellor had been born, on an astonishingly clear winter morning. It had bowed its branches to protect them from the bitter breeze, as Nance had cradled the tiny baby. There had been nothing that she and Nance didn't talk about. It drove May wild.

'Can't you just shut your gobs for half an hour and give us some peace?'

Now there was peace, and Kath was shrivelling with loneliness. She sat on the verandah steps and held out her hand to the dog. Sparks hobbled closer and laid his head in her lap.

36

Sitting at the desk in Eliot's room, Cate rolled the stone from hand to hand as she flicked through his old exercise books. He'd kept some from primary school, the covers made in art class by cutting shapes from potatoes and stamping them in red and green acrylic paint, or by sucking watery paint up a straw and blowing it in spidery patterns across the page. Inside the books were algebra equations, spelling lists with crossed-out words, golden stars and Scratch 'n' Sniff stickers from the teacher, and cartoons he had doodled when bored. Towards the back of his Social Studies book was a piece of comprehension with the heading 'The Australian Aborigines by Eliot McConville', full of spelling errors. Cate smiled as she read it.

'Cate?' Leonora entered and stood beside the desk. She glanced at the exercise books.

'What?'

Her mother fingered her pearl earring. 'There's something I need to tell you.'

Cate straightened, suspicious.

'We've got a buyer for the property.'

'Who?'

'James Rickett.'

Cate remembered a sweaty man with discoloured teeth and strands of black hair pulled across his balding pate, wandering around the stockyards. 'Who owns half of Tumbin?'

'At least he's a local,' Leonora said.

'As if that makes any difference! As if any of it matters. Mum, I don't want to sell.'

Leonora reddened. 'When will you stop being so selfish? It's a generous offer and it'll take care of all of us —'

'Except Eliot and me.' Cate studied her mother's still-luminous, green eyes, the bob of dark hair, which she surely dyed. She added softly, 'And you, Mum. You're only doing this for Dad, aren't you?'

Her mother's lips parted, trying to form words. Then she walked out of the room.

The stone was hot and sweaty in Cate's palm. She realised she'd been gripping it tightly and rolled it across her brother's misspelled piece of comprehension.

After Eliot found the stone, she told him, as they climbed a ti-tree near the house, 'I'm taking it to Mellor to see what it is.'

'When are we going?'

'I'm going tomorrow, after breakfast. You're staying here.'

'Why can't I come with you?'

'I don't want you to get into trouble with Dad.'

'I don't care what Dad thinks! Besides, I was the one who found it.' Eliot was plaintive, picking pieces of bark from the rough trunk.

'No,' Cate said, climbing higher to hide her distress.

They had shown their father the stone a few days before when, after work, he'd sat by the back door and pulled off his boots.

'Look, Dad,' Eliot said. 'Look what Cate and I found.'

He thrust it into his father's hand.

'It's Aboriginal, isn't it?'

Blake turned it over, his thumb sliding over its polished surface. 'Looks like it, mate. Where'd you find it?'

'Harper's.'

Blake frowned. 'What were you doing there?'

'Exploring.'

'It's private property.'

'So? You always let us go where we want.'

Blake pulled grass seeds from his socks.

Cate said, 'I'm going to show it to Mellor —'

'You spend too much time with that lot,' Blake interrupted.

'But Rachel's our friend!' Eliot protested.

'Cate McConville, come here and finish these carrots!' Leonora called from the kitchen.

'What am I, a house slave?' she shouted back.

'Get here this minute, Cate.'

'Why can't Eliot do the carrots? Why does he get out of it just because he's a boy?' she spat, heading indoors.

The next morning, after a breakfast of three Weet-Bix, Cate hugged her brother, pocketed the stone lying on the dresser and ran out to the paddocks. The stone banged against her thigh. Cattle stared, then stepped nervously away. She climbed carefully over the barbed-wire fence and stood before Mellor's access road. She thought of her father's mind, hard and closed like a fist, and set off.

Cate had never been to his place without Eliot. The road was badly eroded at its edges and pocked with holes. In the distance she heard kids squealing and dogs barking. It was impossible to tell how many rellies Mellor had staying. There always seemed to be a different lot of faces in the ute when it drove by. Cate knew Mellor had moved off their property and into town when he was a boy, joining the other rellies who'd been forced onto the settlement on the outskirts of Tumbin when the first white people in the area, the Parkinsons, squatted on the land and then took the Aborigines' hunting grounds so they had to move to the settlement to stay alive. Cate supposed they liked visiting Mellor because it was their old home.

As Cate approached, the patter of running feet, screaming kids, and a hum of conversation, dropped suddenly. Three dogs rushed up, barking, and Cate stepped back, unnerved by their yellow teeth. She wondered where Rachel was, or Jocelyn.

'Cut it out!' a woman yelled at the dogs, coming towards her. The dogs stopped, wheezing. The woman directed her attention to Cate.

'You're the McConville girl?'

'Yes, I'm Cate. I'm here to see Mellor, if he's around.'

The woman scrutinised her, then nodded to the half-built house. 'He's in there. Mellor!' she called.

He appeared at the doorway.

'Cate.' His manner was neither welcoming nor hostile.

Cate's stomach burned. 'Eliot found something at Harper's. We thought you'd know what it was.'

He met her at the bottom of the stairs. He was slightly shorter than her father, his arms stringy with muscle. His denim jeans were faded and dusty, his red flannel shirt so thin it clung to his torso. He smelled of dried perspiration.

Cate handed him the stone. His thumb smoothed over its dark surface, then he held it in his palm. He looked at it for a long time.

'It's an edged tool, Cate. It might've been used to skin animals.' He handed it back. 'Where at Harper's?'

'Under the fruit trees.'

'It would've been disturbed if someone planted those trees. Maybe Harper found it somewhere and threw it away.'

Cate sensed, rather than heard, the rellies listening behind her.

Her fingers tightened around the stone. 'It's Eliot's. I have to take it back.'

Surprisingly, Mellor looked her straight in the eye. 'Let me know if he ever wants to give it to us.'

'Okay.'

Cate turned and baulked. A row of kids was staring at her. The women had returned to the campfire, and a handful of men sat on the bonnet of a rusted car.

'Cate?'

She looked back. 'Yeah?'

'Why didn't Eliot come?'

'I woke too early. Why?'

'You're always together. It seemed strange.'

Cate wandered back through the paddocks, the knots in her tummy loosening. She shielded her eyes from the sun and ran lies through her head, testing their authenticity, in case Blake asked where she'd been.

Up ahead, Eliot sat on the gate, banging his feet against the bars. He leapt off as she approached.

'What did he say?' he asked.

Cate handed the stone over. 'It's an edged tool. Maybe for scraping animal skins.'

'Cool.' Eliot put it in his pocket.

'You didn't tell Dad I'd gone?'

'No.'

'He'd be pissed off if he knew.'

'So? You like pissing him off.'

Cate shrugged. 'Has Mum got any morning tea? I'm hungry.'

'There's coffee cake left over from yesterday.'

They walked over the lawn. Tank was asleep on the wicker chair on the verandah. Cate rubbed under his chin. He yawned and glared at her balefully. She was about to tell Eliot that Mellor had wanted the stone when their father appeared, dressed for the stockyards. Cate tensed, the cat stretched, and Blake went on his way.

Cate placed the stone back among Eliot's underwear, then went to Blake's office and picked up the phone.

When the line connected, she asked, 'Did you know about James Rickett?'

'Hallo, Cate, it's nice to hear from you too,' Natalie said dryly.

'Did you?'

'Yes.'

'And you didn't tell me?'

'I told Leonora it was their job to do that.'

'It was a "job"?'

'You can be a chore sometimes, Cate.'

'Very amusing, Natalie.'

'I'm coming the day after tomorrow. We can sort out things then.'

'There's no point. I'm not agreeing to a sale.'

'It'll be nice to see you, Cate. It's been years. You used to visit me every few months before Eliot disappeared.'

Cate wound the phone cord around her fingers, then hung up.

Her father's desk was littered with bills of sale for stock, invoices for feed and, tossed into the far corner, an envelope stamped with the address of the local doctor's surgery. Beneath it Cate noticed a photograph, its edges curling. She lifted it out. They were all at the school athletics carnival. Both she and Eliot, grinning gappily, held a sheaf of ribbons. Eliot's front teeth had fallen out and were yet to grow again. Blake held Leonora with one arm, while the other stretched around their children. Even with his face shaded by an Akubra, his expression of pride was plain.

Once Cate had been small enough to cling to Blake's leg as he walked across the room and she shouted with delight. He would tickle her and Eliot until they couldn't breathe. That morning, she had heard him making Leonora laugh.

She placed the faded image back beneath the bill.

37

The caterpillars, poisoned by the Mortein Leonora sprayed onto the cedar tree branches, fell overnight. Cate watched them slipping from the branches, tumbling through the air and landing on hessian sacks laid at the tree's base. The muted thuds as they hit the ground woke her up.

She was bathed in sweat. She kicked off the covers, wiped her forehead and switched on the fan. The clock read 3.26 a.m.

When her heartbeat slowed, she pulled on her tracksuit pants and a T-shirt and crept outside to the cedar tree. There were no sacks beneath the tree, nor any caterpillars. Cate ran her fingers over the tree's low, smooth branches.

Nearby, in the chook yard, the chooks sensed her presence and rustled. Eliot, when he wanted to be alone, had a habit of going there. The yard's wire fence was smothered by an ornamental grape vine, the leaves of which were green in summer, then burnished to purples and reds in autumn. In the winter rains, they dropped off, brown and soggy, exposing the chicken-wire fence.

Chooks rushed at her when she opened the gate, but when they saw she had no scraps they went back to scuffing the dirt.

~

'Eliot?' Cate called, closing the gate. There was no answer, though she could see his feet beneath the raised chook house.

'Hi, El.' She bent her head and entered the conical tin shed. She wiped shit off the lowest rung with the sleeve of her old jumper and sat beside him.

The thing about chooks, she thought, watching one peck at a beetle in the soil, was that they were content. Of course, her father shortened their feathers on one wing with a pair of scissors so they couldn't fly, but they seemed happy with their repetitive scratching, pecking and laying of eggs.

'Everything all right, El?' she asked her brother.

'Yeah, just needed some quiet.'

The Christmas when she was thirteen and Eliot twelve, he decided he wanted a chook of his own, and wrote 'speckled chook' on his Christmas list.

'What do you want a chook for?' Cate asked.

'Why do you want the entire series of *Anne of Green Gables*? Each to his own, idiot.'

On Christmas morning, after he'd unwrapped a set of comics and new computer games, they told him to go to the chook yard. The gate creaked as it opened. There was a half-grown speckled chook, a red ribbon tied around its neck. He chased it around the chook yard until he caught it and held it in his arms, stroking the smooth feathers.

Cate and his parents looked on, bemused.

'You're weird, Eliot,' Cate pronounced.

'And you're not?'

The others drifted back to the house. The chook babbled with anxiety. Eliot put it down and followed his family to try out his new computer games.

A few months later, when he walked into the kitchen before breakfast, Blake turned down the radio.

'Eliot, there's bad news,' Leonora said.

Eliot glanced at Cate, mechanically spooning her Weet-Bix.

'It can't be that bad if she's still eating.'

'Cate, stop it.'

She dropped her spoon with a clatter.

'A fox got into the chook yard last night. It ate your chook.'

'What time was this?'

'Early morning.'

'I thought so. I was dreaming about it as it happened.'

He dug out two slices of bread from the bread crock and dropped them into the toaster, watching them cook. Cate wondered if he was hiding his tears. Blake turned up the radio.

As Cate and Eliot waited for Rachel to turn up so they could walk to the school bus, Cate asked, 'What was the dream like?'

'The fox got in, then the air was all thick with squawking and feathers, and then I woke up.'

'Are you upset?'

'About the chook? A bit, but I'm kind of over it now.'

'Why?'

'I liked that they were simple. But now I think they're just plain stupid.'

'Like you.'

Eliot whacked her with his schoolbag.

Cate walked back over the lawn, remembering waking one night from Eliot's screams, 'Cate! Save me! Save me, the bird man's after me!'

She rushed into his room, shaking his shoulder to wake him. When he opened his eyes and recognised her, he relaxed. She curled up next to him.

'It was as tall as Big Bird,' he said, 'but not as friendly. It was chasing me. I had to climb over a fence and that slowed me down. I was so small next to it. It was lifting me up when you woke me.'

Cate flung her arm protectively across his chest and fell asleep again.

38

'Where's Cate?' Natalie asked, as Sally greeted her at the airport. She scanned the heads for the small shape of her niece.

Sally pursed her bright-pink lips. 'God knows. She spends all day in the bush, keeping out of everyone's way. She's stick thin. Won't talk to anyone.'

'You did tell her I was coming today, didn't you?'

'Yeah.' Sally waved to someone she knew, leaving Natalie to wait for the baggage trolley. Natalie guessed Cate was still annoyed with her.

Sally was still talking to her friend when Natalie approached with her bag. She chatted for another ten minutes about rainfall and a local schoolteacher who was pregnant at thirty-eight.

Natalie wished Cate had picked her up.

Once she'd dumped her bags at Sally's house, she borrowed the car and drove to Leonora's. Leonora, wearing her pearl earrings and an apron patterned with chooks, was grating cheese for a macaroni bake for Blake's lunch.

She dusted cheese shavings from her hands on the apron and embraced Natalie.

'Nora dearest, you do look well,' Natalie said.

'You mean, no worse than usual.'

'Is Cate around?'

Leonora's expression soured. 'I've no idea. She comes and goes, all hours.'

'She can't be finding it very easy.'

'Are any of us?'

Natalie didn't reply. She stayed for lunch in the hope that Cate would return, but instead Blake lumbered through the door, silent with pain. She endured Leonora's fussing, and stilted conversation about the price of lambs.

Lying in bed in Sally's guestroom that night, a report unopened on her lap, Natalie felt the old claustrophobia returning, the fear of looking at girls and waiting for an answering, flirtatious glance. Instead there were only ever glazed looks, or an aggressive frown.

She understood why Cate ran, but Eliot – gentle, affable Eliot – had no reason that anyone could see for escaping. To her, that suggested foul play, but the only suspect seemed to be Russell, and when they finally traced him to the other side of the country in Esperance, they found he'd been on the road when Eliot disappeared.

Natalie had pressured to the investigating officer for details.

'He didn't look real happy,' the officer had said on the phone. 'Hangdog, unwashed, unshaven. But the month Eliot disappeared he was trucking down to Melbourne, then to Adelaide, then to Darwin and back down.'

'He couldn't have faked his log book?'

'No, we interviewed the people he delivered his consignments to. They remembered him because he looked so bad.'

Natalie tossed the report aside, overwhelmed with tiredness. She switched off the light and pulled up the sheets. They smelled of the same soap powder her mother had used.

At 6.30 a.m. the next morning, someone shook her arm. Natalie pushed her hair out of her face and saw a skinny figure in shorts and a singlet.

'I brought you some tea, Nattie.'

Natalie struggled up. Cate placed the teacup and saucer on the marble-topped bedside table and hugged her.

'Cate, darling. How are you?'

Cate shook her head, sitting on the bed beside her. 'Not very good,' she answered at last.

'You've lost weight.'

'I've don't have any appetite. I see him everywhere.'

Cate handed her aunt the cup and saucer, and Natalie noticed her forearms were mottled with bruises. She glanced at Cate's legs and found they were the same. Some were dark purple and green, others were small brown circles.

'What've you been doing to yourself?' she exclaimed. 'Those bruises!'

'It's a just a vitamin deficiency, probably vitamin C.'

'You're a doctor, and you're not doing anything about it?'

'It's only because I'm not eating enough. It's stress. It'll get better when I put on weight, eventually.'

There was a frown line on Cate's forehead that hadn't been there before, and a lost look in her eyes. She touched her niece's cheek.

'They want to have a discussion,' Cate said.

'Yes, Sally mentioned that too.'

'They want to sell it to Rickett, but they can't do that without a consensus.' Cate stroked the cotton bedspread, her frown deepening.

'C'mon, let's go riding.'

Cate brightened. 'I'll get the horses ready.'

Natalie began to dress.

39

'Going to talk to Mellor,' May announced, pushing herself up from the sofa. Beside her, Sparks lifted an eyelid.

'But your favourite program's on!'

'It ain't my favourite. It's just the one I watch more than the others.'

May pulled on an old navy army jacket that Kath had found at the Salvos and edged down the stairs. She shuffled along the dusty path to Mellor's shack. Sparks followed, lumbering.

They entered the living room with its weak, yellow light. Stacked around the walls were books, piles of paper and pamphlets.

Mellor sat on the floor, a sheaf of paper held close to his eyes. He glanced up when May entered. The clipped accents of a British policeman on the aunties' TV reached them. It sounded abrupt against the soft burr of crickets and the spirits brushing against the trees.

'Close the door,' he said.

May shut out the sound and lowered herself to an old wooden chair that creaked beneath her weight.

'What you reading?' she asked.

'Stolen Children report.'

'Bringing 'em Home?'

'Yeah.' He put the report down. 'They took these kids by plane in 1949. Everyone freaked out, so they gave the mums material for dresses and tossed sweets to the kids.'

May saw propeller blades, wailing children, and mothers screaming as a hand landed hard against their shoulders, prising kids from their arms.

It had been quiet, in comparison, the day they came to their camp near Musgrove's. It was 6 a.m. and her kids were still asleep. The copper, a slight man whose hair was beginning to silver, had promised her that at the mission they'd be educated like white kids, that she'd be proud of them when they came back. She wanted them to read and write, so she sent them on, but she'd never expected that her kiss to the two sleeping babies in the back seat of a police car would be the last, nor that she'd have no word from her boy for close to twenty years.

'That John Howard, he won't say sorry,' May said. 'And that we can't get Native Title on pastoral land.'

Sparks moved to a pile of papers and sat on them, his tail thumping.

'How do you know that?'

'*7.30 Report*, coupla years back. And listening to the radio, when Kath bakes.'

The accents from the TV, fainter now, turned American as an ad for cars came on.

'We would've been able to do it if we had that tool, wouldn't we, the one the kids found?'

Mellor snorted. 'No, they need way more than that.'

'What about the bora rings? And all our stories?'

'No, they want evidence of our mob here, doing things our way, generation after generation, passing things on.'

'But we couldn't! There was no work for Kath or I, and they might've taken you if you didn't get to school.'

Mellor shrugged.

Sparks stretched out on the papers, sighing.

'All this reading,' May gestured to the room stuffed with books, 'it ain't getting you nowhere.'

Mellor didn't reply.

'But you're cooking something, right?'

He gazed at her, measuring.

When May returned to the shack, Kath was asleep on the couch. May switched off the lights and TV, pulled the eiderdown off Kath's bed, and draped it over her, then kissed Kath's tissue-thin cheek.

40

'What was he like, that Easter in Sydney?' Natalie asked, as they walked down to the dam to round up the house milkers and take them to the shed. She'd wound a white scarf around her smooth, sandy hair, and wore a pale-pink blouse with the collar turned up. The dogs bounded ahead barking, and the ibis at the dam's edge took flight, their wings releasing a rancid smell. A white-faced blue heron remained, stepping delicately among the reeds.

'We weren't completely open the way we were on the farm. Something was wrong, but I couldn't find the words to fix it.'

'What do you mean?' Natalie found a flat stone and brushed soil from it.

'Nothing had been amiss before. We'd no experience of how to mend a breach. It just hung there.'

Ripples appeared in the water where yabbies surfaced and retreated. Natalie skimmed the stone halfway across the dam. 'I don't think that's true, Cate. Things were going pear-shaped when Russell was around.'

Although Leonora, concerned, had hovered after mealtimes to talk to Cate about contraception, and Eliot wandered through the paddocks on his own or worked silently with their father, Cate was unable to attend to anything but her longing for Russell's hands around her waist. He'd pick her up by the side of the road that ran through the property and drive to the bends of the creeks. Sometimes he fucked her on a blanket in the back of his ute and she fought not to laugh as tools and loose pieces of machinery rattled about. She liked it best on the shadowy grass, ti-trees arching above her, a breeze cooling their sweaty bodies.

Afterwards, he never held her, but lay apart, his eyes closed. Cate propped herself upon an elbow, watching the rise and fall of his chest, his ebbing erection, the whorl of hair leading up to his belly button. It was only then that she remembered Eliot and the silences that had fallen between them. She promised herself that on the weekend they would walk to the Falls or go for a ride, but then Russell called.

'Yeah, you're right,' Cate admitted to Natalie. 'Things weren't good with Russell. But by the end of El's stay in Sydney, we were getting on better.'

When Cate met Eliot at the platform at Central Station, he was tall and ungainly, holding his canvas bag over one shoulder. He bent and hugged her and she was surprised by how broad his shoulders had become. For a moment she had to search to see the boy who had followed her through dry creeks.

Then he unfurled his large hand to show her a box, intricately carved with flowers and vines. 'To put your rings in, I guess.'

She kissed his cheek, took his arm and led him through the crowds. On the bus, he was rigid from the people coming and going, the confusion of buildings, cars and crowded roads. She wished she could have held his hand but they weren't children anymore.

She lived in a hovel halfway to Bondi Beach with four other

girls; it was all she could afford on her rural scholarship. She showed him down the hall, hoping he wouldn't mind the sagging couch with its exploding stuffing, the lino in the bathroom stained with streaks of hair dye, the sheets tied across the windows. When they reached the back door and he saw the knee-high grass he asked, 'Do you have a lawnmower?'

'We borrow the neighbour's.'

'I might get onto that tomorrow, then.'

Her flatmates twittered as, wearing his blue Case tractor cap and Bonds singlet, he razed the grass, then raked the clippings into a pile beneath the wattle shrub.

When she took him to bars in the evenings, her girlfriends giggled over his silence. He smiled at them awkwardly, blushing.

'Cate,' they laughed in a lecture the next day, 'He really is such a stud.'

Cate didn't think it was amusing. She couldn't recall him being so morose, and wondered if it was just that the constant smog, noise and movement were so alienating.

'Do you want to go to Ag college?' she asked, as they walked through the Botanical Gardens.

'I dunno.' He squinted at the harbour. 'The waves look like flint, don't they?'

His evasiveness pained her.

One evening after coming out of a bar near Hyde Park around two in the morning, they walked up Oxford Street to the bus stop. Men were pouring from a gay club, hand-in-hand, one or two of them kissing. Eliot almost stopped in his tracks, to the mirth of Cate's friends.

'Guess you don't get that much in the country, eh, Eliot?'

He'd lowered his eyes to the footpath.

The day before he was due to go back, he and Cate went to the local shops for groceries for a picnic lunch. They found a passport photo booth and posed for a strip of silly photos, then caught the bus to Coogee. They walked along the headland, then through the mass of gravestones in Waverley Cemetery to Bronte Park. They washed down their sandwiches with beer, then Cate lay back and closed her eyes. She dozed, despite the cold sea breeze.

'Cate! Cate!'

She sat up with a start, wondering why the breeze was moist and salty, then remembered she wasn't in the hot, dry air of Tumbin.

'Look,' Eliot pointed.

The park was almost empty, but for a man standing a few metres away, a blue macaw gripping his shoulder. Its tail feathers reached down to his knee. A little distance from him was a slight woman in a green tracksuit.

They watched as the man lifted his arm and the bird sprung forth, its powerful wings outstretched, exposing their brilliant yellow underside.

'Oh my God!' Eliot scrambled up, his face bright with elation. 'Cate, did you see?'

The bird settled on the woman's arm. Stronger than she looked, she didn't flinch.

'How do they make sure it doesn't fly away?' Cate asked. 'It must cost thousands.'

Eliot stared intently. 'It's wearing a harness.'

'Do you want to go and talk to them?'

'No! I'm fine to watch.'

Cate felt Natalie's hand on her shoulder and realised she'd been staring at the low hills. They always deepened to indigo as the sun dropped behind them.

She tilted her head. 'Before he left, he said Sydney wasn't so bad – then it felt like we were right, that we had fitted together. But when I came home for the break after my third year of Med, there was a breach again. If I hadn't met Russell —'

'Stop it. Russell was inevitable. If it hadn't been him, it would have been someone else. You were entitled to your life, Cate.'

'But that's just it. I wasn't.' She stared at the heron. 'And then there was the fight with Russell. Eliot disappeared three months later. He must have had something to do with it.'

'He was in Adelaide, Cate. I rang the people he delivered his goods to, and they were absolutely certain it was him.' Natalie added, 'Maybe it's time to accept that there won't be any answers.'

'No.' Cate was abrupt. 'That's impossible.'

'You're as stubborn as your father,' Natalie said tightly. 'Don't you remember how adamant you were that you would never ride? You used to be so scared of horses, and now you can't keep away.'

'Yeah, you taught me on one of the few times you came here.'

Cate, envious of how easily Eliot and Rachel cantered along the roads without her, had stifled her fear of the horses' powerful, curving chests and flinty hooves, and asked Natalie for lessons. With Eliot's encouragement and Natalie gently leading the horse, Cate learnt to walk, to trot, to canter. She never had the same flair as her brother and aunt on horseback, but she came to love the animals' satiny sides, their liquid eyes and patience.

Later, there were rides with Eliot and Rachel wrapped up with wind, laughter and energy. Like Eliot, Rachel could intuit the movement of a herd of cattle and streak ahead to funnel them through a gate. More often than not, it was Eliot on one side of the herd and Rachel on the other, and Cate, bewildered by their speed, pacing her horse back and forth at the rear.

'What're you saying?'

'People can change. If I may be so bold as to present the evidence.'

'Very funny,' Cate replied. 'C'mon, move it!' She clapped her hands at the cows, and they trundled forward.

41

Mellor dragged the old wooden ladder from the ute, laid it against the rainwater tank and shook it, testing that the ropes still held it together. Blake and Charlie were so stingy they wouldn't even fork out money for a cheap aluminium ladder.

He peered through the square of mesh at the top of the tank to see the water's level, then climbed down and rapped the side of the tank with his hand, listening to it echo. It was three-quarters full, nothing to worry about.

He folded the ladder down, fetched his thermos from the passenger seat and sat in the tank's shade. He'd been drinking that same black tea in their humpy near Musgrove's as Joss, Kath, May, his grandparents and cousins clustered around him. By the light of a kero lamp, he read the note that had come from Tumbin. Someone had written it for his father, their pencil pressed hard into the paper. *Nance is sick*, it read. *Wants to see her grandsons. Please come back.*

'That's bad news,' May said. 'Sounds like she's dying.'

Joss leaned against Mellor, her hipbone pressing into his arm.

'If we go, we can't come back,' he said to her. 'What with all that going on in Wave Hill, Musgrove won't want to pay properly. He'd rather sign on whites.'

'I know,' she said softly.

'We're coming with you,' Kath added.

'Are we?' May was surprised.

'Yep. Time we saw our brother Stanley again.'

They pooled their meagre wages and bought train tickets. Mellor and Joss had two boys by then, and Mellor could hardly bear to look at Joss' family as they left the train carriage. Her mother and aunts were crying. The boys, upset by everyone's tears, began wailing as well.

Joss stood at the carriage's tiny window, stretching her hands out to her parents.

'We'll come back,' Mellor said, but it sounded hollow.

It took four days to get to Tumbin on that train. The aunts were exhausted, and the boys just about impossible, when they arrived at the tiny fibro shack.

Stanley's hair had greyed and his eyes were set back in pouches of skin. He held each sister for a long time, greeted Joss warmly, and lifted the two boys into the air.

'Where's Mum?' Mellor asked. 'What's she sick with?'

His father sank heavily into a chair.

'I'll put the boys to bed,' Joss said.

Still staring at the floor, Stanley began to speak. 'She was walking home, couple of weeks ago with her friend Maggie. They were both pissed. Been at the pub. Some white men drove past in a ute, off to shoot roos. They stopped and beat them. Broke Nance's leg so she couldn't get away. Raped her and Maggie.'

'Christ!' Mellor held a hand out to the wall. 'How many?'

'What does it matter, "how many?"' Kath returned. 'As if more of them makes it any worse than one.'

Mellor pulled up a chair.

'She doesn't want to see anyone,' Stanley continued. 'I thought that if you came back, she'd pick up.'

'Can we try now?'

Stanley shrugged sadly. 'Might as well.'

Mellor followed his father to the verandah, where he used to sleep. His mother lay on his old bed.

'Nance, darling,' Stanley touched her wife gently on the shoulder. 'Look, who's here? It's Mellor. Our son. Mellor's come back.'

The huddled shape didn't move.

'He brought Jocelyn and the boys, and my sisters.'

Mellor jerked his head towards the hallway. His father shuffled out.

'Who were they?' Mellor hissed in the corridor.

'Dunno. The police didn't give a shit.'

'I gotta go outside.'

Mellor began to walk the streets, as he had when he was youner. The night air filled his lungs, but it felt dirty.

He applied for a job at the abattoir where his father worked. After the open plains of the north he loathed the cramped tin building that trapped the smell of meat, the blowflies that hung about him as he walked home, and the bloodstained notes he handed to the barman at the pub.

A few months after they'd come back, Mellor sat with a cup of tea next to his mother, who was sleeping on the bed. He contemplated the bare backyard, stretching out to other fibro shacks and corrugated iron lean-tos in the settlement. Swaddled in thought, it was a few minutes before he realised his mother had rolled over and whispered his name.

He spilled his tea in his haste to put it down and kneeled before her. She stretched out her hand and he took it carefully, cradling it between his own.

In a few weeks she was up, the cast cut away to reveal a wrinkled leg. She hobbled around the house and, when the boys were quiet, held them on her lap.

One Sunday they went to church, Mellor and Stanley holding Nance between them. As they passed a white family of four on the path to the church's entrance, Mellor felt his mother stiffen. He looked at the man, who had noticed Nance. The man's expression didn't alter until his eyes met Mellor's. They narrowed, then looked away.

Mellor glanced at his father. He was also looking at the man.

After the service Stanley told the family to go on home. He was meeting a mate for a drink.

'It's Sunday,' Nance reproved him.

'Just go.'

His father wandered into the park next to the church, smoking. The man came out of the doors, squinting at the congregation milling in the sun. Stanley followed him.

Later that week, Stanley cut his hand at the abattoir and couldn't work. Nance wandered vacantly around the house during the day and Stanley couldn't bear it. He stayed in the pub, drinking beer after beer.

Then the coppers came again. May shut the boys in the bathroom with a fistful each of boiled sweets. Stanley was in the lockup, they said. He'd punched a man near close to death. Mellor took his hat from Joss and followed the policemen to the gaol.

His father sat on the cold cement floor, hanging his head between his knees.

'Dad?'

Stanley looked up and, to Mellor's relief, took his son's hand stretched between the bars.

'What happened?' Mellor asked.

Stanley had been buying tobacco from the grocer's when a white car pulled up at the petrol station across the road. Recognising the numberplate, he slipped into the shadow of the street. The man in the car began to drive away, but a couple of metres down the road the car stopped. Stanley stood before it.

The man honked, but Stanley didn't move.

'Get outta the way, you fucker! D'you want me to run over you?' The man slammed the car door, and strode towards him. When he was close, Stanley lifted his fist and punched the man in the temple. The man fell to the ground. Stanley landed on top of him. He punched the man repeatedly until his hand was covered in blood. The police said the man was still unconscious in hospital.

Later, Mellor imagined his father lying on his hard bed, looking at the blueness beyond the three bars of his prison window, thinking of his grandsons, of the unending sky of the plains, of the country from which he'd been exiled, of Nance's cascades of giggles when Mellor, as a child, had tickled and crawled all over her.

He figured it couldn't have been hard, when the prisoners were fixing fences by the side of the road, for his father to coil the rope into his trousers. The officers would have been bored with looking after blackfellas and wandered off repeatedly for smokos.

Stanley would have waited until the time when everyone was deep in sleep. The whites believed this was the witching hour, when the spirits came out, but the truth was, the spirits were always there.

He would have placed a chair on the bed and carefully looped the rope over the beam above his head, the chair wobbling beneath him. As air jerked from his lungs, he would have seen a mass of cockatoos in flight over the treetops of his country, for he was going home at last.

42

At the supermarket in Tumbin, Finch lifted a bunch of dripping chrysanthemums from a bucket by the newspapers. The checkout woman was middle-aged, the roots of her bleached hair showing. She wrapped the stems in newspaper, then brown paper.

'Just passing through?' she asked.

'Yeah.'

She would find out later that he wasn't, and gossip to her friends. She scrutinised him, as though she could eke out more information, but he pointedly returned her stare. Quickly, she opened the cash register.

Finch slammed the car door and accelerated. He had grown up with these people and understood their curiosity, but there was a reason he'd moved to the city. It wasn't just for the money and the jobs.

The place was almost a ghost town, its young people having joined that exodus to the cities. The council had planted trees and erected benches on the footpaths but it still held an air of hopelessness. Finch recognised pubs, schools and solitary, weather-beaten houses. He passed the telephone pole around which Lionel

Edwards, who'd had a death wish, had wrapped his car. Further along was Mae Gregory's cream-and-blue house, shrouded by a box hedge. Paul Gregory hadn't gone far to find his wife; he'd just walked two doors down.

At the edge of Brown Street, surrounded by oleanders, with the garbage and recycling bins still on the road, was his aunt's house. Next to it was the white weatherboard that belonged to Russell and Billy's parents.

As he edged the car into the gutter, the front door opened and Carlotta raced down the steps.

'Look at you,' she said, as he unfolded himself from the car, chrysanthemums in hand. 'You're taller and even more handsome.'

She wasn't much like his mother, whose long frame moved swiftly and strongly. Carlotta was of middling height, and wore ill-fitting trousers and a pink T-shirt. Her unwashed hair was pulled back into a ponytail. Her eyes, though, were the same as his mother's: dark and round, with long lashes.

They'd all been surprised that Carlotta hadn't changed her name when she married.

'And give up being Italian?' she'd retorted. 'No way.'

Sylvia had smiled, secretly pleased. She'd reverted to her maiden name when Finch's father left.

Finch followed Carlotta up the gravel path to the squat, 1920s brick house. The porch was of cement, with white Italianate pillars that Carlotta had instructed Dougie to install.

Inside, her kitchen was gloomy, with a lingering smell of bacon fat. Underfoot the lino was yellow and stained.

'How's Dougie?' he asked, pulling out a chair from the table. She took out an aquamarine ceramic vase he remembered from when he was small.

'Pretty good. Still going at the coalmine. Every few years there's talk of shutting it down but then they seem to find more seams.

Would you like a cuppa?'

'I could do with a drink, actually. Do you have any beer?'

'You bet.'

She reached for two bottles in the fridge. 'How's your mother? Is she ever going to speak to me again?'

'I don't know. She barely even speaks to me. Apparently it was a criminal offence not to ask Aubrey to marry me. Despite the fact that Aubrey didn't want to get married.'

Carlotta smiled. 'Tell me about this woman, Finch.'

For all her untidiness and lack of ambition, his aunt was someone he could talk to. Finch described Aubrey, whose passion for railways had taken her into the depths of Europe. Often, having fallen asleep, he'd wake to find the light coming from the living room. She'd be curled upon the sofa beneath the standard lamp, reading about Hertzian contact mechanics.

'Come back to bed,' he'd implore her, but she'd shake her head, barely glancing up.

'I'm not tired, yet.'

'How can you not be tired?'

'Newton only slept a few hours a night, while George Bush Senior had slept eleven. Note the difference, Finchley?'

He'd stay awake, waiting for her, but sometimes she didn't return until the sky was anaemic with dawn. She often rose a few hours later.

'I swore I'd never be attracted to another neurotic woman,' he said now to Carlotta, 'but it's happened again.' He pushed the beer bottle around on the table, making circles with the condensation.

Finch met Carlotta's gaze. 'I just don't know how Mum did it. The loneliness, not having someone to wake up next to. No one to have coffee with, or to buy flowers for.'

'Your mother was driven,' she replied. 'Especially after your father wouldn't marry her.'

Sylvia Accorso had worked double shifts at Kynidia's hospital to earn enough money to send him to boarding school in Sydney. She caught the train there at the end of each term to pick him up, and attended every annual presentation evening – for he always topped his class in science and maths.

The other mothers whispered, although she was impeccably dressed in a twinset with her cream high heels, her Italian grandmother's pearls and a touch of Chanel No. 5 that was one of her few luxuries. With her height, large sunglasses and the firm set of her pink lips, she was both feminine and intimidating.

'She never seemed to need another man,' said Finch, scratching the damp label off his bottle.

'You need to remember, Finch, darling, that it was frowned upon to be an unmarried mother then. She wanted to prove to everyone that she didn't need anyone else. Also, she couldn't fit in anyone except you; she didn't have time.'

Finch swigged his beer. 'Everything has gone to pot since Aubrey left.'

Carlotta touched his wrist. 'It'll come right, love. Just be patient.'

He looked out the window to the house next door. 'D'you have much to do with the Wakeleys?'

'Nah. I feed their dog when they go to the coast, once a year. Russell's woman, Sonia, brings the boy round when she does her shopping. His name's Johnnie. Nice lad, but mousey. Probably gets picked on at school.'

Finch couldn't bear the cramped room with its orange light any longer.

'Let's go to the pub,' he suggested. 'My treat.'

'Lovely idea!'

Finch waited for Carlotta outside on the dry lawn overrun with bindies and kikuyu. The Williams' yard was bare, but for an ancient mongrel curled up in the shade by a tap. He remembered that dog. His name was Bowser. It had been a puppy when the boys were young, and he was about fifteen. One day they'd tied it up and held it to ransom, and Mrs Williams had come out, drawn by its yelping, and scolded them.

Carlotta appeared in a dress printed with fluorescent hibiscus that his mother wouldn't be seen dead in. He opened the car door for her, as Sylvia had taught him, and drove to the pub.

At 2.00 a.m. he woke on Carlotta's brown couch, his head throbbing. The afternoon had stretched well into evening when Dougie joined them at the pub. Finch stumbled to the kitchen for a glass of water.

The pokiness of the house depressed him. He found a jumper in his suitcase and closed the front door behind him.

The town's stillness was disconcerting, street lamps tipping yellow light onto the pavements. A fox darted across the street, and the rest was silence.

He walked to the other end of town, until the streetlights petered out and he faced the dark paddocks. He'd hated coming back to Kynidia while at boarding school. He had no one to talk too, for he had no friends in the town and his mother was always working. Often, he wandered to the river and sat in a tree, reading. The Aboriginal camp wasn't far away, on the opposite bank. As in Tumbin, they were set up on the outskirts by the river. He would smell the smoke from their fires and hear them singing, or their voices raised harshly in arguments. Sometimes the kids came down to the river to swim or fish. Only once was he seen, by a boy of about seven who stopped in the tall grass.

'Whatcha reading?' the boy called across the water. His friends noticed Finch, too.

'Stuff about dragons.'

'Good?'

'It's okay.'

The boy idly whacked the ground with a long stick he'd found.

'Want to play?' he ventured again.

Finch sorely wanted to romp in a game, but his mother would disapprove. 'Maybe another time.'

'Okay.' The boy walked on with his friends.

Finch headed back through the streets. Distantly, he heard the smash of glass and a guttural cry.

'Those snivelling blacks,' his mother had always said when she saw Aborigines in the street. 'Why can't they get a job and stop sponging off us?'

If she wasn't denigrating Aborigines, it was the 'common people' who pierced their daughters' ears at age five and let their sons' hair grow into mullets, or it was Carlotta who had married a no-hoper and never took any care with her appearance. Eventually, Finch learnt to ignore her tirades and to step away from the arguments.

The sound of glass breaking came again, nearer this time. Finch quickened his pace.

43

Cate paused by Mellor's access road, staring through the trees. She'd seen him earlier that morning, taking a roll of fencing wire back to the shed, so it would just be Kath and May at home.

She walked up the rutted, potholed track. A flock of galahs jumped from the trees like a shredded grey rag, screaming. Cate looked up, and she was in Mrs Davidson's garden, the guinea fowl in the vast oak tree squawking as they roosted for the night. Blake chatted to Mrs Davidson while she and Eliot explored the garden, finding a garden gnome with peeling paint and a fishpond full of tadpoles and goldfish. A grey cat appeared from the oleander hedge and sat beside the pond, watching the fish.

When the light finally fell and the cat went inside to have its dinner, the large, overgrown garden seemed less friendly. Cate was grateful their mother had insisted they wear beanies and scarves. Hers were navy and red, Eliot's green and brown.

Blake crept around the tree with a net. Mrs Davidson was inside with the telly turned low so as not to frighten the birds.

'I saw one!' hissed Eliot. 'It jumped from that branch to that one.'

Eliot's wildly waving arm didn't help, but Cate saw another flapping its wings, then settling.

'It's too far up for him to throw the net,' she commented.

'Keep quiet, kids.'

'That's why he's got a pole,' Eliot whispered.

Their father inched the pole, the net dangling from it, into the tree near the bird. As it moved closer, the fowl flew away, its heavy speckled body roosting higher in the branches.

Their father swore spectacularly, as he did when things didn't go his way.

They waited for a long time. The cold began to eat through their woollen beanies. Their father swayed the net from side to side but the birds kept leaping and flying. Just as Cate, her teeth chattering, gathered enough confidence to ask if they could leave, Blake hooked the net over a bird. It screamed as he upended it, the bowed pole threatening to break. He lowered the fowl to the ground, pinned its wings and called for the children. They ran across to him.

'I need you to get the net off.'

The bird cried hoarsely.

'It's scared, Dad!' Cate said.

Eliot looked equally frightened.

'We'll get it home and then it will be okay.' He glanced at Eliot's white face. 'Cate, can you take the net off?'

Gingerly, Cate peeled off the net, shouting when the bird pecked her hand. Eliot took a step back.

'Now get the box.'

She ran across the lawn, glad of the chance to burn off adrenalin. Mrs Davidson appeared at the door as Cate picked up the wooden fruit crate by the step.

'Everything all right, dear?'

'Yes, Mrs D. We've got one, we're just putting it in this box here.'

'Pity you couldn't get the other two.'

'They're hard to catch. Dad wants me.' She rushed away.

In the car on the way home the bird scratched, rustled and wailed.

'I don't want to hear it,' Eliot said.

'You ought to toughen up, boyo.'

'Shut up, Dad,' Cate said automatically. She licked a finger and wiped blood from the back of her hand.

'Mum will put you two to bed, and tomorrow morning it'll be as happy as Larry, orright, kids?'

The next morning they ran to the chook yard in their pyjamas. The bird wasn't happy. It ran around and around the square pen their father had erected in the chook yard. It ran for three days. On the afternoon of the third day it lay on the ground, panting, and died.

'Stress,' their father pronounced. He chucked the carcass into the sacks for the tip.

A while later, as he was cleaning out the garage, Blake found an old incubator. He decided to try growing guinea-fowl chicks instead.

Leonora was exasperated. 'You're supposed to be throwing stuff out, not keeping it.'

'I've thrown most of it out.'

She looked scornfully at the small pile of dusty books, jars of nails and tins of paint collected in the drive. 'You'll have to do better than that.'

Blake stuck his finger up at her retreating back, making Cate and Eliot snigger. They leaned against him, poring over the round incubator, the lid of which lifted like a shell to reveal six holes.

'Where will you get the eggs from, Dad?' Eliot asked.

'We'll find someone who has guinea fowl.'

'How long will it take for the eggs to open?'

'About a month or so, I reckon. Chooks sit for three weeks.'

A week later, the incubator was filled with eggs and plugged in the laundry.

'Don't touch it,' Blake snapped when they stretched their hands towards it.

'Best leave it alone, kids,' Leonora consoled. 'Your father's broody.'

He was always a bit slapdash in his approach to things and cracked one of the eggs at three weeks. It wasn't ready, and Cate turned away from the muck of blood, yolk and feathers. After that he was paranoid they'd all cook, so he cracked one every few days. Even Eliot, who liked catching tadpoles and watching them grow into frogs and had once kept a hydroponic carrot farm in the kitchen, couldn't stomach it.

'You're a bloody eugenicist, Dad,' Cate said.

'Don't swear, Cate. It isn't ladylike.'

Eliot snorted. 'You'll never make a lady out of her.'

Eventually Blake had three fully-formed chicks, which he kept beneath a heat lamp in a wooden box. When Cate, after much clamouring, finally held a ball of grey-and-white fluff in her hands, her usual look of scorn melted into tenderness.

The chicks' legs grew quickly and Blake built an elongated cage so they could run about. They sped madly from one side to another.

'Are they afraid?' Cate asked one afternoon after tea and lemon cake. Blake tipped out the tea leaves from his cup and Eliot swung silently in the hammock.

'I don't know, love. They aren't the same as chooks,' Blake answered. 'But there you go. You can always do what you want if you set your mind to it. There's no such word as "can't", kids.'

He carried the cups indoors.

The birds looks streamlined, as though they were designed for escape. Cate wondered what they would think of her father's maxim once he clipped their wings.

Something made her turn to Eliot. On his face was an expression of sorrow.

'What's wrong?' she asked.

His eyes met hers. They never lied to one another, only withheld the things they didn't want to say.

'Nothing for you to worry about,' he said softly.

The guinea fowl went into their hut and wouldn't come out.

Cate pressed her hands over her ears, shutting out the galahs and their painful shrieking. She wouldn't be able to hear the aunties among that cacophony. Unnerved, she turned and ran back towards the house, her ears ringing.

44

As Mellor leaned against the motorbike, waiting for Blake so they could begin mustering, he spoke to the crisp air that would later squash them with heat, and the galahs that eyed him from the trees. The dust, now settled and still, would become angry with the stamping of cattle's hooves and the traction of wheels. Even though the whites had buggered the land, it was still theirs, and they weren't themselves without it.

To keep the kids at school and away from the coppers, they were forced into town with a mob they didn't get along with, whose country had been further upriver and with whom there'd been fights way back over hunting grounds and women carried off instead of married to the right bloke. Mellor never paid any attention to Stanley's mutterings about them, but it seemed the other mob hadn't forgotten their history either because, when they drank in the pub to block out the sorrow, they were always picking fights with Stanley's rellies.

When Stanley died there was Nance, Auntie Kath and Auntie May, Joss, himself and their two boys under the one roof. They managed to get work, but it was bad pay. Mellor was still at the abattoir, Auntie May did laundry at the hospital and Kath was a domestic in a bank manager's home. Together they pooled enough to get by, but they rarely had enough food. Sometimes the two boys stole vegies from gardens at the wealthy end of town, or hovered around the bakery, begging for bread. Joss had another two boys but they died young, from scarlet fever. Nance's heart got sick and they had to borrow money from friends and rellies for doctor's visits and drugs. Mostly she wandered around the house, vague, unless she was with Kath and they chatted. Kath could get her to do the dishes, or cut up some potatoes, while they talked.

At night, Mellor would be woken by the drunken cries of men and women stumbling back to the settlement. After what happened with his mother, he worried about Joss, and always went to the pub with her and came home early. She missed her family up north, but she made friends easily. The settlement ran riot with kids and there were always other mums for her to talk to. Sometimes, she said as she lay next to him in bed, they were tired and bruised, and wished they could protect their kids from the shouting in their poxy houses, and play with them in the river instead of slaving over a wringer. They talked wistfully of the new washing machines they saw at Parker's store.

Then Rachel came along and, with her fat brown arms and legs, huge eyes and black wavy hair, she was the prettiest thing they'd ever seen. Nance brightened whenever she held the baby in her lap, while the boys teased and tickled until their sister gurgled. The smell of carcasses didn't bother Mellor so much when he knew that, as soon as he got home, he could hold his little girl in the crook of his arm, and that the evenings would be sweet with lullabies that Joss' mother had taught her.

Mellor heard the drone of the quadrunner and dogs barking. He opened the gate, kicked the bike's motor into life and set off gathering the cattle.

Blake wasn't in a good mood. He gunned the quadrunner, choking the engine. When the cattle broke away he swore viciously, taking off after them. Heat began to pound upon their shoulders. Blake's face darkened beneath his Roundup cap and the dogs cringed when he shouted at them.

Beneath the bleating and barking, Mellor heard the clomp of a horse's hooves. He glanced about, wondering if it was a spirit, then his shoulders relaxed. It was Cate, on Sally's horse Biscuit.

'Mellor!' Blake roared, angry with him for having slowed. Mellor pointed at the horse and rider in the next paddock over.

Blake stopped the quadrunner, staring. When he saw who and what it was, his body and face softened. Then he twisted the accelerator and sped off.

Cate trotted through the open gate. Eliot and Rachel had been the more natural riders, but Cate, though she was a late learner, had been good on a horse too. Mellor waved to her.

Cate waved back. She looked at the mass of cattle, then kicked the horse into a canter towards the weakest part. Slowly, with the bikes and the horse pressing in and the dogs nipping at strays, they urged the cattle into a tight circle, forcing them through the gate. Once on the other side, they spilled out, and the process had to be repeated.

Cate cantered through the gate, Blake behind her. She veered to the left, her father to the right. Mellor closed and latched the gate. Blake's face, he noticed, was clear of clouds. Cate knew how to manage a herd, that was for sure.

45

Evening was falling as Cate walked along the edge of the paddock. Her father's dogs bounded through the wheat stubble, sniffing for lizards and mice. Cate loved this time of day, when the dense smell of earth rose through the still air and crickets' songs took the place of birds. Once the sun dropped beyond the hills, the sky flushed a pale pink and the ti-trees lining the creek became looming silhouettes. If she didn't know the country so well, Cate would have found the dark shapes threatening, and expected bunyips to creep out of the creek, setting off the dogs.

From Rachel she'd learned that bunyips liked swamps and waterholes, that they were terrible creatures with dank, dripping hair and haggard faces. Eliot loved the bunyip stories and pestered Rachel for more, but Cate found them unsettling.

She headed towards the house, but instead of the increasing gloom she saw the bright light of a winter's day, the sky a startling blue beyond the pale eucalypts. She, Eliot and Rachel watched Leonora bringing a quiche, individual strawberry tarts, a chicken salad, bread rolls and passionfruit fizzy drink from the boot of the car.

'How long 'til lunch, Mum?'

'A few hours. It's only ten o' clock.'

'A few *hours*?'

Their mother dug into her large leather handbag and dropped dollar coins into their hands. 'Go and put some money on the horses.'

A cork whizzed from a bottle and their father squealed with laughter. The kids ran past the streaky white buildings to the racecourse.

The dusty grass beneath the bookies' stands was littered with slips of paper. Women picked their way across the soil in large hats and colourful, strappy sandals, their dresses rippling in the light wind. Men laughed, bottles of beer in hand, rocking back on their heels or leaning on upturned petrol drums scattered with pencil stubs.

Cate pored over the program, reading out the colours of the riders. Rachel decided on a horse with pink and green, Cate picked one that was red and yellow. Eliot, scorning this selection method, settled on a horse according to name.

'Thunderbolt?' said Cate snidely. 'How long did it take them to come up with that?'

Eliot punched her in the shoulder.

They handed their cash to a balding bookie, his pate red from the sun already. Over his shoulder he'd slung a satchel, crackled with age. He glanced briefly at Rachel as he took her coins and didn't make eye contact again.

They wandered to the track's fence. Rachel wore a denim dress of Cate's over a pink corduroy shirt, with an electric-blue headband Cate had bought for her from the Tumbin chemist.

'You look nice,' Cate had said when Mellor dropped Rachel off that morning.

Rachel beamed. Beneath the band, her dark hair was bound

into plaits and knotted with pink ribbons. Leonora had wanted Cate to put on a dress but she adamantly refused, pulling on moleskins and a white cotton shirt so she resembled Eliot as closely as possible.

The kids clung to the fence as people gathered around them, the excitement of the crowd thrumming through their skin. The starting barrier lifted and the crowd surged closer. Commentary blared from old, crackling speakers.

'I can't understand what they're saying,' Cate complained.

'Mine! Mine's coming first!' Eliot jostled against the fence.

A man with binoculars leaned into Cate's view.

Rachel peered. 'Number twenty-five is first, then thirty-one, then nine.'

The man lowered his binoculars, staring at her.

'So, El, you're not winning. None of us are now.'

'How can you see that?' Cate asked.

'Good eyes.'

The horses rushed past in a cluster of muscle, divots spinning from the earth. A woman behind them screamed, and Rachel winced.

The day passed quickly. Eliot ate too many tarts and whinged to Leonora about feeling sick. She told him it was his own fault. Charlie won money in the 3.00 o' clock race and shouted everyone beers in the corrugated-iron shed that was the bar.

By evening, the adults were raucous. The kids sat around the campfire eating sausages snuggled into white bread that stuck to the roofs of their mouths, while the men roared and bellowed over jokes. Leonora's friend from town, Jane, tottered in her purple sandals and squeezed her husband's backside.

'You enjoying yourselves, kids?' Blake barked, looming over them.

They looked up from their sausage sandwiches, nodding.

'What about you, Rachel? Not often that the likes of you get to places like this.'

'Shut up, Dad.' Cate was sharp.

Blake blinked at her uneasily, then turned away.

Cate took her friend's hand. Next to her, Eliot was frowning.

The adults went off dancing and drinking in the area cordoned off with metal fence posts and hessian sheets. The kids chased each other around the cars with green glow sticks Leonora had given them, then sat by the fire with the children of their parents' friends. They toasted white and pink marshmallows on twigs until white goo dripped into the fire, and tried to scare each other with ghost stories.

'I've got a bunyip story that's scary,' Rachel said.

The kids fell silent.

'Yeah, you coons would know all about that,' said David, a boy with red suspenders clipped to his jeans.

'Take that back,' Rachel said.

'What?'

'That word. "Coon."'

The fire rustled. The kids' eyes were large.

'Sorry,' the boy mumbled, sitting on his hands.

Rachel began, 'Once there was a tribe, and the young men of the tribe who went hunting and fishing never returned. Their tracks, when they were followed, ended at the edge of a lagoon. The men stopped fishing at that lagoon and found other waterholes, but one young woman was in love with a man who hadn't come back. She was brave and curious, so she went to the lagoon and dived into it to search for him.

'In the lagoon, she felt the water move, and a big black shape rose beneath her. The girl leapt from the water and looked back. It was an animal three times her size with long thick hair, tusks like a boar's and teeth like a fox's. It paws were tiny, like a kangaroo's, but as it stretched them out she saw it had long, sharp claws.

'She screamed!' Rachel shouted. The children jumped. 'Then she ran along the edges of the lagoon, where she noticed a line of footprints. She followed them to a cave, which was full of bones. They crunched beneath her feet and she knew she was going to die.

'Just then, something came out of the darkness and hugged her. It was the man she loved! Then the rest of the missing men appeared. The bunyip was roaring, trying to get into the cave, so they picked up the bones and threw them until it jumped back into the water. Then they all escaped.'

The silence around the fire was palpable. The kids shifted on the canvas chairs, making them creak.

'I think that's bollocks,' said an older boy.

'Yeah,' the children chimed.

Rachel shrank into her seat.

Eliot spoke up. 'You're all just frightened, aren't you? If it's not true, then you don't have to be scared of it.'

The bag of marshmallows crackled. Someone told a story of the night their grandfather saw a ghost in the silo, but it was lacklustre against that gnarled creature that surely lingered in the shadows between the gum trees.

It was almost completely dark. Cate realised the dogs were no longer close by, and called for them. She waited, listening, then was reassured by the rhythmic sound of their lolloping. She set off across the paddock to the house, where the windows shone with light. They reminded her of James Rickett's teeth, bared in a yellow, unctuous smile. Angrily, she picked up sticks and threw them as she walked. The dogs chased after them, thinking it a game.

46

Finch wiped his palms on his jeans as he stepped from the street's glaring light into the gloom of the pub. As his eyes adjusted he recognised Cate, sitting before an ancient computer. Her hair was pulled into a ponytail, loose strands falling against her cheek.

The publican was watching him. Finch made his way to the bar to order a beer. As the barman tipped a glass beneath the tap, Finch watched Cate from the corner of his eye. Her body was still, every muscle seized with attention.

'You were here the other night?'

'Yeah, with my aunt.'

'What's your name?'

'Finchley Accorso.'

'Sylvia's son?'

'Yeah.'

'She left before I got here, but Carlotta talks about her sometimes.' The barman picked up a cloth and resumed his polishing of the glasses.

Finch angled himself so he could watch the TV above the bar and keep Cate in view. Shortly, she clicked the browser shut and stretched. Finch swivelled back to the bar. As Cate stood beside him, dragging coins from her wallet, his face grew hot from the closeness of her skin.

'Any luck?' The bartender asked as he took her coins.

Cate shook her head.

'Hey, this fellow here, he's come home after a long time too.'

Finch didn't know whether to love or hate the bartender. He looked up.

She frowned, immediately suspicious. 'What are you doing here?'

'You two know each other?' the bartender interjected. 'Geez, this place is smaller than I thought.'

'My aunt. I came back to visit.'

Her face hardened. 'You told me you hadn't been back for twenty years. You hated it here.'

'That was Kynidia.'

'This is virtually the same town.'

He should have known he'd be trapped by her ruthless intelligence, and didn't know what to say next. To his relief, she walked away.

The barman polished pointedly.

Finch watched through the old, rippled glass windows as Cate flung her handbag and folder into the passenger seat of the car. Her mouth was a tight, thin line.

When he arrived back at the house, Carlotta was yelling into the phone, her face brick-red. 'I haven't encouraged him to do anything! He came here off his own bat.'

Finch closed the screen door.

'He's here now. You talk to him.' Carlotta thrust the phone at him. 'It's your mother.'

'Hello, Sylvia,' he said, taking the phone.

'Finchley, what exactly are you doing in Tumbin?'

'Visiting Carlotta.'

'Why?'

'She's my aunt.'

'Jack said something about a woman.'

'And?'

His mother was silent.

'Carlotta shouldn't have encouraged you.'

'Carlotta had nothing to do with this.'

'She told you the woman was there.'

'So what?'

'She has no sense, Finchley! And you're not showing any, either. You need to let go of Aubrey.'

'What's that got to do with the price of fish? You miss her more than me – you were bucketing tears when I told you she was leaving for Europe!'

'No, Finchley. I was only upset because your heart was breaking.'

Finch slammed the phone down.

'Wow,' Carlotta said. 'You beat her to it. She always liked to hang up first. It made her feel like she'd won.' She tried to smile, but her face was white.

'Let's put the kettle on,' Finch suggested.

'That's the first time I've heard her voice in years.' She followed Finch into the kitchen. 'I'm kind of glad, even if she was yelling at me.'

Carlotta slumped into a chair at the kitchen table. From the cupboard, Finch took down a mug printed with Mickey Mouse and another with Roadrunner.

'She never got over me marrying Dougie,' Carlotta commented.

'She never liked anyone who didn't reek of class or money.'

'Your father had money,' she added glumly. 'And look where it got her.'

Finch made the tea and brought it to the table. 'It looks like I'll be going back to Sydney, anyway.'

'The doctor didn't recognise you?'

'The opposite. The doctor has a memory like a hard drive and recognised me immediately, and in the next second realised I was stalking her.'

Carlotta patted his hand. 'At least you tried, love. You can't regret trying.'

They both tipped three spoonfuls of sugar into their tea and stirred thoughtfully.

47

Nance died from the cocktail of drugs for her heart in 1974, leaving Kath both brimful with stories and as empty as an old tin can. She still missed Nance standing next to her doing the dishes, creaming butter and sugar for a cake while Rachel played at their feet, waiting for a sugary wooden spoon to lick.

Kath bunged the baba tin, full of chocolate-cake mixture, into the oven, then began searching through the cupboards in her room for her address book.

In Tumbin, Mellor and Kath used to sit outside at the end of the day with a case of beer, yarning while Jocelyn put the kids to bed. Then, when Nance died, Mellor was so muddled with memories of her that he forgot to talk to his aunt. Kath left it for a couple of weeks. When she started going spare with no one to speak to, she asked Mellor to tell his stories again. As she listened, she found his father's stories of their country surfacing. The plains their ancestors had smoothed out between the hills replaced conversations about his mother.

'Something's bothering him,' Kath said to Joss as they hung out the washing.

'Something's always bothering him,' Joss replied impatiently.

'Maybe it's the same thing as always.'

'Which is?' Jocelyn flapped out a pillowcase, spraying drops of water.

'Country.'

'He's always banging on about country. He just sits on his arse and thinks about it.'

'Maybe it's not in him to do anything, Joss. Maybe we need to help.'

Jocelyn placed her hands on her hips, squinting against the sun. 'I'd better work something out.'

A few weeks afterwards she set off in a crisp white-cotton blouse and floral skirt to the Country Women's Association meeting. She had her handbag in one arm and a cake tin in the other.

Kath minded Rachel until she came back.

'What did they say?' she asked breathlessly, as Joss walked through the front door.

'Some didn't like it. Some said right out they approved of blackfellas getting ahead, 'cause Aboriginal women are country women too. Leonora McConville liked my sponge cake, and that's all that matters.'

Jocelyn's cakes and slices found their way into the CWA fetes. They asked her to stand behind the cake stall to sell the goods, using her as an example of successful assimilation. She was polite and cheerful, she remembered the names of people's children and she often baked extra to give away for free.

'Why you doing all this white women's crap?' Mellor demanded, when she didn't come home from a meeting until late Saturday afternoon and his lunch was late.

'I'm doing it for you.' Tight-lipped, she slapped sausages and potatoes onto a plate.

'How?'

'Watch.'

After a few months, she overheard Leonora McConville complaining about being run off her feet by the children, and unobtrusively offered her services.

Leonora looked at her, surprised.

'And my husband, Mellor, he could help out on the farm if you like. He lived there until he was nine, and his father Stanley worked for Mr McConville. They left in 1948, and moved into town.'

Leonora's expression became appraising. 'I'll talk to Mr McConville and see what he says.'

When Mellor came home that evening, Jocelyn said, 'Just a matter of time, now.'

The following week they borrowed May's car, bundled Rachel in the back and rattled across gravel roads for forty minutes, arriving at the McConville's mid-morning.

It was, as Jocelyn later told Kath, Rachel that decided it. They'd left their two older boys behind because they were rowdy, but Rachel was dressed up in a spotted navy dress with a white sailor collar, pale-blue ribbons in her dark plaits, and white bobby socks with frills around the rim.

Cate and Eliot looked at her, fascinated, until Cate asked, 'Do you want to play in the tree house?'

Rachel stared at them solemnly, then she beamed. Cate and Eliot took off and she followed without looking back.

Over cups of tea, Mellor worked his hands and looked at the floor, while Joss held her teacup properly and complimented Leonora on her caramel tarts.

Eventually, Blake took Mellor outside, where he breathed more easily in the fresh air.

From the tree house in the apricot tree came the children's

prattle. Mellor said later he was surprised to hear Rachel's voice so clearly. Usually she was so shy or overwhelmed by her brothers that she didn't say anything unless pressed.

'You done any cattle work?' Blake asked.

'Yeah, up north. I was mustering.'

Blake rolled a rock beneath his boot. 'I remember your father, he was a good worker. My pop used to say he was sorry to see him go.' Blake kicked the rock. 'So I reckon, if Leonora's happy, I'll be happy too.'

'Thanks, Mr McConville,' Mellor muttered.

When they drove away, Rachel's cheeks pink with merriment, Mellor took Jocelyn's hand and gripped it. Jocelyn later said it was worth all the snubs of the white women of Tumbin to see joy shining through Mellor's skin.

When Mellor and Jocelyn left, Kath's loneliness seemed to make even that small house cold. She missed Rachel's scampering and laughter so much that she went and found Sparks in a litter of puppies that her cousin was going to drown in the river. When it looked like Mellor could stay for good, she and May moved to the farm.

She watched Rachel grow into a skinny, lively thing. When the girl came home from school, Kath gave her biscuits or a slice of cake, made sure she did her homework, then let her run back to the McConvilles to play with Cate and Eliot.

In the evenings, Kath would sit on the verandah and listen to Joss reading to the girl before she went to sleep. Sometimes, in the mornings before the sun was up, Rachel would cross the yard into their house and climb into her bed, wrapping her skinny arms around Kath's neck.

Having pulled out all her jumpers, Kath still couldn't find her address book. She tried the bookcase beneath the window, running her hands over the volumes to check their size because she couldn't see them clearly.

'What're you doing?' May's voice was curt, her hands on her hips as she surveyed the floor covered in jumpers.

'Looking for me address book. Can't find it anywhere. What's Rachel's number?'

'Yer cake's burning, Kath.'

'Christ!' Kath clumsily pushed herself up and hurried to the kitchen. She pulled open the oven door. 'You don't know nothing about cooking, May! It's hardly half done.'

'Smelled like it was burning.' May came into the kitchen. 'And I won't eat burnt cake.'

'Help me with these effing dishes then.' Kath filled the kettle from a bucket of water and put it on the stove. 'Hell, I wish we had running water in this kitchen.'

48

Cate pushed the brush over Biscuit's flank, smoothing her hand over the sleek hair, then pulled it through the horse's rough mane.

'Hey, Cate.'

The soft-shouldered form of her uncle was silhouetted in the stable door.

'Hi, Charlie.'

'How was the mustering?'

'We got them all in the yards. No breakaways.' Cate slid her hand from the brush. Horsehair stuck to her fingers; she wiped it on her pants.

Charlie sat on an old wooden crate outside. Cate joined him, leaning her head back against the slabs of the stable.

'I've missed the horses,' she murmured.

'That so?'

'Yeah. I've missed a lot of things.'

At the crinkle of plastic she lifted her head. Charlie was rolling a cigarette.

'I thought you'd given that up?'

'Sally told me to give it up. There's a difference.' He flicked his lighter and lit the tobacco. 'And don't you go on, young lady. I'll quit soon.'

She wrinkled her nose at the acrid smell of smoke. Charlie drew a few puffs then crushed it out beneath his boot.

'Do you remember your dad talking about the Italian POWs who worked here during the war?' Cate asked.

'Yeah, there were two of them. They were so homesick they ran away, but they only got as far as the train station before someone brought them back.'

'Could they speak English?'

'Not much. Mum once said she had to go to hospital with Dad because he'd broken his finger and she couldn't take Blake – he was only six months old – so she left him with the Italians. She was a bit worried, but when she got back one of them was walking the baby in the pram up and down the driveway, singing songs to him in Italian.'

Cate smiled. 'One must have stayed, because there's an Italian family in Tumbin.'

'Oh, the Accorsos.'

'I met one of them in Sydney. He came to my surgery. Finchley Accorso.'

'His mother was in Kynidia. A nurse. I think his father left not long after he was born. Somehow she sent the kid to boarding school in Sydney. The father was wealthy, but he didn't give them a cent.'

'He said his aunt was in Tumbin now.'

'Carlotta. Nice woman. Bit on the common side.'

'You shouldn't say things like that, Charlie.'

'Ah.' Charlie pocketed the dusty butt, then cleared his throat. 'Catie love, I don't care either way whether we sell this farm or stay, but your dad's not well.'

Cate pulled her head away from the wall. 'They should have

come to me about his hip. I would have been able to sort it out more quickly.'

'It's not just that. It's in his head. He's finding it difficult.'

'Aren't we all?' Cate snapped. 'Except you and Sally, who want Rickett's money.'

Charlie's hand moved back towards his pocket.

Cate stood. 'Tell Sally I won't stay for dinner.'

'D'you want a lift home?'

'No thanks, I'll walk.'

She headed off down the hill, kicking stones as she went. At the bottom she paused, wondering if she should go back up and apologise. Instead she walked along the gravel road. Finchley Accorso had held himself quietly at the pub, his hands bunched in his pockets. He was a tall, trim man with curling black hair and brown eyes shaded by long lashes. His skin was olive-gold and he smelled of soap and aftershave. Cate remembered the springy hair of his chest beneath her hands as she felt for the infection in his lungs, the way he'd hailed a taxi after their dinner, and opened the cab door for her. She wished she had thanked him.

Cate kicked another stone into the long grass.

49

'Cate, darling, you need to eat more.' Leonora picked up Cate's plate, half of her food untouched.

'Mum, if I wasn't so stressed, I'd have more appetite.'

Blake pressed a hand over his face.

'Can you take the plates please, Blake?' Leonora asked. She returned to her daughter. 'At least have some dessert.'

'What is it?'

'Butterscotch pudding.'

'That was one of Eliot's favourites.'

Blake took the plates from Leonora to the bench and left the kitchen, banging the back door.

'Yes,' Leonora said carefully. 'It was. Would you like to have some with ice-cream?'

'Okay,' Cate relented. 'But only a bit. It's so sweet.'

As Cate ate her pudding and read a magazine at the table, Leonora filled the sink and rubbed a cloth over the plates, suds collecting between her fingers.

When Leonora looked at her daughter, she couldn't help but think of the sparrow they'd found in the roof when Blake was laying bait to kill the rats and possums. He had descended the ladder, holding it in the palm of his hand, and called for the kids.

The bird's feathers had fallen away, but the dry air had preserved its brown, wrinkled skin, the curved claws and its beak. There were hollows where its eyes had been.

Eliot was fascinated. He shifted it onto a sheet of cardboard and spent an afternoon taking photos of it. Cate left him to it, disgusted.

Leonora wiped the cutlery clean. Cate brought her empty bowl to the sink. 'Thanks, Mum, that was good.'

'You're welcome, darling.'

A few minutes later, Cate was on the phone in the office to the fellow doctor at her surgery, her voice clipped and matter-of-fact.

Leonora heard the back door close and glanced up as Blake came in. He wrapped his arms around her waist and laid his chin on her shoulder.

'Not too much longer,' Leonora said, reassured by his bulk and warmth.

'God, I hope not.'

Leonora shifting, facing him. His chin was speckled with a day of stubble. 'Sometimes I think you hate her.'

'Don't you?'

'No! She irritates me, but she's our daughter. I couldn't hate her, ever.'

Blake released his hold, heading for the brandy decanter on the sideboard. Leonora stared, suds dripping onto her shoes.

50

Cate woke at 5.10 a.m., dawn filling the room. The apostlebirds were calling from the apricot tree. Eliot used to sing with them, maintaining that they were calling his name with their three-syllable song: *El-i-ot*. She made a cup of tea and sat outside on the verandah. Out of the brittle light, Tank appeared, striding boldly across the lawn.

'Tank!' Cate called.

He rubbed his cheek against her calf. Cate picked him up. His fur was cold and the pads of his paws damp and dirty; he'd been out in the paddocks that night. He leapt into her lap and she stroked his head. She wondered if he was too old, now, to hunt enthusiastically.

The stars were absorbed by growing daylight. Eliot, obsessed with cosmology, would sit on a camp stool on the lawn on summer evenings with a telescope, a torch and a book of constellations. He would locate each one, page by painstaking page, and once stayed up all night to watch Halley's comet pass by.

She smelled the figs on the breeze again and closed her eyes.

Russell had been over; he and Eliot had returned from shooting rabbits on the property and the three of them were making their way to the creek to sit in the afternoon shade and drink beers. When they stepped into the paddock, harvested a month before, they saw snakes in the grass, so Eliot went back to the house for their guns. Cate, dozy already in the heat, watched him go. Fruit flies from the fig tree hovered. Cate waved them lazily from her face.

She was startled when Russell grabbed her, kissing her roughly on the mouth and jerking her to him so she felt his hard, insistent cock.

'Quick, under the fig tree, before he gets back.'

'No, Russell. He'll find us. I don't want to.'

'I do.'

He pulled her by the wrist under the tree, stopping to take off his shirt and place it beneath her. He tore off her shorts and undies and slipped his fingers, briefly, up between her legs. The pleasure was intense, and she lay back as he unbuckled his jeans and tore off the top of a condom packet. He lifted her hips and thrust himself into her. Cate couldn't keep from crying out. She was saturated by the smell of figs.

She sensed her brother standing nearby before she could see his boots, the ends of the guns resting beside them.

'Stop, Russell,' she gasped. 'Stop.'

'What?' he groaned, pushing himself in one last time, and exhaling.

Cate heard the crunch of wheat stalks as Eliot walked away. She laid her head on the ground.

'Why did you want me to stop? You sounded keen.'

'Eliot saw.'

He made a noise. She didn't know if it was laughter or embarrassment. Her eyes filled with tears.

Carefully, Russell pulled off her T-shirt and unclasped her bra.

He tugged lightly at her nipples with his teeth and fluttered his tongue over her swollen clit. She didn't want to come, but pleasure was already rolling through her body and washing over her. She dug her nails viciously into Russell's shoulders, marking him.

This was what shame was: the smell of overripe figs and sex, and wave after wave of orgasm as her brother walked away.

That night, Eliot didn't come home for dinner.

'We, uh, had an argument,' she told her mother.

Leonora frowned. 'That's not like you two.'

Cate selected knives and forks from the drawer to lay the table.

'Do you want to talk about it?'

'No.'

'You sure?'

'Yes, Mum. Contrary to popular opinion, talking doesn't solve all the world's problems, okay?'

Cate lay awake once her parents had gone to bed, staring at the ceiling. Bats flapped to the fruit trees. The next morning they would find some entangled, hissing, in the nets Leonora threw over the trees. At 12.10 a.m. she heard the sound of Eliot's sneakers pressing across the grass. She listened to the front door swing, the fridge's seal unsticking, the pouring of a glass of cold water.

When the lamp clicked on in his bedroom, she opened the door between them.

'I'm sorry you saw that, El.'

He sat on his bed and unlaced his shoes.

'Russell was so sudden, I couldn't stop it.'

'Was he violent?'

'No, I wanted it. Though not at first.'

'He's been like that to other women.'

'How do you know?'

'I've heard.'

'From whom?'

Eliot shook his head.

'I won't see him again.'

'Why not?'

Cate tried to find her words. 'He was supposed to be your friend, too. He should have shown more consideration.'

Eliot snorted. 'I hardly think he's that kind of guy, Cate.' He pulled off his socks, wriggling his toes. 'Besides, it's your life. You can do what you want.'

'It's not just my life,' she said faintly.

Eliot's expression softened. 'Don't worry about it, Cate. Go to sleep.'

Cate crawled back into bed but she couldn't sleep, even after Eliot had switched off the light.

The next day, when she called Russell and ended it, she was astonished by the vitriol that he hammered down the phone.

'But I'm leaving for uni in a month, you knew that all along,' she told him. 'And I'd rather spend that month with Eliot, not you.'

He didn't stop swearing, so Cate hung up. Although, for weeks afterwards, her body craved him like salt; she refused to pick up the phone.

Tank was kneading her legs, his claws pricking her skin. Cate pushed him from her lap and went into the kitchen to find him some cat food. On the bench were quiche, flan and roasting trays for the lunch her mother would make. Everyone was coming, and they wanted her to sign the contract with Rickett.

A few hours later, when the roast was in the oven and the flan and quiche pans lined with pastry, Cate pulled on her sneakers. She hoped to get out of the house without her mother knowing, but the creak of the screen door gave her away.

'Cate, is that you?' her mother called from the kitchen.

Cate waited until Leonora came to the door. 'I left a note on my table.'

'Where are you going?'

'Running. In the back paddocks.'

Her mother frowned. 'How long will you be?'

'Hours.'

'But we need you here, Cate, to talk about what to do and sign the papers.'

'You know what I want. I'm not selling.'

'We've been through all this! You said you'd decided —'

'I didn't *say* or *decide* anything; you inferred it all.' Cate closed the screen door between them.

'Cate McConville, don't you dare leave!'

Cate ran away from it all, losing her frustration in the rhythm of her breathing and the measure of her stride.

51

Sally and Charlie pushed open the screen door as Leonora turned the potatoes in the roasting pan.

'G'day, love,' Charlie hugged her, his jacket smelling of the exhaust fumes from their motorbike. Sally kissed her cheek and lifted a basket onto the bench. She wore her favourite fob chain and had swept her hair back from her face with a black-velvet headband.

'Nat will be around in a bit.'

'Where's Blake?' Charlie asked.

Leonora opened the oven and pushed the roast back in. 'He's out the back, mending his motorbike.'

Charlie disappeared.

From the basket, Sally took out two bottles of wine, rounds of brie and packets of crackers and Arnott's assorted biscuits to have with coffee.

'It's nice to have Nat here again.'

'Yes, she and Cate have their conversations while I cook in the boiling kitchen.'

'They don't see each other often, Nora.'

'And when they do, they're like this.' She crossed her third finger over her second, then rinsed dust from the wine glasses.

'Chardonnay?' Sally asked.

'If you dry these, I'll find a bottle opener.'

Sally wiped the glasses with a tea towel printed with drawings of the Anglican church in Tumbin. 'Where's Cate?'

Leonora swished the implements in the drawer. 'Running.'

'When's she coming back?'

She found the bottle opener between a knife and the barbecue tongs. 'I've no idea.'

'But the deal won't go through without her —'

'I know. I've told her that.' She slammed the door shut.

'We shouldn't have let the kids become partners.'

Leonora peeled off the black wrapper from the bottle's neck and forced the screw into the cork. 'You were part of that discussion too, Sally. You were more than happy then to sign them into the partnership so Eliot could work the farm, and you and Charlie could stay here. We can't do anything without a consensus, remember?'

'Here's Natalie.'

Leonora heard relief in Sally's voice, and pulled the cork.

Natalie urged Charlie's old ute up the hill, through the gate and beneath the peppercorn tree. She switched off the engine and stepped out in pressed camel trousers, a cream cashmere jumper and ballet flats. Her white blouse was too long and hung beneath her jumper, and her sleek sandy hair was pulled back into an untidy knot.

'How can she look messy and classy at the same time?'

'Money,' Leonora replied grimly, taking a mouthful of wine.

Natalie leapt up the steps, all smiles and light perfume, to meet Leonora and Sally on the brick patio.

'Hi again, Sal.' She stooped and pecked Sally's cheek. 'I fed the chooks and I cut some roses for the vase in the bedroom.'

'Not my Grand Galas, I hope. I was saving them for Amy Farrer's birthday.'

Natalie followed the women to the kitchen. 'Where's Cate?'

'Out running somewhere.'

'I was looking forward to seeing her.'

'You needn't. She's being a surly bitch.' Leonora opened the oven door and checked the roast chicken.

'Nora! You shouldn't be so hard on her.' Natalie poured herself a glass of wine.

'I have to be hard. She won't sign otherwise. I told her to be here and she bloody well left.' Leonora closed the oven door. 'Besides, it's easy for you to be sympathetic: she's not your daughter.'

In the dining room, the table was laid with plates and cutlery that Leonora and Blake had been given on their wedding day. Leonora removed Cate's plate, glass and cutlery and took it into the kitchen. No one commented. They seated themselves, and Blake sliced the roast chicken. Leonora passed around the porcelain gravy boat, embellished with roses and ivy, and the white ceramic bowl of crisp potatoes. Although she tried to resist it, fury rippled beneath her skin like a grass fire.

'Beans, Nora?' Charlie was asking.

'Please.'

Charlie sat in the same seat Eliot had occupied the last time they'd eaten together like this. It was the Christmas before Cate began her third year of university. Natalie had flown up from Melbourne and was staying with them. Cate, excited by the prospect of going back to the city, was chatty and lively.

Eliot, meanwhile, spent most of his time in the hills, shooting.

'He's been very quiet,' Natalie commented as they drove to Tumbin for groceries the day before. 'More so than usual.'

'Cate's going to Sydney soon to do some temping before uni starts. He gets upset every time she leaves.' Leonora slowed as a car passed, enveloping them in dust. 'I think he imagined she'd always come back, but that's looking less likely every year.'

'Maybe I'll have a chat with him.'

'Good luck. I've tried, but he just evades my questions. He's become very skilful at it.'

Leonora never asked if Natalie had spoken with him. Perhaps her sister-in-law had decided it wasn't needed, for on the day of the lunch, Eliot was cheerful again, diligently refilling the glasses and carrying dishes back and forth from the kitchen. They pulled bonbons left over from the previous year's Christmas, and Eliot arranged the plastic toys that fell out – a hairclip, a tiny hourglass, a pair of dice – in a row along the kitchen windowsill.

'Delicious chicken, Nora,' Sally was saying. 'Which recipe did you use?'

'The *Women's Weekly* one,' Leonora answered automatically. 'I put red wine in the gravy. It makes it richer.'

After lunch, Natalie watched Leonora's gloved hands washing the dishes. 'Cate's not going to come back for a while, is she?'

Leonora sighed. 'Probably not. We'll have to schedule another meeting.'

'You might not be able to make her change her mind. She's stubborn, like her father.'

Plates clacked as Leonora slid them onto the draining board. 'She has to do it, unless she wants to look after Blake and I in retirement.'

'Surely it's more complicated for her than that.' Natalie found the jar of coffee in the fridge and spooned it into the percolator. 'She's already lost a part of herself. If the farm goes, she loses even more.'

'Don't we all?'

'Blake has you, Leonora, so he already has more support. The person Cate loved most was Eliot —'

'She has us.'

'Not in the same way.'

'It's been eight years, Nat. She should be getting over it by now.'

'She might never get over it.'

Leonora shook her head, pulled off the gloves and took down the brown ceramic cups from the dresser for coffee.

When they entered the dining room, the table was clear and the white sheets of Rickett's contract lay against the dark, smooth wood. Blake stood by the window, staring at the low hills in the distance, deep blue in the summer haze. His shoulders were pulled straight by his hands, knotted behind his back. Leonora placed the cups carefully on the table and touched his arm. He looked down at her, a frown scoring his forehead.

He nodded at the table. 'Everyone's name is on it except Cate's and Eliot's.'

'It won't take long,' she said, beneath the sound of Natalie pouring the coffee. 'Then you can do the ploughing and listen to the radio in the tractor.'

He nodded, unclasping his hands. They hung loosely by his side.

52

Mellor waited by his ute. The flies, his dog and the dry heat waited with him. It was at times like this, he thought, that people liked to smoke. They couldn't see the breeze stroking the wiregrass, breathe in the hot, dusty smell that rose from the soil, nor watch the faint tracks left by tiny lizards going about their business. He wiped his palms on his shorts and shifted his backside against the door.

When Cate had passed him at this spot a few weeks ago he'd sensed a harshness that hadn't been there before. She used to be such a mischievous girl, with a playful glint in her eye. It was still there, still sharp, but now bitter. He remembered her bloodshot eyes following the pair of rosellas flying overhead in a flash of green and red.

Once Mrs Mac had asked him to pick up her kids from the bus stop. She'd been called into town at short notice and Joss had taken Rachel up north to see her rellies. He'd lifted Eliot onto the motorbike before him, while Cate sat behind, rubbing her cheek against his flannel shirt.

He'd let them into the house, made a cup of tea for himself and found packets of chips for them in the cupboard. He took them outside. Eliot, singing, climbed into the hammock while Cate slipped into the tyre that served as a swing, demanding to be wound up. Mellor whirled her round, the rope twisting, and when it would tighten no more he released it. Cate spun quickly, shrieking with delight. As the tyre slowed, Cate told Mellor about her day in a patter of, 'He said Mrs Smith said she said and I said,' as gentle as rain on a windowpane.

When Mellor heard the crunch of the car's wheels in the drive and said, 'Mum's coming,' the kids didn't move. It was only when the back door opened and Mrs Mac appeared that they emerged from their worlds. Mellor had putted home through the paddocks on his motorbike, the kids' trust sitting in his veins like gold.

His palms were sweating again. Ever since that day a few weeks back, when he'd stopped by Mrs Mac's for a cuppa and she told him Cate was coming home, he'd felt leaden, carrying those ugly details around with him. It would be a relief to give them up.

He stiffened. The sound of magpies cawing disappeared and a heavier footstep was coming, breaking twigs and grass as it found the earth.

53

When she saw Mellor at the bottom of the hill, resting against his ute, Cate wondered if it was *déjà vu* or if, after eight years of insomnia, she was finally hallucinating. She didn't know how long she'd been running, but it must have been about an hour, for her socks were furry with grass seeds and the sun was directly above her head.

Mellor pushed himself away from the ute. She jogged towards him, slowing to a walk to get her breath back. Sparks scuttled up and bounded towards her. She let the dog sniff her hand, then patted his head.

'Everything all right, Mellor?' she asked.

'Yeah,' he said, looking to the right of her shoulder.

'Is your ute busted?'

'Nah, it's fine.'

She took off her cap and wiped her forehead, then jumped. The dog was licking sweat from her legs, liking the salt.

'Sparks, here.' Mellor's tone was sharp.

'It's okay.'

The dog looked up, tail wagging.

'How's the business?' Mellor gestured in the direction of the house beyond the paddocks.

'I'm avoiding it.'

'How long you going to keep running?'

'A couple more hours.'

Mellor flicked his hat, startling Sparks into the shadow of the ute. 'Can you last that long?'

'I think so.' Cate watched sheep in the adjacent paddock making their way to the dam. Unsettled by Mellor's silence, she put her cap back on.

'I'll be off then.'

'Cate, don't go.' Mellor put his hand on her shoulder. Surprised, she stood still.

'I need to talk with you.'

'Right now?'

'Yeah. I think you should come back to my place for a cuppa.'

'Why can't it wait?'

Mellor dropped her hand, gazing at the hills beyond, the clouds dotting the expansive blue sky, then returned to Cate. 'It's about Eliot.'

She started. 'What about him?'

'We need to have a cuppa and talk.'

Heat rushed through her body, prickling her scalp. She reached out and found the side of the ute. 'Mellor, do you know where he is?'

He didn't respond, looking down at his feet.

Cate studied him, her throat dry, then said abruptly, 'Okay, let's get moving.'

Mellor drove along the dirt road for five minutes then turned up a track that wended past Harper's. They passed the empty, shambling weatherboard with its flaking paint. Cate gripped her knees.

The track became rougher. Spanners and screwdrivers at Cate's feet clanked against each other as the tyres dipped into potholes. In the side mirror she saw Sparks pressed against the side of the tray, sniffing the wind.

When they pulled up at the house, Cate expected kids and dogs to come running out, the way they used to, but instead it was silent.

An old woman wearing a beanie hobbled out of the second shack, which was listing so much it was propped up with posts. One eye was brown, the other cloudy with a cataract.

'Here's Auntie Kath, you remember her?'

'Of course I do.' Cate recalled sitting in Kath's broad lap, her low voice vibrating through their bodies. She crossed the yard and kissed Kath's cheek.

'We're having some tea,' Mellor said. 'You aunties can join us later if you like.'

Inside Mellor's house, Cate leaned against a door jamb as he rustled in a cupboard, tapping her foot. Dust had collected in the corners of the room and the lino was lifting, cracked and stained at its edges. On the bench was a row of battered enamel tins labelled *Tea*, *Sugar*, *Coffee*. The windowpanes were marked with dirt splashed from the sill during storms. She remembered the place being spotless when she'd visited as a child, but Jocelyn had been alive then.

'Do your rellies still visit?' Cate asked.

'Yeah, but hardly ever. There's no kiddies for them to play with.'

'What happens when the aunties get sick?'

'I take 'em into town. They go to the doctor every couple of months anyway, for check-ups.'

'Kath needs that cataract removed.'

Mellor clanked two aluminium mugs together. 'I know, but somehow blackfellas never move up the waiting list. She's been on it for a year, now.'

He put a saucepan of water on the gas ring, then pulled out an old tin tray from the cupboard and arranged the cups and spoons on it. Cate studied the checked shirt hanging from his stooped shoulders, worn jeans held up with an old plaited belt and his cracked dusty boots.

She glanced behind into the sitting room. The floorboards were bare; a television and a tattered couch sat in one corner. All around the edges of the room were stacks of newspapers, folders and files.

'I'll see if I can do something,' she added.

'You and Eliot,' he said quietly, 'you were good people. Always helping.'

The water in the pot boiled quickly, spattering onto the gas flame with a hiss. Mellor switched off the element and, with tea towels in both hands, tipped the hot water into the teapot.

He fetched a carton of milk from an old Kelvinator fridge, which growled when the door was opened.

'I'll take the tray,' Cate offered.

He shook his head. 'Get the door, we'll sit outside.'

Cate followed him to a rickety bench in the shade of the house. The seat swayed beneath their weight, but held. Crickets purred nearby. Sparks pushed himself up from the aunties' verandah and hobbled down the steps towards them. He sniffed Cate's shoes. Mellor lifted the pot and poured tea into the chipped mugs.

'Drink up, Catie. You'd be thirsty after all that running.'

Obliging him, she cracked open the tin and spooned sugar into her chipped mug. The dog sighed and flopped at Mellor's feet. Two rosellas perched in the tree above, eyeing them. A trail of ants wended through the bindies.

When Mellor spoke, his tone was cold. 'You know anything about Native Title?'

Cate, surprised, shook her head. 'Not much. Bits and pieces that I've read in the paper.'

'Do you know that game, "Paper, Scissors, Rock"?'

'Yeah, Eliot and I used to play it on the bus going to school. With Rachel.'

'That's the game the government plays with us. Paper covers the rock. That's what all this Native Title is. We need mountains of paper to prove an unbroken connection to our land. Your father's country.' He sounded mocking. 'That's how whitefellas see their country. Something to be owned, to be passed down through sons, or sold off to a mine. But how can you sell something alive? Something that breathes, speaks and takes care of you?'

Cate pushed a hand across her forehead, feeling her pulse pumping through her temples.

'You know how every corner of the paddock, and the tracks and the views from the hills, they all have memories?'

She nodded, scuffing her shoes in the soil.

'Except that it's not just memories. It's the spirits in everything. Cate, when they took away our land they made us feel just like you do now. Like a part of you has gone.'

'What are you saying, Mellor?' Her ears rang with a strange pressure.

He reached into his pocket and took out a Swiss watch with an inbuilt compass, the silver spotted and corroded.

Cate snatched it from him. 'Where did you get it from?'

Mellor pressed his lips together, shaking his head.

Reverently, Cate ran her fingers over the links and the square, glass face. It had been a sixteenth birthday present from their parents before Eliot went jackarooing for a summer. He wore it proudly, his shirt sleeves rolled up to set it off. When he was bored he would slant its face to reflect sunlight into Cate's eyes, annoying her.

'You've got the scissors, Cate.'

'Pardon?'

'You can cut through all the bureaucracy.'

'You'll have to explain.'

'Give me your land, Cate, and I'll tell you where Eliot is.'

Cate sprang from the bench. For a moment she wasn't sure if Mellor had actually said the words, or if they were part of those that she had imagined a thousand times before.

'Is he alive?'

Mellor didn't avert his gaze.

'Mellor! I must know! This is killing me.'

'Is it really? You've had a good life all these years: a doctor in Sydney, making more money than most of us could imagine —'

'A good life? I work like a dog because as soon as I stop I think about Eliot. Every time the phone rings I think it's him. Each boy with dark hair I touch on the shoulder. I would have done myself in a long time ago, except for the thought that he might come back and find me gone. I've been waiting for him to come home for eight years. This isn't a "good life", Mellor.'

She tried to read his face, but there was nothing – neither compassion nor anger – in his eyes nor in the shape of his lips. 'Please, is he alive? Can you tell me that?'

'I can't tell you anything until you give me the land.'

She dropped to the bench. The old dog, sensing her distress, began to whine. 'I haven't, for one night, slept properly since he disappeared.' Her voice began to waver. 'Why can't you just tell me?'

'Because you're white, and white people don't keep their word.'

'I'm not them!' she shouted.

The air was very still, and Mellor's voice was clear. 'You'd be surprised, Cate, how much you are like them. They're your family, after all.'

Cate bent her head into her hands.

'Mellor!' She heard Auntie Kath call. 'What the hell are you doing to that poor girl?'

Soon Kath was sitting beside Cate, wrapping her comforting, fleshy arms around her as she had when Cate was a girl.

'There, there,' she hushed. 'We all got our griefs, Catie. All of us.'

Cate pressed her cheek against the old woman's chest.

54

Long after the rest of the family had driven away, Leonora sat on the verandah behind the gauze, listening to crickets whirring and fruit bats flying overhead. The smell of wet earth still hovered after she'd watered the row of terracotta pot plants lining the front of the house. She crossed her legs, webbed with thin varicose veins.

'I've had a gutful of that child,' Blake had spat as he slowly stepped out of his trousers and pulled on his nightshirt. The pain had become so ferocious that afternoon that there was nothing he could do except go to bed with a sleeping pill. 'Five people wanted this to go ahead. She's the only one holding it up.'

The sun began to drop. Leonora thought of the sound of Cate's violin reaching her as she'd dug up carrots for dinner the other evening. She'd gathered the carrots by their hair and carried them inside. None of the lights had been switched on. Silently, she left the carrots in the sink and brushed her hands on a tea towel. The music began again, a piece that Leonora recognised as one of the children's favourites. It skipped and burbled like a creek, then fattened like storm water and spread calmly out to sea.

She stole to Eliot's bedroom. Cate stood by the window,

looking out to the hills as she drew the bow across the strings. The moment had been worth the years of timid phone calls, of her daughter's abrupt replies, of staring out windows and waiting for Cate to come up the driveway or walk across the lawn.

Mrs Emerald had once told her that teaching the children their duets was simply a technical exercise. She supervised their hand placement, suggested pieces for them to play and translated the Italian musical terms, but the music they produced needed no directing. Individually their playing was competent, if lacklustre. Eliot showed promise, but needed application. Cate practiced hard but had little flair. Together, however, their music was transcendent. To Leonora, they both sounded beautiful.

As she'd listened to Cate, she saw her children chasing each other in the twilight around the old gum tree; Eliot, at age four, whacking the soil with a trowel while Leonora planted potatoes; Cate learning to walk, refusing help and pulling herself around the kitchen by holding onto the cupboard doors; both of them cradling a frightened bunny that Blake had brought home after its mother had been caught in a trap; hot summer afternoons where the temperature stretched into the forties and it was too hot for the kids to do anything except sprawl like starfish on the kitchen's slate floor and sleep. Sometimes there'd be three of them, with Rachel there, especially on the days Jocelyn worked, and from the garden would come a voice counting as they played hide-and-seek.

Leonora missed Jocelyn and their nattering over cups of tea. Once she'd moved to the farm Jocelyn kept going to the CWA meetings, even when there was hostility towards her. Leonora reminded the ladies that the CWA was about extending help to all women, not just the white ones, and they bitched about her for that, too. It helped that Joss had a biting sense of humour, and sometimes they joked about Faye Brendan's garlic breath or Pauline West's sultana biscuits that were so hard you could break a tooth.

The bowel cancer had been a dreadful way to end, especially for a woman who was always tidy. Jocelyn gave up work, though Leonora visited often and slipped her money for the chemo. In the end, Leonora thought, Joss was glad to be relieved of the indignity of it. Only after she'd gone, and the house no longer sparkled even though Leonora took hours with it, did she realise how much she missed her old friend.

She heard the faint clink of a gate and sat up, the chair creaking. Soon Cate appeared, her expression drained, her shoulders hunched.

Alarmed, Leonora hurried out to the lawn. 'What's happened to you?'

Cate ignored her.

'Have you been running all afternoon? It's far too much strain on your body. You'll have a heart attack. I spoke to Jane about it, her cousin's a doctor.'

Cate stumbled up the step and Leonora reached out to her.

'Mum, go away, please. I don't want to hear it.'

She followed her daughter into the house. 'Don't ignore me, Cate,' she said quickly. 'Cate!'

Her daughter closed the bedroom door against her, bolting it.

Leonora studied the door's wooden grain. When the sound of crying reached her, she leaned her forehead against the door and closed her eyes.

55

Finch sat in Tumbin's only cafe at a wooden table with a bung leg that made it wobble, reading the local *Tumbin Independent*. It had gone upmarket from the days when it was a booklet of photocopies stapled together, the copying sometimes so dark it was hard to make out the pictures.

The waitress, a crust of pimples at the side of her mouth, brought his coffee.

'You the new bloke who's staying for a bit?'

'I'm going back tomorrow.' He turned the pages of his newspaper and she walked away.

The coffee was insipid. In a few days he would get a proper latte from Café Brioso. Jack would tell him to buck up because it was his own fault for pursuing difficult women, and would pester him to go out with his mates again.

Cate was across the road in the pub. When he saw her car as he walked down the street, his pulse began its familiar banging. He wandered into the chemist's beauty section to find a gift for Carlotta, and by the time he came out he was calmer.

He heard loud voices outside and, pulling back the lace curtains at the window, saw a stringy white man bellowing at a shorter, muscular Aboriginal man on the pavement. The white man had a bottle of beer in his hand. The Aboriginal man shouted back, spittle flecking the other's cheek. The white man bent down, slammed the bottle on the ground and rammed its broken neck into the Aboriginal's face.

Finch shoved back his chair, its legs shuddering. He threw open the door, the bell on its handle rattling insanely, and sprinted to the pub.

'Cate! Cate!' he bellowed.

She knocked her stool over in fright. 'What is it with you?'

'There's a fight across the road. Glassing.'

In the seconds Finch had taken to get Cate, the white man had thrust the broken bottle into the Aboriginal man a second time, then taken off. Blood leaked from the man's throat and the air smelled of beer. A crowd of people had gathered. Two other men pursued the white man down the road.

'Stand back!' Finch shouted. 'Here's a doctor.'

Cate kneeled beside the man, the wings of her shoulderblades showing through her white singlet. She pulled out a folded handkerchief monogrammed with 'EM', laid it on the gash and pressed hard with both hands. 'Where's the nearest ambulance?'

'Kynidia,' said the waitress, picking at her pimples in distress.

'We'll have to take him,' Cate told Finch. 'Can you lift him? I can't let go.'

Finch scooped up the bleeding man and drove them to Kynidia as Cate sat in the back of the car, her hands and jeans wet with blood. As she continued to apply pressure to the man's neck, she talked to him about Rachel and her brother riding horses on the farm.

Later, she and Finch sat in the waiting room while the man lay in the operating theatre.

'You don't have to stay,' the nurse said. 'We've found his family and they're coming.'

'We'll stay,' Finch replied automatically. He glanced at Cate. 'Unless you want to go home, in which case I can call you.'

Cate shook her head. 'I'll stay.'

'Would you like a coffee?' Finch asked.

'That would be good. Just milk, please. I'd better call my parents; they freak out easily.'

She was waiting, hands pressed between her knees, when he came back from the cafeteria. Her hands shook as she took the coffee.

'You okay?'

'Yeah, it's not this that's upset me. It's ... stuff at home.'

'Get the coffee into you. It'll put hairs on your chest.'

Cate smiled, and Finch was gratified.

Half an hour later the man's mother and relatives arrived.

'We're here for Rob Donoghue,' they said to the nurse on reception, loud with distress. 'Is he gunna be all right?'

'Because of that young lady,' the nurse nodded to Cate, 'he should be. She's a doctor. Knew to keep pressure on the vein to stop the blood.'

Several pairs of eyes turned towards Cate, who looked tiny and gaunt. She rose unsteadily. Rob's mother, a plump woman with thick, curly black hair, embraced her.

'What's your name, love?'

'Cate McConville.'

'Mellor's mob!' said a girl who looked around fifteen.

'Rachel and I grew up together.'

'We gotta call Rachel.'

'Not now.' Mrs Donoghue's voice was grave.

One of the men asked Finch, 'The bloke who did it, what did he look like?'

'Same height as me. Square face, long brown hair. Tats on his left arm.'

'Doesn't sound like anyone we know. Must've been someone from out of town, Mum, a random.'

'It's never fucking random,' replied Mrs Donoghue.

The family sat in the waiting room, talking among themselves until there was nothing left to say. The plastic clock on the wall ticked.

When the surgeon came out, Cate was falling asleep, her head on Finch's shoulder. Finch gently shook her arm. Cate blinked against the fluorescent light.

'He's all stitched up now.' The surgeon was squat, with a thick moustache, his speech direct. 'He'll be okay, but he needs to stay for at least a week.'

Mrs Donoghue clutched the surgeon's arm. 'Thank you.'

'No need for that. If it hadn't been for Doctor McConville, he wouldn't be here.'

'What can we do?' one of the brothers asked Cate.

'Nothing. I would have done it for anyone,' she replied tiredly.

'We need to go,' Finch intervened. He wanted to put his arm around Cate but was wary of her prickliness. Instead he placed his hand in the small of her back. She felt as fragile as a bird.

As the car approached Tumbin, Cate said, 'You're too exhausted to drive me home, and so am I. If you leave me at the pub, Harry will give me a bed.'

'Don't be ridiculous. Carlotta has a spare room. It's a bit poky, but it'll be quieter than the pub.'

He took Cate's silence for assent.

As he opened the front door, Carlotta appeared wearing only a T-shirt of Dougie's covered in holes. When she saw Cate, she disappeared and returned in a different T-shirt and pair of shorts.

Finch introduced them. 'Cate's sleeping here tonight, if

that's okay?'

'Of course.' Carlotta smiled avidly.

Finch opened the door to the spare room, showing a white, girlish bedspread patterned with pink blossoms. Carlotta fetched her a towel and a nightie printed with a giant koala.

'The shower's down there, love,' she said, pointing to the end of the hall.

'Sleep well,' Finch added.

'I think, just this once, that I will.' Cate closed the bathroom door.

Finch turned and found Carlotta beaming at him.

56

Half an hour out of town, Cate pulled the car to the side of the road. Paddocks of rust-coloured sorghum stretched on either side. To her left was the familiar cluster of long, white weatherboard buildings, their corrugated iron rooves glinting in the sun. Adjacent to the buildings was an overgrown racetrack surrounded by a post-and-rail fence.

Finch parked behind her. Cate wound down the window.

'I just need a few minutes to collect myself,' she said when he appeared.

'What's going on at home?'

She looked at him, this strange man with dark-brown eyes and thick, waving hair who had followed her into the country. That morning, she had been at the breakfast table in the koala nightie when he walked in. He was clean-shaven, his hair wet from the shower, T-shirt clinging to his chest.

Carlotta, chatting nonstop, laid an enormous plate of bacon and eggs before her. Cate looked at it with dismay.

Finch laughed. 'She can't get through all that.'

'Look at the size of her!' Carlotta gesticulated. 'She wants feeding. I thought you said she was pretty, but she's downright scrawny.'

'Don't listen to her,' Finch apologised to Cate. 'It's an Italian thing – you have to be plump to pass muster. I'll take that. What would you like?'

'Toast with jam, please.'

'You heard her, Carlotta.'

'I'll get it!' Cate sprang up.

'Don't be silly. Sit down.'

After breakfast Finch had walked Cate to the car. She had borrowed a T-shirt and shorts from Carlotta. The shorts came down to her knees. In the car, Cate reached for the ignition, then paused. Peering through the passenger window, she said, 'Do you want to come with me?'

'To the property?'

'Yes.'

'Why?'

'It will unsettle them. I need to buy some time to make a decision.' Cate flicked the beads dangling off the key in the ignition, watching him.

'I'll tell Carlotta,' he replied.

Now, looking at his intelligent face, she saw that, even if he had some screws loose, he was a kind person.

'It would take too long to explain what's going on,' she said.

'It's not as if I've got much to do in Tumbin.'

'Let's go for a walk.'

The grass, which hadn't been slashed since the last race day, swished against their legs. Sunlight fell onto their necks and dripped down their backs. They passed the long, low buildings with peeling walls and came to a burnt-out circle of earth where there had once been a campfire.

'Eliot had a fight here, with Russell, your aunt's neighbour.

Russell was trashed. It was the picnic races. There was always a lot of drinking.'

The wind that night had made the trees bristle. She and Eliot sat by the fire with beers, warming their legs and waiting for their parents to finish dancing and come home.

Russell had been hanging around with a bunch of blokes from Tumbin. Cate, hearing his raucous laughter throughout the day, had ignored him. Now, she saw a rangy figure walking out of the light of the hessian-enclosed dance floor, weaving through the trees towards them. She sighed.

'What is it?' Eliot asked.

'Russell.'

'Hello, youse two,' Russell pulled out the chair next to Cate. 'Got any beer?'

Reluctantly, Eliot reached into the esky beside him and chucked Russell a Foster's.

'Youse not kicking up your heels tonight?' He jerked his head to the lights and noise beyond the hessian.

'No, we don't mind being here.'

'You two never needed anyone else, did you?' Russell broke open the can with a crack, beer spilling over his knuckles. He wiped them on his moleskins, which, Cate noticed, were dirty and stained. 'Not even old Russell, here.'

Cate was disappointed that what had been a pleasant day, with clear winter light and a few wins for Eliot, was going to be marred by Russell's boorishness.

He drank the beer greedily, wiping the back of his hand across his mouth.

'So you too good to talk to us, Catie? Now you're a doctor?'

'I won't be a doctor for another three years, Russell, and I said hello to you this morning.'

He laughed, spraying beer. His voice hardened. 'That's just common courtesy, Cate.'

Cate raised an eyebrow.

'So, you got anyone fucking you in old Sydney Town?'

'Stop it, Russell,' Eliot warned.

'Oh! Little brother is standing up for big sister, now,' he said mockingly. 'We've come a long way since then, haven't we?'

Cate folded her arms, staring steadfastly at the trees.

'Now that we have a black bitch and all —'

Eliot's chair hitting the ground behind them, then his hand connecting with Russell's stomach, was so swift that for a few seconds Cate had no idea what was happening. She saw Russell groaning at her feet, blood leaking from his nose. Eliot's face was white with fury.

'Leave now,' he snarled, 'unless you want me to kick you into the fire.'

Russell groaned, unmoving, and Eliot's boot landed in his stomach.

'Get up!'

Russell dragged himself to his feet, swaying. Eliot gripped his arm and punched him in the eye.

'El!' Cate snapped out of her shock. 'What are you doing?'

Russell staggered, a hand pressed to his face. He lurched between the parked cars, steadying himself with a hand on a bonnet, and vanished into the darkness.

'What on earth did you do that for?'

'He's a nasty prick. You should know that.'

Cate sat cautiously, waiting for an explanation, but none came. Three months later, Eliot was gone.

~

'Did the police talk to Russell?' Finch asked.

Cate looked up. 'Yeah, but he was away trucking when Eliot disappeared. I always had a feeling that he was involved, though, because Eliot's reaction to him was so completely out of character. I've been trying to track him down for years, but I haven't had any luck.' She traced a pattern in the ashy soil with the side of her shoe. 'Let's do a circuit of the track.'

As they climbed over the post-and-rail fence, brushing its flaking paint from their clothes, and stepped through the grass, Cate explained about her father's hip, Rickett the buyer, and Mellor's promise. They finished up at Finch's car, leaning against the doors.

'Have you told them about Mellor?' Finch asked.

'No. I know Blake won't negotiate, so I need to work out a strategy.'

'I'm good at those.'

Cate tilted her head, trying to recall why. 'Ah, the rescuer of ships.'

'That's one way of putting it.'

'Aren't you supposed to be on call?'

'Only for two weeks at a time. Not at the moment.'

Cate pushed herself up. 'We'd better get going. I'm warning you, though, they'll be all over you like a rash.'

After ten minutes, they rattled over a cattle grid, through a creek and up the road that led to her mother's green oasis. Cate eased the car through a gate and the dogs bounded out, yelping. Her mother and father unfolded themselves from their white wicker chairs as Cate parked the car beneath the peppercorn tree.

She opened Finch's door and said, tight-lipped, 'Here we are. Home.'

57

'For God's sake Mellor, can't you sit yourself down?' Kath snapped, as she greased a baking tray with butter. 'You're driving me crazy.'

Mellor didn't want to be in his own house with piles of paper full of government jargon. He sat on the rickety chair on the aunts' small verandah and tried to keep still. Sometimes the mess got to him, because it reminded him that Joss had gone. She hadn't liked the Native Title politics and papers.

'Isn't it good enough that I got us out here?' she fretted. She liked Leonora, and didn't want to upset her.

There'd had been no smell of baking that afternoon fifteen years ago in Tumbin when he came home with a parcel of cutlets from the butcher. It was so hot the telephone poles wavered in the distance and the tarmac was hazy. He was tired, longing for a swim in the river with his boys.

'Hello?' he called when he came into the kitchen. He opened the fridge. Its racks were bare. 'Mum? How come there's no food?'

He put the meat in the fridge.

The rooms were silent. He tramped through them, angry for a response, and found Nance lying on her bed, back to the door.

'Why hasn't anyone done the shopping?'

She didn't stir and he registered that the room was quiet. His mother could keep a house awake with her snoring.

'Mum?' He stepped closer. There was a bottle of pills beside her head and a half-finished cup of tea on the bedside table. He touched her shoulder.

'Mum! Wake up!'

He shook her hard, even as he knew it was too late, that it had been too late since his father hung himself in his cell.

Sparks barked and Mellor jolted. The dog ran suddenly into the bush. Mellor stood and leaned over the verandah railing, then paced for a while, then sat again. May came outside, having woken from a nap. She rubbed her eyes with the heels of her palms. Her long hair was unravelling from its plait.

'Not allowed in the kitchen,' she commented. 'She's antsy.'

Mellor nodded, unable to repond.

'You didn't say anything to her?'

'No.'

May rested her hand on his shoulder.

58

'I thought we might go to the Falls,' Cate suggested, as they sat with Leonora among the remains of a late lunch. Blake had left to round up some sheep for crutching. He nodded to Cate and Finch as he left, his face a mask.

'What a lovely idea!' Leonora burst out.

Cate ignored her.

'Where is it?' Finch asked.

'A twenty-minute drive up the road. We used to go there when we were kids.'

'I'd like that,' Finch answered.

Leonora's smile was so bright it was painful. 'Shall I pack a thermos for you, and some gingerbread?'

'If you want to, Mum.'

Immediately, Leonora rose and switched on the kettle.

When they went on family excursions to the Falls, Cate and Eliot would jostle in the back of the ute as it bucked in and out of potholes. The dogs barked, running from one side of the tray to the other, dripping slobber onto their bare calves. Cate whinged as pieces of straw, left over from carrying bales to the hayshed, whirled into her face and made her nose run. She rubbed her itchy eyes until they became red and watery, her irises a luminous green.

After three gates and two creeks, they parked halfway up a hill amid the scent of eucalyptus blossoms and the thick drone of cicadas. They jumped off the tray, hauling out baskets covered with tea towels, Eliot's schoolbag packed with plastic plates and cups, an old, blackened billy and buckets filled with balls of twine and fishing nets.

If it wasn't a drought year, the creek would be running, water scalloping around rocks. They crossed by leaping from one exposed rock to another, and ran through a tunnel of ti-trees. If it was summer and their legs were bare, they were careful of stinging nettles; a brush with the soft green leaves raised a nest of welts.

Then the air cooled, the sound of rushing water became louder and the dirt beneath their feet changed to pebbles. There was the rock, a cliff of granite with water either dripping or churning from the top, depending on that season's rainfall.

While Blake, Leonora, Sally and Charlie shook out rugs and unpacked plastic wine glasses, Cate and Eliot attacked a ball of twine, cutting off lengths and tying them to small chunks of kangaroo meat. They scuttled to the water's edge and tossed in their strands, telling each other to whisper lest the noise scare the yabbies. But nothing could silence them when Eliot, feeling tension in his string, pulled the crayfish in, at the same time sliding a net into the water. With a whoop he scooped up the creature in the net, screaming, 'I caught one!'

Cate stared at the pool. The breeze brought out goosebumps on her skin.

'Come on,' she said to Finch. 'Let's go up to the top.'

Halfway up, they came to a rusty wire fence. Finch held down the top strand, the way Eliot used to do, to help Cate over.

She led him through a thin crop of gum trees until they reached the top of the Falls, bordered by granite that had been stroked smooth by water. The Falls were fed by the creek that emerged from a copse of ti-trees. Clumps of long grass and moss grew where water lapped the stones.

Cate walked to the edge and lay on her stomach, peering at the pool three hundred metres below. Finch crawled down beside her. She turned her head, squinting. Finch's face was framed by the brilliant blue sky.

'I think the only thing I can do is to buy them out,' she said.

Finch exhaled. 'My aunt said they wanted something like one and a half million.'

'That's right.'

'How much is your apartment worth?'.

'Four hundred thousand.'

'And what do you have in shares and savings?'

'About half that. I've worked a sixty-hour week since I left uni, usually more. My only costs have been the apartment and looking for Eliot. I haven't had a holiday, I've hardly ever left Sydney because that's where my GP training was, and I don't go out much. I don't even have a car; I don't need one.'

She watched Finch running the numbers through his mind, no doubt the same way he weighed up a ship's cargo. 'Do you trust Mellor?'

'I don't really have a choice.'

Cate closed her eyes, the sun pushing through her eyelids, making her vision red. She remembered Sally, her mother and Natalie sitting on the rocks upstream in their bathers, Eliot slipping on algae-covered rocks and yelping at the icy water. The creek was always cold, even in summer. She felt Finch get up.

'Cate.'

'What?' Her irritation resurfaced.

'Come away from the edge.'

She was about to tell him to bugger off, then saw his outstretched hand. When she grasped it, he pulled her close.

Cate had touched thousands of patients over the years, probing muscles and joints to see where they hurt, lightly stroking rashes to feel their change in texture, gently manipulating limbs to see how they released pain, yet she was struck by the heat of Finch's body. Unnerved, she stepped aside. 'Let's eat Mum's cake.'

She sat on the sun-warmed stone, digging the thermos and cups out of her backpack. She cut slices of gingerbread and offered a piece to Finch. Instead of taking it, he gripped her arm and turned it, exposing the white skin spread with bruises.

'What's this?'

'It comes when I'm stressed and don't eat enough. It's just a vitamin deficiency.'

Finch brushed his thumb over the discolouration. Cate pulled her arm away, left the cake for him on the stone and unscrewed the thermos. 'Your aunt said your girlfriend left you.'

'You didn't waste any time in getting to know each other.'

'I hardly invited the conversation. She started talking as soon as I got up.'

Finch grinned. 'She likes company.'

'Why did your girlfriend go?' Cate poured tea into the two plastic cups.

'Her work was more interesting than me, that was all.'

Cate handed him the tea. 'So you know what it's like, then.'

'What?'

'Searching for her in every crowd. Trying to tell yourself to get over it. Being hurt by the places where you were together.'

Finch looked at her properly. 'Yeah, it's like that,' he answered at length.

Cate's mouth was dry.

A while later, as she backed the ute down the gravel road eaten by erosion, the picnic basket placed between them, Cate asked, 'Would you like to stay until tomorrow? I need to get them together for a meeting. If you're there, it will keep them on the back foot.'

Finch gazed out the window at the hills rocky with granite, the powdery soil and green-grey trees.

'But if not, I can drive you back to Tumbin when we get back. It's up to you.'

'I'll stay.'

After dinner that evening, Leonora proudly retrieved her scrapbook from the bookshelf in the living room.

'Look,' she said, turning the large pages with newspaper clippings glued into them. 'They won the duet division in the Tumbin and Kynidia eistedfodds every single year, from 1977 to 1987.'

There were pictures of them becoming taller, their teeth straighter, their postures more adult. In each photograph they held their violins protectively.

'Do you have to, Mum?' Cate protested. 'Look, I've got braces on in that one. And a perm. It's hideous.'

'Don't be silly. You were always beautiful.'

'What, even with zits?'

There were other articles, too, on Cate's academic success: topping the region in English and Science tests, and sometimes winning long-distance running races.

After the duet photos was an article declaring *A Regional Phenomenon*. On the next page was the heading *Local Boy Disappears*.

'Put it away please, Mum,' Cate said quietly.

Leonora, her face colouring, took the book to the living room.

Finch gathered the empty plates and stacked them on the sink.

'Finch, you mustn't,' Leonora cried when she returned to the kitchen.

'Mum, let him. It makes him feel wanted,' Cate said, allowing her humour to surface like a platypus in the river at dusk.

Leonora's face split with a smile.

59

Finch woke in the guest room just after sunrise. The kitchen was full of light, the wooden table trapping it. There was a note on the table: *Gone running. Leonora in town. Blake at work. Back by lunch, having family meeting. Cate.*

He padded around the kitchen, making tea. In the fridge was a blue-and-white striped jug of milk. Finch thought those things only existed on the set of *A Country Practice*. He took the *Tumbin Independent* to the verandah with his tea.

The cat had taken a liking to him. As he sat in a chair it ran across the lawn to meet him, placing its wet paws on his shins.

'Get off,' he said, kicking it away.

It glowered at him, then began its elaborate routine of personal maintenance, starting with the chest where his shoe had made contact.

A cool breeze fluttered the wisteria leaves, while Monarch butterflies dipped and eddied above the garden. It beat a fortnight of twelve-hour days before a computer screen, and nights of being on call. Jack would have told him he was being a doormat. Yet if it was a choice between being used or facing the long, lonely drive back to Sydney, he would opt for the former. Besides, Jack wasn't exactly an authority on successful relationships himself.

The cat stuck out its leg and began to work on its thigh. Finch drained his cup and closed the paper. On the front page, a farmer sat on bags of wheat beneath the heading 'Grain Glut'.

Finch stretched and went into the house to look for some cereal, but found himself in the living room. It was dim, the only light coming from the windows to the verandah. In the bookshelves were old farming and rainfall almanacs, a set of encyclopaedias and rows of romance-fiction titles.

Lower down were the photo albums. Finch kneeled and pulled one out. Here they were, freckled, dark-haired, wearing plastic Dracula teeth. Here was Cate as a cheerleader with a red wig and red jumper, a 'C' of masking tape stuck to it, and a pregnant Eliot with a pillow stuffed beneath an awful sky-blue dress, wearing a wig of thick yellow plaits.

He pulled out another album. There were few photos of the children on their own. Both of them were blowing out candles on a cake, jumping off bales in the hayshed, laughing at the Tumbin show with fairy floss and heart-shaped balloons. In all of them Cate was happy and relaxed, with that impish grin Finch had only seen a few times. The last photo was a strip from a photo booth, Eliot with a silly grin and Cate with crossed eyes. Eliot had dark fuzz on his cheeks; Finch guessed he was sixteen or seventeen.

He put the album back and pulled out the green book of clippings, looking again at the photos of them posing with their violins, at first with gappy teeth, then tight lips covering their braces, then proud smiles.

Finch turned to the last two articles. In the first, dated 5 January 1988, Cate leaned against a jacaranda tree, a certificate in her hands. She'd topped the state in physics, chemistry and maths for her final exams. Finch, unsurprised, turned to the next article. It was dated

25 November 1991. Eliot had been missing for two months. He was last seen by his parents in the afternoon. They assumed he'd gone roo shooting, because his gun was missing too. Any members of the public with information were encouraged to contact the police.

Finch turned the next page and found it blank. The pages were bowed, however, by something resting at the back. He lifted them and discovered a plastic sleeve full of more newspaper articles. He supposed they were pieces Leonora hadn't yet pasted in her clippings book. The first article was headed 'Bringing them Home.'

Frowning, he lifted out the thick sheaf. There were articles from the *Sydney Morning Herald*, *The Australian*, and the *Australian Women's Weekly*, each dated in Leonora's neat hand, with some paragraphs underlined.

A stolen girl at Cootamundra Domestic Training Home for Aboriginal Girls was tied to the old bell post and continuously beaten. She died that night, still chained. Boys at Kinchela Boys Home near Kempsey were whipped with a hose pipe. Mothers and fathers travelled hundreds of miles across the state to visit their children in the homes. Kim Beazley broke down in tears as he called on the government to apologise. Schools, the police, state and federal MPs, academics, parents and citizens associations and church groups all apologised to the stolen generations, but John Howard walked out of the chamber when the Opposition read out descriptions of the experiences of Aboriginal children. Some mothers waited years for their children to return. Many turned to alcohol to obliterate their despair.

Finch carefully slid the clippings back into the sleeve, placed them in the album and closed its covers. He wondered if Leonora knew what Mellor had said to Cate. Walking back out into the light of the morning, he looked for the cat to stroke for reassurance, but it had disappeared.

60

'What do you reckon about this chap of Cate's?' Charlie asked his brother in the stifling tin shed where they kept their tools.

Blake shrugged, poking through greasy pieces of machinery. 'She says he's a friend.'

'Sally was all set for them to get married.'

'Women! Marriage and babies, it's all they think about.'

'Cate doesn't.'

'Ha! I knew we had one.' Blake held up the spare part.

Charlie followed his limping brother to the tractor and helped him fold back the engine cover. 'She mentioned him once before. He's the grandson of the Italian POW who used to work here.'

'Interesting.' Blake measured the part to check it fitted.

'He's pretty quiet,' Charlie continued.

'That's an asset.'

'Except Cate isn't a talker either, though I suppose she used to be.'

'Yeah, she used to be a lot of things.' Blake began loosening bolts with a spanner.

'Will she agree to sell to Rickett?'

'I don't know. Nora won't talk about anything else.' He wriggled the decrepit pipe. 'She thinks it's the dawn of some new bloody age. That Cate will sell, marry her man and produce grandchildren who will visit us in a house by the coast. I don't even know how long he's been around.'

He wrenched the pipe out. Together, they peered at the corrosion.

'Pretty old,' Charlie commented.

'Yeah.' Blake threw it at the old bin beside the shed full of discarded sheet metal and wire. It missed and hit the side with a clang. 'Anyone with half a glass eye can see that Cate's stalling over something and she wants him here to help. That's why she wants this meeting, I'd say.'

'Have you spoken to her?'

'No, I hate talking to her. She's like a snake in the grass. Always was.'

Charlie wondered again if he should point out that Blake had always favoured Eliot. Perhaps it was too late. 'What will you do if she doesn't sign?'

'Take her to court.'

Charlie was aghast. 'You can't do that! She's your daughter.'

Blake looked directly at Charlie. 'No daughter of mine would refuse to talk to her father for nearly a decade.'

He took the part and wriggled it in. Charlie rubbed his beard and studied his brother's back, how his hips tilted to favour his good leg.

'There, she's right to go.' Blake finished tightening the bolts. 'I'll plough the Black Horse Paddock. You going to fix that roof?'

'Yeah.'

'I'll see you at this lunch, then.' Blake folded down the cover, handed the tools to Charlie and stiffly hauled himself up into the cabin.

Charlie returned to the shed to cut sheet metal for the leaking roof of the shearing shed. He pulled on his visor and switched on the lathe. It screamed through the metal and the dark room flowered with sparks. He wondered how, exactly, Blake could go to the courts, because Natalie would take Cate's side.

The metal pieces clattered to the floor, smoking. Charlie switched off the machine, his ears ringing in the silence. He knew he should find Natalie and speak to her. He picked up the pieces from the floor and prepared to cut them again.

61

The smell of frying sausages wreathed in the air. Blowies circled the butter and bread on the table. The women drank a bottle of champagne Natalie had brought. Blake handed Finch a Tooheys. Finch would have preferred the champagne but he didn't want to make ripples. Besides, it was unnerving, for there was nothing to celebrate.

Charlie remembered Finch's mother.

'Look.' He rolled up his trouser leg to show a long, puckered scar. 'She helped sew me up.'

'Small world,' Finch said, forking potato salad onto his plate.

'Fell off my motorbike when I was nineteen and split my calf. Mum drove me to Kynidia Hospital and Nurse Accorso was on hand with the catgut and needle. And I remember your grandad. Very heavy accent. Good worker, though.'

'He died when I was a boy. I didn't know him well.'

Cate, sitting next to Finch in the shade of the liquidambars, had crossed her legs and folded her arms. Finch ate his salad and lamb chops, listening to a litany of the district's teenage pregnancies and a story about the minister's wife spilling a packet of white sugar in the supermarket aisle. Finch wondered how Jack was getting on. The house would be littered with pizza boxes, the couch ringed by empty beer bottles and the shower would be clogged with his girlfriends' hair.

'I think it's time you did something about this, Cate. I'm sick of you dragging your bloody feet.'

Finch looked up. Blake was standing at the table, his face red. Cate placed her champagne glass on the table.

'If you don't agree to this,' Blake continued, 'we'll sort it out in court.'

'Blake!' rasped Leonora.

Cate faced him. 'And how do you propose to do that?'

'Blake, why didn't you discuss this with me first?' Leonora's voice was high and urgent.

'I told Charlie.'

Charlie glanced guiltily at Sally.

'This is our *daughter*,' Leonora snapped.

'I can't believe you're springing this on me!' Natalie was flushing.

'I was going to tell you before we got here, Nat,' Charlie said, scratching the back of his head, 'but I didn't know where you were.'

'I've been here for a week! Besides, it was Blake who should have spoken to me.'

'We have to sell it!' Sally was shrill. 'We haven't got time to go to court. Rickett will lose interest.'

Finch watched Cate trying to pull the words from her thin, tired body. Her muscles strained, the cords of her neck prominent.

'Mellor knows where Eliot is,' she finally blurted.

'Jesus Christ, where?' Blake slammed his hands onto the table.

Again, Cate tried to form the words, but they wouldn't come.

Finch forced himself to be calm, the way he did when the phone calls came telling him a ship was sinking on a reef, and there wasn't just the cargo to save, but the delicate ecosystem around it.

'This is the problem,' he said evenly. 'Mellor won't tell Cate where he is unless Cate does an exchange.'

'What kind of exchange? I'm not giving that Abo any money, they just piss it up the wall —'

'Shut up, Blake!' Leonora screamed. 'Didn't you hear what he said?'

Blake sat abruptly, blinking. The sparrows in the nearby banksia rose fell silent. Finch poured a glass of orange juice and handed it to Cate.

'Mellor wants the property,' he said simply.

The sparrows began to twitter again.

'What, the entire place?' Sally cried. 'He doesn't have a cent, let alone one and a half million. We can't just give it to him.

'Don't any of you want to know where Eliot is?' Cate's tone was chilly. 'How can you put a price on that kind of knowledge, Sally?'

Sally twisted her fob chain, the silver links tinkling.

'What's your solution, Cate?' Natalie asked.

'I'll buy you out. I'll sell my apartment, get a mortgage and give you the asking price.'

'Cate, you can't do that!' Leonora protested. 'You'll be in debt forever. Surely there's some way you can convince Mellor —'

'There's no bloody way that boong is going to have my land —'

'Actually, Father, it isn't your land. For one thing, it originally belonged to the Aborigines and the government took it and sold it to the squatters. For another, I'll never agree to sell to Rickett.'

Blake snorted, opening his mouth to retort, but Finch spoke. 'You have two options. Either you agree to let Cate buy you out, which would be the same as selling the property to a third party as you intended, or you take Cate to court. You don't have to decide anything now. I'm taking Cate to Tumbin and in a day or two you can talk about this again.'

'I should've known she'd end up with some bastard who'd fuck us over.' Blake sprang to his feet and seconds later doubled over, grabbing his hip.

'Blake!' Leonora cried.

'Get away,' he hissed, squeezing his eyes shut.

Finch took Cate's arm and led her to the house. As Cate packed, he sat on her bed, surrounded by girlish books and dolls. After a few minutes she zipped up her suitcase and said in a small voice, 'I'm all done.'

62

Leonora put Blake to bed with a sleeping pill and painkillers. She ignored her own throbbing head and sat at the dining-room table with a tumbler of sherry, the bottle beside it. Light poured from the overhead lamp onto her scrapbook of clippings about their children. She read each article carefully again. The newspaper reporters always had a chatty tone, whether they were noting wins at the eisteddfod or a maths competition in which Cate had topped the region.

She drained her glass and poured another, the rim sticky.

When Blake had righted himself, fighting off their attempts to help, he sat at the table, white and sweating.

'What are we going to do now?' Sally was close to hysteria.

'Shush, Sal.' Charlie placed a hand on her knee.

A breeze sprang up, rustling the liquidambar. They heard Finch's car start and drive away.

'I'll put the kettle on.' Leonora hastened to the kitchen.

When she returned with the tray of tea things, Natalie was talking to her brothers and Sally in her measured, lawyer's voice. Leonora had never loved her sister-in-law as much as she did then.

She set out saucers and fitted cups into each one, then poured the tea, tipping in milk and sugar as each person liked it.

'I don't think we want to fight this in the courts,' Natalie was saying. 'Anyone can see that Cate is close to falling apart.'

'Why is it always Cate we have to think about?' Blake said. 'What about the rest of us?'

Leonora bit her lip. She knew Blake's pain sometimes made him irrational, but his resentment of their daughter was disturbing.

Natalie talked long into the afternoon, outlining the litigation procedures they could take. Finally, she concluded, 'We all need this to be finished.'

'How do we know he's not lying?' Sally asked.

'We don't. If he is, that's when we go to court.'

Leonora capped the sherry bottle. She came to the blank pages of the clippings book, the thick wad of loss behind them. She'd begun cutting them out when the stories first appeared a few years before. As she read the mothers' transcripts about having their children taken, she understood how these women ached for their sons and daughters, as she did when Eliot wasn't in his bed one morning and never returned, and when Cate never called her back, nor ever came home.

Her son, with his cordial nature, had always brought out the sweetest parts of themselves. She liked to think that, for his sake, she, Cate and Blake had preserved some of their goodness, like peaches soft and mellow in a jar of syrup. She picked up the phone and dialled Cate's mobile. If Blake was going to be an arsehole, so be it, but she wasn't going to lose her daughter as well.

63

The dawn was breathing, its pink exhalations settling on the hills. In the ute, Mellor and Cate were silent, but the space between them seemed more intense. Cate realised there were no tools bouncing at her feet; Mellor had cleaned up. She sat on her hands, unsettled by his sense of ceremony.

They turned off the main road at the machinery shed, with its familiar smells of spilled oil and wheat rotting in the grain shed. When the crops were good and the wheat piled high in the shed like a dune, she and Eliot would scramble to the top and slide down it, laughing until chaff crept beneath their clothes and began to itch.

Mellor drove along the edges of the paddock and passed the 1920s Holden abandoned in a ditch by her great-grandfather, then slowed at a gate. Cate slid out and opened it. The rising sun shone into her eyes. As they continued up the paddock, she said, 'We're going to the volcano, then.'

Mellor didn't reply.

They walked up the incline, passing the place where the family had celebrated Australia Day by the trig station. The further east they walked, the more panicked Cate became. The second old, rusting pyramid came into view, its severe edges rearing against the sky. Cate wiped her hands on her shorts as they passed it.

'Those bora rings?' she asked. 'Is that where we're heading?'

Mellor seemed to shake his head, but it was so imperceptible Cate couldn't be sure. She felt stones beneath her shoes and heard a galah pouring out its hoarse song. Breezes stroked the eucalyptus trees and flies dipped in and out of tussocks of wiregrass. Cate longed, as she always had, for Eliot to come running out of the bush, grinning wildly and calling her name.

Instead, at the base of an outcrop of granite, shrouded by a gum tree and overhung by a jutting slab, lay fragments of a ribcage, a skull sunk into the soil and delicate shards of finger bones, all stained by years of wind and dirt. A rusting rifle lay beside them.

Cate fell to her knees, rocks piercing her skin. The breeze turned sharp, scraping against her arms, and the light was so bright she could barely see.

'How do you know it's him?' she cried, at the same time that she saw, resting among the weathered bones of his clavicle, three turquoise beads. They once were strung on two strands of leather that he'd worn around his neck, a gift she'd given him for his fifteenth birthday. The leather had worn into nothingness.

She heard Mellor's footfall. He touched her shoulder but she shrugged his hand off. There was blood on the soil from her knee.

'Catie, come away, it's bad for your memories.'

'Leave me alone!' The smell of the bush was suffocating. 'You brought me here, and now you tell me not to look?'

'Cate.' Mellor's voice was so soft she could hardly distinguish it from the breeze. 'When a person dies, their spirit goes back into the land. Can you understand, now, why you mustn't sell?'

The winter when she and Eliot were thirteen and twelve, it had flooded. They had waited impatiently for the waters to recede, checking the levels from the fence by the fig tree. When most of the water had gone, they stomped through the paddock towards the creek, mud sucking at their gumboots. They discovered a channel that they'd never seen filled with water before, and busied themselves with building dams and banks to make it wilder and faster. They ran boat races with twigs and leaves, and Eliot jumped and whooped when he won. Cate stalked sourly towards the creek.

'Cate!' He called after her, his tone excited rather than indignant. She turned to find him bent over something on the ground.

'Look, a spoonbill. It's dead.' He lifted a muddied wing.

They crouched over it and Eliot prised open the odd, rounded beak.

'What a weird bird.'

'It must've drowned,' he said, peering down its throat. 'Let's take it home.'

'I'm not carrying it.'

Eliot tried to drag it by the feet but it was too heavy. He dropped the bird, downcast.

'Get a bucket,' Cate suggested.

He ran away over the boggy ground, returning ten minutes later with one of their mother's white plastic buckets, originally full of fertiliser and now used for carrying grass cuttings and weeds to the compost.

'Help me get it in, Cate.'

Gingerly, she picked up a wing. The bird was heavy and, although decay hadn't set in, its feathers smelled rancid.

Eliot could barely lift the bucket, so Cate grabbed part of the handle and they hauled it across the paddock. They left it on the tank stand where the dogs couldn't reach it and showed it to their father when he came home.

'The bird eats by sifting mud through its beak and swallowing the insects and grubs,' Blake explained.

Fascinated, Eliot opened its beak again.

By morning the bird was stinking. Their mother wanted to throw it into the creek but Eliot wouldn't let her, insisting instead that it be buried in the vegetable garden. The next year their potatoes were enormous, jostling for space in the soil.

Cate became aware of Mellor's joints cracking as he kneeled beside her. He took her hand, his fingers rough with calluses.

'How do we know it wasn't murder?' Cate asked.

'They wouldn't have left the gun,' he replied.

'They might have wanted it to look like suicide.'

Mellor stroked her hand. 'What reason would anyone have had?'

'If I didn't know him well enough to keep him from suiciding, how could I have known what other life he had?'

Mellor lifted her from the ground and wrapped his arm around her shoulders. She gripped him spontaneously. In the ute, as he turned the key in the ignition, they could barely hear the motor turning beneath the sound of her cries.

64

Cate was stunned by the number of people at the funeral. Girls she hadn't seen since school appeared with kids that stared at her with enormous, unblinking eyes, their tiny hands grabbing fistfuls of their mother's skirts. Cate nodded as people spoke at her by the church doors. She couldn't register what they were saying. They smiled at Finch, curiosity lighting their eyes, but kept their questions to themselves and filed into the building. There was always the chance to find out about him later, their whispers circling the room like blowflies.

Who knew, Cate wondered, that death could be so tedious. All she wanted, now, was to be left alone. Her parents talked, but words had deserted Cate. There was no longer the gentle, supporting hope of 'If Eliot comes home', but only the undeniable weight of past tense.

She closed her eyes briefly. When they opened, Russell was before her.

Heavy lines gouged either side of his cheeks, his hair was grey at his temples and pouches sat beneath his eyes. He was still thin, his skin parched and wrinkled at his neck, but his checked blue shirt and black pants were clean and pressed, his shoes shining.

'Russell,' she said stonily.

'I'm real sorry, Cate.'

She was surprised to hear the raggedness in his voice, the splayed ends of his words. 'I've been looking for you for years,' she replied.

Russell studied the brickwork of the church behind her. 'I get around a bit. Trucking, you know. I like to be on my own.'

'Free spirit?'

'Yeah.'

'I'm being ironic.'

He glanced at her, guarded.

'Let's have a drink, after.'

'I'll see, Cate. I gotta get on. Gotta load to deliver.'

Russell sloped into the church, his shoulders hunched. Cate recalled his easy posture as he'd ferried them about in his ute, his confident, wide smile.

Later, she found the hollow sound of soil hitting the casket sickening. All those years ago, she had shouted at her father to let Eliot be, but she'd been just as much to blame. In showing Eliot her life in Sydney he had shrunk away, perhaps knowing that he couldn't be part of it, and perhaps not brave enough to say.

The mourners drifted away. She heard Leonora begin sobbing again. Cate wanted sleeping pills and oblivion.

'Cate, love.' Someone touched her arm. She recognised from the perfume that it was Natalie.

'I want to go home.'

'Just have one drink at the pub, Cate. Finch has gone to find Russell.'

'I can't remember what the minister said in the service.'

'It was some bullshit about Heaven.'

'Eliot wouldn't have liked that. He would have wanted a

cremation. Why else would he have shot himself up there? He wanted to be part of the land.'

'I know, but it's done now, Catie.' Natalie led her to the car.

65

As the minister rambled in a nasal monotone, Finch's thoughts drifted to the rocks beside the hot, dusty plateau where he'd watched a forensic pathologist label the remains of Eliot's bones, which somehow hadn't been carried off by foxes, before a woman took photographs of them. There was a bullet hole in the top of Eliot's skull. He must have placed the rifle beneath his chin and pulled the trigger. With gloved hands, the officers tried to check that the rifle was discharged, but it was too clogged with dirt and rust.

Later, Blake acknowledged it was the same one Eliot used for roo shooting. He'd been angry, too. 'Why didn't you blokes look up there the first time round?'

'It's a pretty big property, Mr McConville. I'm sure we did look, but the body was fairly well obscured.'

Blake had turned away in disgust.

They were rising, now, the congregation rustling and opening their hymnbooks. Finch found the page for 'Nearer My God to Thee', a hymn he remembered from boarding school. Cate, on his left, stared ahead. She had wanted a cremation so that Eliot's ashes could be scattered on the property, but with both Blake and Leonora pitted against her, she'd had to back down. Finch, understanding it was none of his business, had taken a glass of whiskey outside to the hammock, stroking the dog that sat at his feet, its ears pricked to the harsh voices.

The hymn finished and the minister said a few more flat words. Then the coffin was carried out by Charlie, Blake, their old friend Paddy the barman, and the husband of Leonora's friend Jane

As the congregation watched, Finch saw a skinny girl standing beside Mellor. An Aboriginal woman, obviously her mother though a little darker, stood on the other side of her. When the girl noticed him watching, she drew herself up and lifted her chin with the same haughty, hostile expression that Cate had when she was pissed off. Finch smiled with amusement and the girl, disarmed, smiled back with a mischievous flash of teeth.

Later, as the soil was turned, Finch watched Russell leave the funeral, and followed him between the gravestones to the car park. When Russell had pulled out in the wide purple Ford that must have belonged to his mother, Finch turned the key in the ignition of his own car.

Russell was leaving, Finch realised, as he turned into Brown Street and glimpsed him going indoors. His truck was parked on the opposite side of the road, taking up two driveways.

Finch pulled into his aunt's, noting with relief that she wasn't there. He switched off the motor. In the stillness, he heard another car coming around the corner too quickly. He glanced out the rear window and saw the police.

They strode up the garden path and rang the bell. Finch carefully wound down his window. Mrs Wakeley opened the door.

'Russell!' she shouted, her voice a mixture of exasperation and anger.

Russell appeared, changed into a shapeless T-shirt, baggy jeans and trucker's cap. He took the cap off when he saw the cops.

'Just got a couple of questions to ask,' said one of the policemen. 'About Eliot McConville.'

Russell crushed his cap in his hands. They went indoors.

Finch decided he couldn't stay where he was and went into Carlotta's house. He waited for twenty minutes, watching the Wakeley's porch from the kitchen window. The cops came out. Russell was nodding. The police nodded too, then they walked back down the path. They didn't seem tense.

Finch folded and unfolded a tea towel printed with kittens, calculating what to do next. Russell appeared again, a small backpack in hand.

Finch stopped him just as he was opening the truck door.

'Russell. Finchley Accorso, friend of Cate's. My aunt lives next door to you. I was just grabbing some stuff.' He gestured to the house. 'Say, do you want to come to the pub? Cate would love to see you. She's a bit knocked around, but still, she'd like to chat.'

'Sorry, mate, I got to get going. This wasn't a scheduled stop, see.' Russell tossed his backpack into the passenger seat. 'You know, the first time I saw them was at this B&S in the middle of nowhere. They had the same freckles, same brown hair, even the same way of standing. It was fucking eerie. Tell Cate —'

Something caught his words, trapping them in his throat. He tried again. 'Tell Cate I'm real sorry. And tell her, it wasn't her and me that upset him, or the fight at the races.'

Finch stepped forward. 'What was it, then?'

Russell, lifting himself into the cabin, didn't answer.

'Have you a number she can call you on?'

Russell shook his head. 'No, mate. No number.'

He turned the key in the ignition.

Finch stepped back as the vehicle, with its heavy load, crunched onto the tarmac and drove away.

He found Cate staring into space at the pub, unaware of the sobbing around her, and pulled up a chair. 'Russell's left town.'

Her bland expression collapsed into disappointment. 'I needed to talk to him.'

'The cops beat you to it. They went to his place to question him. I spoke to him after they left. He wasn't going to tell me anything. The only thing he said was it wasn't you and him that made Eliot leave, or the fight.'

Cate scrutinised him, taking in the information.

'We can call the cops in the morning.'

'Yeah.' Cate pressed her hands against her eyes. 'They've questioned him before, and I don't think he'd have turned up if he knew he could be convicted, but he did know something. Why else would he have stayed away?'

66

Kath and May drank too much beer, and by the afternoon, May was sleeping on a chair on the verandah and Kath had flopped onto the couch inside. She dozed, listening idly to Mellor's chat on the phone to the rellies, outlining his plans for the land and telling them they could come home. Then something occurred to her. She looked at Mellor, who was off the phone now, staring out the window and drumming his fingers on the sill.

'Did you call Rachel?' she asked.

'Yeah, it was the first thing I did.'

'And you told Cate?'

He frowned. 'Cate knows.'

'About the baby?'

'No, I never told her that.'

'When are you going to tell her?'

Mellor walked outside.

'Mellor!' she followed him to the verandah. 'She's lost her bloody brother, she has to know!'

Mellor climbed into the ute and drove away, leaving Sparks barking.

Kath scowled at her sister slumped in the chair, snoring through the racket.

'And you're just as useless as he is,' she snapped, heading indoors.

When he was older, May's son Dan had told them how, in the home, they were woken on cold mornings by the brothers clanging saucepan lids. He had often wet the bed and they belted him across the calves for it, darkening bruises that were already there. Then they forced him to scrub the sheets in the bitterly cold washhouse and, shivering, to throw them onto a washing line he could barely reach.

He had ached for his mother's arms and their language, but there was only the angularity of English drummed into them day after day as they read the Bible and listened to sermons. The brothers rapped their knuckles with a ruler if the children ever spoke in their own tongue, seeking out some morsel of home.

Kath knew all this worried Mellor, but she still turned things over as she tried again to find her address book. She shook out the contents of her sister's bag, showering the floor with torn dockets and lolly wrappers.

'Stupid, selfish black bastards,' she muttered.

Then she noticed the *White Pages*, sitting beneath a pile of newspapers, topped with a pair of gumboots.

'Ha!' She thumbed through it, peering closely with her good eye, until she found the McConville's number. With care, she pressed the buttons of the phone.

'Hello?' It was Leonora, her voice flat.

'Mrs Mac. This is Kath, Mellor's aunt.'

'Yes.'

'Can I please speak to Cate?'

'What's it about?'

'Her friend, Rachel. Mellor's kid.'

'I see. I think Cate's asleep.'

'Can you wake her up? It's important.'

Leonora grunted. The phone rustled as she put it down. After a few minutes, Cate picked it up.

'Hallo?' She sounded groggy.

'Catie, this is Auntie Kath.'

There was silence. Kath figured Cate was trying to remember who she was. She pressed on. 'Cate, I got something to tell you.'

'What's that?'

'You've gotta go and visit Rachel.'

'Why? Where is she?'

'In Tumbin. Here, I'll give you the address.'

'Why do I need to see her?'

'You'll understand when you get there.'

Cate sighed. 'I wanted to visit her anyway. I saw her at the funeral, but it was too difficult. What's the address?'

When Kath hung up she found May leaning against the doorway, frowning.

'Who were you talkin' to?'

'Cate.'

'What for?'

'I told her to go to Rachel.'

'You silly bitch!' May shouted.

'What's so wrong with that? She deserves to know!'

'Don't you see? She'll take the child.'

'She wouldn't do that.'

'Kathy, she's just about out of her tree. Who knows what she'll do? We wanted to wait until she went back to Sydney.

'Well, there's more than two of us in this family,' Kath snapped. 'A helluva lot more.'

She slapped the *White Pages* shut.

67

Cate lay on the prickly rush matting beneath the stars Eliot had stuck onto the ceiling, listening to the house creaking and ticking as it released the day's heat.

She had always imagined that, once she found Eliot, sleep would return, soothing and stroking like a lover. Yet here she was, staring at the ceiling after another sleepless night. There were cobwebs in the corner and cracks in the paint. She thought of her anaesthetised flat in Sydney, with the one room that had been alive.

'Cate?'

She turned her head. Natalie was in the doorway. 'I need you to go through the contract I've drawn up, so you understand it.'

Cate slouched at the table. Finch was already there, twisting a paperclip into shapes. Natalie began to read out what she'd written on her laptop. Cate looked vacantly out the window.

'Cate, are you listening to me?'

'Yeah.'

'What did I say?'

'It was in legalese. I didn't understand.'

Finch sighed.

'What?' Cate demanded.

'Nothing.'

'Look, I'm not some goddamned boat you can steer into a harbour.'

'Cate, be civil, would you?' Natalie was sharp.

'Why should I? Mum and Dad are hardly civil to me. They can't bear it that I'm here and he's gone.'

'That isn't true, Cate,' Finch interrupted, shifting in his seat. 'Maybe you haven't seen it, but your mother is overjoyed that you're back.'

'Mum thinks the sun shines out of his arse,' Cate said snidely. 'Then again, any man who even looked at me would be good enough for her, least of all one who was insane enough to follow me from Sydney.'

'Christ, I don't need this. I'm going back.' Finch pushed back his chair and walked out, slamming the front door.

'Finch, I'm sorry!' Cate ran after him, but he ignored her, reversing out the driveway and driving fast down the road, dust and stones spiralling behind the car. When she trudged indoors, Natalie looked at her with a hard, analytical gaze.

'No wonder you keep winning court cases. You look like Medusa.'

'You're not a child anymore.'

'So my father keeps telling me.'

'I mean it. We all hurt, Cate. It doesn't give us the licence to act badly.'

'I can't help it.'

'Of course you can.' Natalie was impassive.

Cate stared at the table, its surface dotted with the marks she and Eliot had made when they were children, jamming their pencils into the wood to annoy their father. Her eyes filmed with tears.

'You've finally let something good happen to you, Catie.'

Cate nodded. 'I'll call and apologise.' She wiped her nose on her sleeve and gestured to the contract. 'Can you start at the beginning of this thing, and go slowly?'

68

Cate pulled up beside the kerb of number seventeen in a street where dogs lazed on lawns and old cars were parked in the dusty front yards. As she walked across the dried patch of lawn over which bindies stretched their tentacles, silhouettes appeared at screen doors and kids stopped playing their soccer games. She felt uncomfortable in her dark-blue jeans and black blouse.

Pots of sunburnt geraniums lined the front of the house and a blind was lowered over the front windows. She pressed the doorbell.

'I'll get it!' a girl called, opening the screen door.

Cate stared at her. She knew those eyes. The girl stared back, apprehensive.

'Who is it, El?' An older woman's voice came from the hallway.

Cate's pulse rushed. She saw Rachel, that lithe, laughing girl, exchanging smiles with Eliot across a herd of cattle.

'What's your name?' Cate whispered, short of breath.

Rachel appeared, wearing a red-and-white cotton dress. When she saw Cate, she snapped at the girl, 'Go to your room.'

'But —'

'Now. Take your homework.'

Rachel waited, hands on her hips, her legs astride. The girl slipped past her and they heard the thud of her door.

'If you want some kind of custody, I'd think twice. This street's full of Mellor's mob.'

Cate stretched out a hand to the doorframe. 'Eliot and I were the same. If I upset her, I would only hurt myself. And I didn't know until I saw her just then.'

'I'm sorry.' Rachel's mouth twisted. 'She's all I have.'

Cate stepped forward and embraced her old friend, feeling Rachel's stringy arms encircle her.

Although Rachel was still slender, she'd aged swiftly, with long shadows beneath her eyes, a downturned mouth and threads of grey in her hair. Cate narrowed her eyes, wondering if it was the strain of secret-keeping.

'Did Mellor tell you he knew where Eliot was?'

Rachel shook her head. 'I found out after you did.'

'May I see her again?' Cate asked.

'Soon. Come inside. We both need a drink.'

She led them into the cramped house. In the living room, laundry was piled on the couch, spilling onto the floor. Magazines and an exercise book lay open before the TV. Beyond that was a bedroom, the beds unmade. The girl's door had a wooden 'E' circled by a fairy stuck in the centre.

Yet the kitchen was tidy, with large windows looking out to the dry backyard, in which grew a straggling gum tree. A girl's bicycle lay in the dirt and clothes flapped on a Hills Hoist. Plates were stacked neatly on the draining board, the lino smelled of Mr Sheen and newspapers were folded beneath the fruit bowl. Cate suspected Rachel was too oppressed by the malaise of every single mother – overwork and exhaustion – to clean more than one room at a time.

Rachel stood on a chair to open a cupboard above the stove. She rustled among bottles of cough syrup and packets of paracetamol until she found a half-empty bottle of Scotch.

'Medicinal,' she said grimly.

On the fridge was the most recent missing-persons ad Cate had placed in the paper.

'So you were looking, too,' she said.

Rachel didn't answer, taking two plastic tumblers and a thick envelope from the cupboard. She handed the envelope to Cate. Inside it, Cate found hundreds more ads.

Rachel sloshed Scotch into the tumblers and gave one to Cate, who gulped down a mouthful.

'Let's go outside, I don't want her to hear,' Rachel said. 'Besides, she'll come out soon. She hardly ever does what she's told.'

They sat in the scattered shade of the gum tree on white plastic chairs. Kids yelled further down, a car revved and soccer balls thudded.

'When did it start? Cate asked.

A currawong cried out from the tree.

'I think the first time he came over was when he was ten. He brought the edged tool that he'd found at Harper's, and that you hadn't wanted to give to Dad because it was Eliot's to give. He couldn't leave it with us without you knowing, but from the start there was a sense of – I don't know how to say it – trying to make amends, I guess.'

'Why didn't he take me?'

Rachel gazed at Cate. 'He asked you that question once, too.'

Cate tipped back the rest of the Scotch and reached for the bottle at Rachel's feet, her throat and belly searing.

'He didn't come that often. Maybe once every few months. He asked Mum and Dad and the aunties about our people. It upset him, listening to the stories of what had been done to them.

He liked Mum. He used to make her tea and do the dishes while she put her feet up. Once, though, she teased him about his voice breaking and we didn't see him for about eight months. Mum just about cried when he came back.

'He went jackarooing that summer when he was sixteen, remember? He came home tanned and muscular, trying to be brash like a country bloke, though we all saw through it. And that's when he and I stopped being kids. We went to Harper's and tidied up one of the rooms. We'd pick the fruit and eat it. He was always just so gentle and considerate.' Rachel's voice lost its firmness.

The Hills Hoist turned slowly. It was pegged with a small yellow frock with a Peter Pan collar, a row of tiny white socks, a pink towel and two face cloths.

'After a while he began to worry about his father. His fears would grow in his head until he couldn't make decisions. He thought he'd be disinherited, and he really loved the land. And then you left, Cate, when he was seventeen. He wasn't a cheeky bugger anymore. He came by less often. My brothers were around for a bit that year and he used them as an excuse to keep away. Then he went to Sydney to see you and when he came back he was more distant than ever. He dug out those pamphlets from his music teacher and began to talk about going to the Conservatorium.

'I never doubted that he loved me, but he was frightened of where we were heading, and of having to disclose it to Blake.' She looked directly at Cate. 'He missed you too, terribly, and then there were the periods of depression, when he wasn't himself at all.'

'I knew it was bad now and then,' Cate said, 'but not that it was debilitating.'

'He was good at hiding it. I think it's why there was no note when he shot himself. It was just too hard to describe.'

'Why did he do it, then?'

Rachel tilted her head and drained her tumbler. 'He made up

his mind to move to Sydney, and almost at the same time I found out I was pregnant. As if that wasn't difficult enough, at the same time Russell started harassing me. I think he felt that, in attacking Eliot, he was revenging himself on you.' Rachel refilled the tumbler. 'He followed me home from work, made crass comments. Sometimes he parked outside the house all night. There was no point in going to the cops, 'cause they'd never believe a black woman. Then he threatened to tell your father about us. It was just too much – El was depressed again. He disappeared three weeks later.'

Cate's skin crawled. 'To think I was infatuated with him.'

Rachel laid a hand on her arm. 'We all do stupid things when we're young. Although I would never say Eliot was a mistake.'

Cate looked at Rachel's hand, with the thin fingers that Eliot would have held, and the skin that he would have stroked.

'Why didn't he tell me?' she demanded.

'Sometimes we need to have our secrets, to make us feel like we own ourselves.' Rachel reached for her hand. 'That's how he felt when you were with Russell.'

Shocked, Cate pulled away. 'So it was my fault, then.'

'No! Cate, no. It was inevitable.'

'Nothing is inevitable! If I'd paid more attention he would still be here.'

'Mu-um?' The girl had opened the back door and hovered on the threshold.

'I knew she wouldn't stay in there,' Rachel said.

'Mum, can I come out now?'

'You're already out, aren't you?'

'My feet are still inside.'

'Come here. I want you to meet this lady.'

Eliot wasn't just there in her eyes, but in her height, her long arms, the hesitant way she stood before them. Cate felt tears start behind her eyes.

'Elinor, this is Cate McConville. Your father's sister.'

Elinor. As close to her father's name as possible. Cate stretched out her hand. The girl took it, and smiled.

'I'd like to take you home,' Cate said. 'Back to your country.'

69

Leonora sat on the verandah, a glass of gin on the coffee table beside her. Tank stretched out at her feet, watching bees hovering from flower to flower.

Although it had been terrible watching Cate come back with Mellor so distraught that they'd needed Finch to help carry her inside, Leonora hadn't been completely surprised that it was suicide. She'd known that Eliot was missing his sister, but when he never improved, she'd sensed that there was another weight on him. She wished he had spoken to her, the way he used to when he was little, crawling into her lap and complaining that Cate had hit him, or pinched his textas and wouldn't give them back.

Then, a week ago, Cate had returned from a trip to Tumbin and, around the dining table with Blake, Natalie, Charlie and Sally, had announced, without embellishment, that Eliot had a child.

Leonora's eyes widened. 'Who on earth with?'

'Rachel,' Cate answered.

'That's bullshit!' Blake puffed with indignation. 'There's no way Eliot could have been with a gin. You're just saying this to wind me up, the way you always do —'

'Stop it!' Cate looked at her beefy, red-faced father. 'Just stop.'

Leonora had tried to drink from her glass of water, but her hands were trembling. Cate put the glass on the table and took her mother's hands between her own.

Blake sank into his chair, a bull in the ring that had been prodded too long. Leonora couldn't compel herself to break Cate's grasp and comfort him. When he began to sob, it was Natalie who led him from the room.

A few days later, after they'd dropped Natalie off at the airport, Leonora told Blake, 'Rachel's bringing our granddaughter to meet us at lunchtime.'

'Don't count on me being here.'

'Suit yourself.' Leonora concentrated on putting together a lamb roast and instructed Cate to make a lemon-delicious pudding.

'Mum, you're going to too much trouble. They'll be intimidated.'

'Too much trouble?' Leonora was incredulous.

Without another word, Cate went outside and picked lemons from the tree.

When Rachel came up the drive in her Honda, Leonora hung back and let Cate greet them. Elinor was a slip of a thing, with Rachel's narrow body. She had Eliot's shyness too, and pressed against her mother's side.

At Cate's suggestion, they sat outside beneath the liquidambars. Leonora could barely take her eyes off the little girl, but she was careful to keep a distance between them.

Cate strove to keep the conversation going, but after a while it faltered, and a pair of willy wagtails filled in the gaps.

'How old are you, Elinor?' Leonora asked at length.

Elinor glanced at her mother, who nodded encouragingly.

'Six-and-a-half.'

'And what sort of books do you like to read?'

'Mem Fox,' she said, emphatically. 'And books about Possum and Echindna.'

'I'll have to get the titles off you,' Leonora murmured to Rachel.

Once they'd eaten Cate's lemon-delicious, which Leonora thought bitter from too much lemon rind, Mellor appeared in the distance, walking across the paddocks towards them, the dog by his side.

'Sparks!' Elinor shouted, and ran to the fence.

'She's more excited about the dog than her grandfather,' Rachel said dryly.

Cate went indoors. When she came out, Mellor was standing beside the table and Elinor had buried her face in the dog's neck. Cate handed Mellor a black stone.

'I should have given it back at the start,' Cate said.

'What's that?' Leonora asked.

'It's from Harper's. Eliot found it years ago. It's an Aboriginal tool.'

'Thank you,' Mellor said gruffly.

Only then, when they were leaving to head to the aunties, did Leonora allow herself to stroke Elinor's long black hair. It was thicker and stronger than Cate's or Eliot's had been. The girl smiled at her properly, and she was Cate all over again in a naughty mood.

'Is she a handful sometimes?' Leonora enquired, as Rachel opened the car door.

'You bet, Mrs Mac. But when she's reading and she's still, well, it's lovely.'

Leonora sipped her gin. Sally had sent Charlie to the real-estate agent's in Tumbin and was putting things in boxes in a frenzy.

Leonora knew she ought to be packing too, but she'd only got as far as pulling the suitcases from the cupboard. When she thought of making cuttings from all her plants, and peeling Eliot's stars from his bedroom ceiling, she felt too heavy to move.

She heard a motor in the distance. It wasn't the ute; it sounded like a motorbike. It appeared from the creek and Leonora recognised Mellor's white hair.

She knocked back the gin and went indoors to put the kettle on. When she came out with the tea things Mellor was sitting in the wicker chair, teasing the cat with a twig.

'The cake's a bit old,' she apologised, setting the tray down. 'I haven't felt like baking.'

She poured Mellor's tea. The cat chewed on the twig. Sparrows jumped out of the thick jasmine vine.

'How's Blake?' he asked.

Her husband had risen before dawn, white with pain. Unspeaking, he took the Nurofen she offered. 'Not very well.'

She handed Mellor his tea and they sat in silence. Tank clawed Mellor's bootlaces.

'Mellor, when did you find Eliot?'

He cleared his throat. 'That day I stopped by and you told me Cate was coming home. I'd taken Sparks up the hill in the morning to visit our sites. Sparks made a racket when he reached those rocks, so I went to look.'

Leonora nodded, lifting the teapot over her own cup.

'I came to ask you to stay, Mrs Mac.'

Her hand jerked, spilling tea streaming from the teapot's mouth. She set it down. 'Where?'

'Here, in this house. We can take Sally and Charlie's place, and maybe build another for the rellies and kids who come to stay. Then Cate can still visit you, and so can Rachel and Elinor.'

Tank sprang from the verandah to stalk a cricket hopping

through the lawn.

'Blake wouldn't stand for it,' she answered, pushing crumbs around her plate. 'But then, I'm wondering if he should go with Sally and Charlie to be closer to the hospital.'

'You're not splitting up, Mrs Mac?'

Leonora tipped the spilled tea from her saucer over the side of the verandah and refilled her cup.

'I loved and supported him, but the way he treated Cate —' She broke off, pouring in milk. 'That's not the man I married. Besides, he would never have anything to do with his – our – granddaughter.'

'It can make you act badly, Mrs Mac. All this mess. Maybe take some time.'

'There isn't an excuse,' she said. 'I've had enough. For now, anyway.'

Tank pounced at the grasshopper but it evaded him, flying away.

'It would be nice to see the aunties,' she said. 'I've lost touch with them. We could have a yarn.'

Although Mellor's old, spotted hand gripped the saucer firmly, the teacup rattled loudly.

'How about I get you a mug?' Leonora suggested.

'That'd be good, Mrs Mac.' Mellor placed the cup on the table with obvious relief.

70

They had all signed the contract Natalie had draw up, and now Blake limped heavily across the paddock. His hat had blown off and the midday sun was scorching.

The previous few days Cate had been walled up in his office, putting her apartment on the market, selling shares and organising a loan with the bank. In a few weeks, when some money came through, they would need to walk, and the land would be Mellor's. Then the fences would collapse and foxes would breed. Mellor didn't believe in killing, except for the odd kangaroo for dinner. Blake's paddocks, of which he'd taken such care – making sure they fallowed so they would renew themselves for the next season, unlike other farmers who ploughed them with chemicals – would revert to useless grass. Mellor and his rellies would take over Sally and Charlie's house, drinking and pissing in the bedrooms.

Blake stopped, finding himself at the boundary between his and Harper's land. He leaned on the fence, remembering Eliot as a teenager, gangly-limbed and uncoordinated, sitting with him on the verandah after work. They sat in companionable silence as Blake unlaced his boots and peeled off his socks. Then Eliot asked, his breaking voice strained, 'Did you have a good day, Dad?'

Blake looked at his awkward, gentle son with affection. 'Yes, thanks, mate, I did. The lambs are going well.'

When Cate came back to the house with Mellor after they'd been up to the volcano, she couldn't get out of the ute. Leonora had flown to Blake, crying. He'd folded his arms around her, watching their daughter, and quashed his tiny hopes: that one day he would round up the cattle with Eliot again to take them to market, that they would come to know each other closely enough to work without speaking, that men in the district would be proud of his son, who rode a horse easily and worked hard.

Blake's legs buckled and he fell in the soil, his palm landing in a patch of burrs. After they'd signed, Mellor said, 'Mr McConville, I won't be kicking you out. I've said to Mrs Mac that you're welcome to stay in this house.'

'We can't. It's not our place.'

'It is, Blake,' Leonora replied. 'This is where Eliot is, and where Cate will come back to. This is our home.'

'But Mellor owns it. He's taken everything. There's nothing left.'

'I'm staying, Blake. You can go with Sally and Charlie until you work out what you want.'

Blake saw they'd already discussed it.

It wasn't possible for him to be on Mellor's land, even if it meant never hearing Leonora singing like a canary in the mornings, nor storing away terrible jokes to make her laugh. He hung his head between his knees, the sun beating through his cotton shirt.

He wasn't sure how long he kneeled there, but when he looked up at the sound of a motor, his neck was stinging with sunburn. He squinted, eyes adjusting to the light, and saw his brother getting out of a ute.

'C'mon, now.' Charlie's shadow hovered over him. 'We can't have this. Let's get you up.'

His brother hooked his hands beneath Blake's armpits and pulled, helping Blake stand. He brushed the burrs from Blake's hand. As they walked to the ute, crows cawed overhead from a gum tree.

Charlie was talking to him. 'Y'know that place by the river with all those bloody roses? Sally's already made an offer and it's not even for sale. It's gunna take two men to put in the irrigation pipes, that's for sure. Let's hope a drought doesn't come or Sally will have our guts for garters.'

Blake climbed into the passenger seat, barely listening. He remembered Leonora spinning in her yellow dress at the party near Bromley, and the radiance of her wide smile.

71

Cate picked her way down the narrow street in Paddington, a bunch of blue hydrangeas cradled in one arm. Her green silk dress, which brought out her eyes, rippled against her calves. Halfway down she reached a two-storeyed terrace with a wrought-iron balcony, shaded by a big eucalyptus that was breaking up the footpath. The tiny porch before the door was patterned with a mosaic of black-and-white tiles. Her heels echoed as she mounted the steps. She wiped her sweaty hands on her dress and rang the bell.

When the door was opened by a skinny, dishevelled man wearing just his jeans, she wondered if she had got it wrong from the start. Finch lived in Paddington, after all.

'Good morning,' she said politely. 'Is Mr Accorso home?'

The man stared at her, then at the bunch of blue hydrangeas in her arm, then back at her face.

'Are you the doctor?' he asked slowly.

'I am a doctor, yes.'

He sprang to life and sprinted down the hallway and around a corner.

'Finch! Finchley!' he yelled. 'It's the doctor!' He knocked

furiously on a door.

In a minute he was back, grinning broadly. 'He's just coming.'

'Thank you,' Cate replied. He continued to smile at her.

Cate shifted the flowers to her other arm, relieved when Finch came into view, wearing a faded T-shirt and tracksuit pants, his feet bare.

'Jack, you can go now,' he said quietly, as he brushed past the man.

Jack hesitated, then rushed up the stairs to the next floor.

Finch leaned and kissed Cate's cheek. His skin was rough with stubble. 'Sorry about my flatmate. He's not the sharpest knife in the drawer.'

Cate handed Finch the hydrangeas.

'Beautiful,' he said, his face illuminated with pleasure. 'Would you like coffee?'

'Please.'

His kitchen was well lit and clean, but for a stack of cardboard pizza boxes pressed behind the rubbish bin.

Finch switched on the coffee machine on the bench. Beside it was a window looking out to a courtyard surrounded by lilies. Cate counted arum lilies, day lilies and Madonna lilies. Finch found a tall, white vase and stripped leaves from the hydrangea's lower stems, then placed them in the vase with water. He set it on a small table in the hallway.

As he came back into the kitchen, Cate drew in his smell of aftershave, the clean scent of his clothes.

'You're looking better,' he said. 'No bruises. More weight. Carlotta would be pleased.'

'Thank you,' Cate smiled.

He filled two mugs with hot water from the machine and rattled coffee beans into the grinder.

'I'm sorry I was unpleasant to you,' Cate said.

She wasn't sure if he had heard her, until he turned and said, 'That's okay.'

The warmth of his expression was unexpected. Cate glanced away.

He switched on the bean grinder, filling the air with noise and the rich aroma of coffee. Cate watched ropes of muscles in his forearm rippling as he moved, the veins crossing his large hands.

When the grating sound of the machine stopped, Cate took a step closer. 'Why did you follow me?'

Finch spooned the ground coffee into the filter. 'I thought that, if I had you, I could have Aubrey back.'

Cate couldn't quell her bitter disappointment. She looked at the floor. The boards were so polished she could see her reflection in them.

Finch put the spoon down and dusted his hands on his pants, then placed them on her shoulders. Cate lifted her head and met his gaze.

'But now I've realised how much more I gained.'

He kissed her lightly and Cate felt shot through with sunlight, the way she had when she and Eliot held hands and ran between the tall eucalypts, their laughter tangling in the trees.

ACKNOWLEDGEMENTS

Writing this novel has been an absolute joy, not least because it was produced when I was back in Australia after a long, homesick stint overseas. On a practical level, I am grateful to Anne and James White, Rebecca White, Wesley Aird and Simon Prendergast for putting a roof over my head while I wrote, and to Dr Jill Ashburner for being a very accommodating boss.

I am deeply indebted to Michael Aird and Sarah Martin for their conversations and resources on Indigenous culture and history, and to Frank Russo for his editorial suggestions. Thanks are also due to Dr Lisa Phipps for advice on medical matters, Dr Briony Croft for her railways expertise, and to Christopher Daniel and Philip Cohen for details regarding the Ship Emergency Response Service.

Thank you to my wonderful agent, Pippa Masson, my efficient and committed editor Rachel Scully, and the brilliant team at Penguin, including publishers Kirsten Abbott and Ben Ball, for bringing this novel into being.

Finally, thank you to Hadley, my closest friend, right-hand man and other ear, and the best brother a girl could ever wish for.